Meet Me in Winterberry

Meet Me in Winterberry

Karen Liszewski

Book Cover by Jillian Liota, Blue Moon Creative Studio.

Edited and Formatted by Miranda Joy.

ISBN: 979-8-218-30913-8 (ebook)

979-8-218-30914-5 (paperback)

First edition 2023.

To Joey and Olivia, my entire world.
This is for you.

Contents

"From the cold crisp air,

I know you will keep me warm my dear.

Because I can feel the magic with you here,

This Christmas time."

Samantha Hooey and The Idol Club, "This Christmas
Time"

Chapter One

Penelope

"You can't be serious," I mutter, gaze glued to the tabloid in front of me.

Staring back at me is a picture of my fiancé Drew sucking face with another woman. Above the photo a headline reads, "*Drew Henry Gets Cozy with Mystery Woman Who Isn't Fiancée Penelope Maxwell.*"

My palms grow damp as my hands begin to tremble. This can't be real. He was cheating on me?

Only six months ago, that man—who was caught in a serious lip-locking session with someone else—was on one knee asking me to marry him. Now, I get the delightful news that my fiancé is a cheating scumbag, along with the rest of the world. What the hell did I do to deserve this?

With my iced coffee in my hand, I walk over to the floor-to-ceiling windows, and gaze down at 5th Avenue. This has always been my favorite spot in my penthouse. The corner fireplace and built-in bench with the cream cushions are perfect for relaxing and watching the sunset over Manhattan. When I first saw this view, I knew I was home.

I always imagined making this my home after marriage, raising a family to fill the three empty bedrooms and crafting countless memories within these walls. But, thanks to Drew's inability to keep his hands to himself, it looks like that dream isn't coming true.

People mill about the red-and-white decorated streets below, clearly taking advantage of today's Black Friday sales. They pop in and out of the storefronts, laden with shopping bags. Loved ones hold hands, parents work to get a handle on their kids, everyone is apparently getting into the festive mood. From this height, it's like peering into a snow globe.

My heart constricts at the sight of so many people making beautiful memories with their loved ones while I'm up here. Alone. While my world crashes down around me.

I wrap my arms around myself and take a few deep breaths, trying to center myself. The tell-tale signs of a panic attack threaten to push through the surface. I fight to keep it away, focusing on each breath.

After a few minutes, my heart rate evens out, and I stand. Straightening my spine, I take a sip of my coffee through the aluminum straw. A single tear clings to my eyelash before streaking down my cheek. Using the sleeve of my robe, I quickly wipe it away.

A lump forms in my throat as a sob threatens to escape, but I take a few deep breaths, steadying my mind.

"That's enough Penelope," I tell myself. "You got this."

My solo pep talk works, and I stop the sea of tears from falling. At least for now.

But as I watch the world go by from my window, I realize I haven't checked my phone yet today. It's still on the charger. All I've done is make coffee and discover Drew kissing another woman.

After a few more minutes, I drag myself from the window and make my way through the living room, sighing at the feel of the thick Persian rug beneath my feet. The large cream-colored couch sitting off to the side, so fluffy it feels like a cloud, suddenly seems too big and ridiculous for just me.

Honestly, the vibe and decor in my place isn't what I would've chosen, it's too cold, but the interior decorator talked me into it.

Thinking about my little trinkets and personal items sitting alone in storage, my heart squeezes. It hits me how cold and inauthentic my life has become. There are so many Christmas decorations from when I was little that have never seen the inside of my apartment.

I head into the kitchen, which is one of the largest kitchens I've seen in NYC. It's a shame, considering I don't cook. I'm more of a take-out and leftovers type of woman. With gray-colored cabinets that line both walls, marble countertops, state-of-the-art appliances, and an island that makes all my friends jealous, you'd think I'd utilize the gorgeous space. It was less for me and more for the family I envisioned. I figured I could hire a personal chef or learn to cook when the time came. So much for that.

My phone sits in a holder on the counter, and as I approach it, it lights up with a message. And another message. And another.

An endless barrage of notifications flood in, covering the picture of me and Drew on my lock screen.

I hesitate as I reach for the phone, almost aborting the mission, but I'm going to have to look at it eventually. Might as well get it over with. The moment I unlock my phone, I regret it.

Hundreds of notifications from all my social media platforms await my attention. I scan a few, catching glimpses of the tabloid cover, videos speculating on my relationship, and a slew of opinions from strangers all around the world. My text messages and DMs are flooded, everyone I've ever met reaching out to check on me.

"Oh. My. God." A cold sweat forms on my upper lip and the back of my neck.

I can't believe how fast the news has spread. Once I silence my phone, putting it on vibrate instead, morbid curiosity gets the best of me, and I do the worst thing I can—search on Google. I type in "Penelope Maxwell" and an onslaught of articles on all the gossip websites show up. And the headlines are all similar:

"Drew Henry Caught Kissing Mystery Woman"

"Playboy Drew Henry Shows His True Colors"

"Actor Drew Henry Cheats On The Gorgeous Penelope Maxwell"

"Penelope Maxwell Heartbroken Over Drew Henry Scandal"

I frown at that last one, clicking on the article to read what people are saying. Apparently, I've been seen crying at the cafe around the corner. I literally *just* found out and haven't even left my place yet. Unbelievable.

After reading a few more articles, I'm ready to throw my phone out the window, but it starts ringing with a call from my agent, William. My thumb hovers over the green button, but I don't press it. I'm in no mood to deal with anyone, not even him. And I *like* him.

Thirty seconds later the voicemail notification lights up.

"Penelope, darling. I've seen the news," he says with an English accent. William grew up in England and moved to the United States when he was twenty-one to follow the American Dream. Now he's an agent to the stars. Over the years, he's also become a friend.

"Darling, I need you to call me back. We need to get ahead of this and get a statement from you to protect your image." There's a brief pause. "Don't worry about him, Pen, you'll find someone way better than that douchebag. Okay, call me."

There's no way I'm calling him back, as much as I may adore him. I don't care about my image. I care about my *heart,* which is now broken into a million pieces. Some people may not have thought the relationship was real, or that we were in love, but I was.

Truly in love.

From the moment my parents died when I was thirteen, my life hasn't been my own. I was forced to move in with my Gran who lived right outside of New York City, in a small town in New Jersey. I knew no one, didn't make friends easily, and couldn't wait to leave.

Gran tried the best she could, but she was in her eighties and didn't have the patience for a teenager. With no siblings or other family members to set an example, I fell into the wrong crowd in high school. I was rebellious and stupid, partying in the city and failing my classes. By the skin of my teeth, I graduated. A week later, Gran died.

For the first time in my life, I was eighteen years old, out of school, and completely alone.

Her house was paid off, so luckily, I was able to live there until I figured out what to do. To make ends meet, I waitressed at a local restaurant and worked inside the Gershwin Theatre on 51st Street as an usher. It was there that I fell in love with acting and performing.

A couple years later, I started taking more waitressing shifts so I could afford acting classes. Once a week, I would take the train into the city and attend an early morning improv class. It was the best hour of my week.

In fact, that's where I met my best friend Georgia, who was also interested in becoming an actress. She went a different route and became a social media influencer while I took any role I could in movies and TV shows on the East Coast. Yep, I was definitely a person murdered on Law and Order: SVU before I got my big break.

For years, I sent in my headshot and went on auditions, even when I knew I'd never get the part. Deep down inside, I knew that eventually, someone would see my talent. I knew I was meant to be an actress, and the right role was out there for me.

Finally, at twenty-five, I landed a starring role in a popular superhero movie and my career took off from there.

I was thrust into the spotlight that I had desired for so long. I walked red carpets, wore designer clothes, had thousands of followers on Instagram, and earned more money than I thought was possible.

I was happy.

But it was also a lonely life. Always on the road, living out of hotel rooms more often than not, and surrounded by people who I never truly got to know.

Until I met Drew.

I'll never forget the day I first laid eyes on his handsome face. We were on the set of a movie that I had the lead role in, and he played my love interest. I was so taken aback by how incredibly good looking he was that I forgot my lines. Literally. My mind went completely blank, and I just stood there like an idiot.

At the end of shooting, Drew asked for my number, and we went on our first date a week later. The internet went crazy when we debuted as a couple—on the red carpet of the movie premiere—and we were the new It couple. We couldn't go anywhere without paparazzi behind us or fans wanting to take pictures with us to post on social media.

We got completely swept up in the madness and were engaged two years later.

I thought I had it all. Everything I could ever dream of. But now, I wonder how much of it was actually real.

I ball my hands into fists so tightly that my nails dig into my palms, and I shake them at the ceiling.

"Real funny, Universe," I yell. "I've had about enough with you!"

With a sigh, I tug on the belt of my robe to tighten it around my waist, my phone vibrates in my pocket, and I pull it out to see who's calling. When I see Drew's name, an unfamiliar sound, like a murderous growl, escapes me. I can't believe he has the audacity to call me.

The asshole has something to say apparently. As much as I'd love to answer and give him a piece of my mind, I ignore the vibration and let it go to voicemail. I can't give him any more of my time. He doesn't deserve it.

Against my better judgment, when the voicemail icon pops up, I hit play and put it on speakerphone. His voice fills the penthouse and sends chills up my spine.

"Hi baby, it's me—"

I hastily tap the delete key before I hear another word.

I should've never listened to it. The familiarity of his voice strikes me in the gut. My eyes start to water and tears slide down my cheeks. Mindlessly, I throw myself onto my oversized couch, letting the cushions envelope me as I sob.

Chapter Two

Penelope

I snag my phone and scroll through my contacts until I locate Georgia. It rings twice then I hear her voice. My tears start to dry up and my breathing becomes normal.

We've been by each other's sides ever since the day we met. She always makes me feel better just by being there, and right now, I need her.

And honestly, I don't have anyone else.

"Georgia…." I try to get the words out but my voice cracks.

"Do you want me to come over?" She knows me too well.

"Please."

"Let me get dressed and I'll be right over. Are there any paparazzi outside the building?"

"Oh God, let me double check, I didn't even think to look for them."

I climb off the couch and quickly cross to the windows, peering out to see if there's any paparazzi at the entrance to the building. Sure enough, a crowd of people stand on the sidewalk, aiming their cameras at the building.

"Ugh, there are. What am I going to do?"

"Don't worry, I'll stop by the store and grab some food, so you don't have to leave," she says. "I'll bring pajamas too and we can just veg. You shouldn't be alone right now. Is there anything specific you want from the store?"

"You're the best. How about some Ben and Jerry's and peanut M&M's? Not part of my diet, I know, but I don't care right now."

"I got you. Be there in a little while." She hangs up.

I hold the phone to my chest for a few minutes before putting it back in the kitchen.

Trying to pass the time before Georgia arrives, I decide to clean up my closet. Surrounding myself with my vintage and designer pieces normally makes me happy.

When I open the closet door, I gasp at the sight in front me. On display is the cream, floor-length Chanel gown that Drew had surprised me with on the night that he proposed.

I'd been on set filming my newest movie when I got a call from him, informing me that a car was coming to pick me up and take me to a surprise location. The gown and shoes were inside. It was at our favorite restaurant in the city that he got on one knee and asked me to marry him.

It was a no-brainer when I said yes to being his wife.

It was the happiest moment of my life.

Now, standing here in front of this symbol of joy, all I feel is rage. And pain. And disappointment.

It fills me up until I'm bursting at the seams, needing a way to let it all out. Quickly, I turn on my heel and dart into the kitchen, throwing open the junk drawer and grabbing my scissors.

My heartbeat thumps in my ears as I rush back to the closet. I rip the dress off its hanger and wipe the sweat from my brow. Before I can second guess what I'm about to do, I take the scissors and slice the fabric.

I slash and rip.

Strips of fabric drop to the floor, each one representing a shredded piece of my heart. And the love I thought I had.

Tears stream down my face.

I keep cutting until all that is left is a heap of jagged fabric and I'm so out of breath that I'm forced to sit down to avoid passing out. Letting out an animalistic scream, I pull my knees to my chest and try to ignore the ache in my stomach.

The sound of my penthouse phone pulls me out of my fog. I make my way to the ringing, grabbing it off the wall by the elevator door, and putting it to my ear.

"Miss Maxwell, you have a visitor," Frank, the doorman for the building, says. "Can I let Miss Georgia up?"

"Frank, thank you. Please let her up."

"Have a great night, Miss Maxwell," he says before hanging up.

I don't even know what I look like, but it's Georgia, so I'm not worried about it. She's seen me when I was broke, trying to make enough money to eat, and she's seen me walk the red carpet at award shows.

She's seen it all.

I close the door to my closet so she can't see the mess I made in there. She wouldn't judge me but I'm keeping that to myself.

The elevator dings as it reaches my floor. When the doors open into my foyer, Georgia rushes out and throws herself at me. She wraps her arms around my neck and my knees buckle. I'm so glad I'm no longer alone.

"Let it out girl," she says into my hair.

And I do. I let it all out. It comes in waves of tears, screams, shaking, and tons of cursing.

"I hate him," I say through my sobs. "How could he do this to me?"

"He's a jerk Pen and he never deserved you. Never. You were always too good for him."

"I never felt that way," I get out through my tears. "How did you get past the vultures downstairs?"

"Those guys didn't stand a chance against me." She laughs. "They didn't recognize me in my sunglasses and hat. I hope they leave tonight and give you some peace."

We pull apart and she wipes the tears from my face. Even through the pain, a smile forms on my face. I'm so lucky to have her.

"Okay, let's stuff our faces with some ice cream and watch reality TV."

Grabbing my favorite blanket, our ice cream, and the remote, we settle on the couch. For the next few hours, we completely zone out.

And it's everything I need right now.

Nothing matters.

Not my phone buzzing in the other room, the paparazzi downstairs, or my broken heart.

After a few episodes of my most beloved Real Housewives show, I glance at the window and notice my reflection in the dark glass. Checking the time on the TV, the clock reads 12:30 a.m.

Sitting up, I stretch and put the empty ice cream container on the coffee table. There goes my waist and all those hours in the gym.

"If you have to get going, don't feel bad," I say. "I know you have to be on set early tomorrow morning."

"Are you sure? I can stay a little longer. I wish I could stay overnight."

"I'm sure. You are the best friend any girl could ever ask for, Georgia." A fresh wave of tears fall. "I'll be fine, I promise."

She stands up and pulls me in for one last hug. "Okay, call me in the morning so I know that you're alright. You know I'm here for you."

As I walk her to the elevator, she grabs her big hat and sunglasses, even though it's nighttime, and we say our goodbyes. Once the door closes and the silence fills the space, I'm not sure what to do with myself.

Do I go to bed? Should I clean up the scraps of my dress from the floor of my closet? Do I take a shower?

After a few minutes, I head to my bedroom, get into my comfiest pajamas, throw my hair on top of my head, and cuddle on the couch with a book. Reading has been my escape since I was little when I would hide under the covers with a flashlight.

I love getting lost in a good book in between shoots or when I have downtime on the plane or in the car.

I grab the romance novel I'm reading, settle in, and forget everything that is going on around me. What I wouldn't give for real life to be like the sweet books I love so much.

The next thing I know, I'm opening my eyes to a dark room. The crick in my neck screams at me for sleeping on the couch. I glance at the clock and notice that it's only 4:30 a.m.

"Ouch." I sit up and rub my neck. Add this to the list of crap I'll have to deal with today.

Shuffling across the ground, I head into the kitchen and pick up my phone. Hundreds of notifications, phone calls, missed Facetime calls, and social media comments fill up my screen. I watch the numbers continue to rise, it practically burns my hand and I immediately turn it off and put it in the junk drawer in my kitchen.

I'm completely overwhelmed, hurt, and I can't deal with the outside world knowing all of my business right now.

Walking over to the picture windows overlooking the city I love so much, I take a peek at the front of the building and catch sight of the paparazzi still outside the building. I guess they never left last night.

What am I supposed to do now?

Panic starts to creep in as my heart begins to beat against my chest and my breathing becomes shallow.

With nowhere to go and nothing to do, I return to my favorite spot on the couch and pull the blanket up to my chin and get as comfortable as my broken heart will let me.

Three days later, I still haven't left my apartment. I haven't showered, changed my pajamas, or turned on my phone. My stomach has been in knots since Friday, and I've barely eaten.

Stretching and removing myself from the spot I've been sleeping in—that is now an indent of my body—I do what I've done every morning and check to see if the coast is clear outside the building.

It's easy to spot the paparazzi, with their large cameras around their necks. I watch as they stop residents who are leaving the building, probably trying to figure out if they've caught a glimpse of me.

"Vultures," I say.

I can't stay cooped up in this apartment. I'll go stir crazy if I sit here a moment longer, wallowing in my sorrows. I need to change my clothes and brush my hair. That would probably be a good idea.

The mere thought of doing any of that makes my stomach muscles clench, and the overwhelming urge to snuggle back into the couch takes over.

"Enough of this!" I slam my fists against my thighs. "You're Penelope Maxwell. You're better than this."

Sadness morphs into white-hot, anger, threatening to explode if I don't move.

I take a few deep breaths and do what any sane person would do—I march into my room, collect my laptop and iPad, throw them into the closet and grab my Louis Vuitton suitcase from the top shelf.

I briskly navigate the room, throwing clothes, jewelry, makeup, and other necessities into the suitcase.

I struggle to drag the luggage out of my bedroom. It takes thirty minutes to get the bags to the foyer elevator, and my back is not pleased. I call the front desk, hoping Frank is working early today and can help me load my car.

Frank answers and I breathe a sigh of relief.

I hang up with him and set the code to the safe, change into leggings, throw a hat over my hair and wait for Frank to come up on the elevator.

I locate a piece of paper and scrawl a note to Georgia. I'll ask Frank to give it to her so she knows I'm safe and sound.

Hey Georgia,

I've decided to get out of the city for a few days to clear my head. I left my phone here but I promise I will call you when I get home.

Love you.

Pen

At the last second, I run into my office, grab a few books, stuff them inside, and run back to the door in time to greet Frank.

"Frank, can you do me a huge favor please?"

"Sure, Miss Maxwell. What can I do for you?"

"Can you make sure this note gets to Georgia?" I hand him the piece of paper. "Also, if anyone else comes looking for me or asks where I have gone, can you please not tell them anything?"

"Of course, Miss Maxwell. And if you ask me, Mr. Henry never deserved you." He winks and tears threaten to spill over again.

He gingerly takes the bags and loads them onto the cart, and we make our way into the elevator to go downstairs. When we reach the underground parking garage, we load everything into the trunk of my white Porsche Cayenne Coupe. Frank gives me a nod goodbye, and I buckle into the driver's seat.

Freezing, I realize that in the time it took me to decide I was leaving and pack my things, I never actually picked anywhere to go.

"Really, Penelope," I say. "How are you going away when you have no idea where you are going to go?"

Then it hits me.

I'll drive north until I get tired or feel like stopping. Wherever I wind up, that's where I'll stay. Maybe I'll even see some snow. It's well before rush hour, so hopefully not many people will be on the road yet.

As ridiculous as the plan sounds, I'm happy with it. I start my car and edge out of my spot, exiting the garage. Glancing at the swarm of paparazzi waiting on the street, I barely pay them attention as I head into traffic.

Here goes nothing.

Chapter Three

Brent

"Dad. Dad. DAAAAAAAAD!" Small fists thump my chest as Nora screams in my face. "Dad, if you don't wake up and get your grumpy butt out of bed, I'm gonna be late for school!" She's a little terror who doesn't want me to sleep.

"Okay, okay I'm awake," I say through a sleepy haze.

Slowly, I open my right eye to peek at her. She stands next to the bed, hands on her hips, staring daggers into my soul. Grunting, I open my other eye, so she knows I'm awake.

"Dad, you're killing me," she says like a thirty-year-old who's trapped in a seven-year-old body.

With her bright green eyes and headful of blonde curls, my little girl is so beautiful that sometimes it hurts when I look at her. Oftentimes, I find myself staring until she gets annoyed and tells me to stop.

Yep, she gets her spunk from me.

As soon as she's convinced I'm awake enough, she stomps out of the room, calling over her shoulder that I have ten minutes before we have to leave.

"Crap," I mutter as I rub my hand over my face, willing myself to wake up.

I'm not a morning person. Not even a little bit. But the last thing I want is to make Nora late for school, so I pry myself out of bed and proceed to the bathroom before heading downstairs.

Christmas tunes blare from the inn's speakers, invading the guesthouse Nora and I call home. There should really be a limit on how early Christmas music can be played.

If it were up to me, Christmas music wouldn't be played at all.

I used to play Christmas music all the time with my wife Michelle before she passed away from breast cancer when Nora was three. We'd been married six years when Michelle got sick, and six short months later, she was gone. It's been me and Nora against the world ever since.

It was one of the hardest times in my life and I'm not sure I've truly recovered yet. Or if I ever will. Michelle was my best friend and losing her gutted me.

A little over a year ago, Nora and I moved back to my hometown in Winterberry, Vermont. We were in our little shore town in New Jersey, in the same house we loved and lost Michelle, when my parents called me out of the blue one day and told me they needed help at the inn. It was in trouble and they were struggling. Nora and I made the move.

Was it my first choice to move back to my hometown and live with my parents at the age of forty-two? Hell no.

Do I regret the decision? Not for a second.

They've always been there for me, and to be honest, it's nice to have help with Nora.

The Butterfly Inn is situated not far from Main Street in Winterberry. It was my parent's dream for as long as I can remember to own a bed and breakfast in this quaint, quirky little town. When old Mrs. Weatherby passed away ten years ago, and the inn was for sale, my parents took all the money they had and purchased it.

It needed some repairs, but it's a cozy and welcoming spot where tourists and families come to spend time together. It's a popular place to take in all Winterberry has to offer, especially for the holidays. And there's a *lot* to take in.

Unfortunately, with the amount of money it has taken to fix up the inn, it hasn't been an easy time the past couple of years for my parents, but things are turning around.

I do repairs when needed, little odds and ends around the property, like the landscaping, and whenever it gets busy, I help at the front desk. I also opened a small law practice right in town. I'm usually there three days a week. For the other two, I work from the guesthouse so I'm more accessible to my parents.

In my other life, before coming back to Winterberry, I was a very sought-after lawyer who wore suits every day to the office and worked on high-power cases.

Today, I dress in jeans and a black hoodie with my black work boots. I make myself a black cup of coffee, and head across the lawn to grab Nora and take her to school.

The guesthouse came with the purchase of the inn and looks exactly like a dollhouse. It's light blue on the outside, with a small front porch painted white and a little swing that Nora loves sitting on when she reads her books.

Inside the house, there are two small bedrooms and one bathroom, a kitchen, and a small living room. It may not be much, and it definitely has no manly character to it, but it's home.

I trudge across the lawn, and as I get closer to the French doors that lead from the backyard into the mudroom at the inn, Mariah Carey's famous hit "All I Want for Christmas Is You" grows louder, mingling with the distinct voice of my little girl belting out the tune.

Nora takes after Michelle in the Christmas department.

She's all in, every year.

From traditions and music to every single event in town, Nora is about it.

There used to be a time in my life when I was the same way. Michelle and I would decorate the house from head to toe. And then when Nora came along, we spent every day of the Christmas season trying to make it as magical as possible for her.

Now, I grumble through the holiday season, trying to keep up with Nora. She counts down to the holidays, and I count down until they're over.

Stepping inside the inn and out of the cold, I kick off my boots, take a very deep breath and walk into the Christmas hell that waits for me.

"Wow what a beautiful voice you have," I say as I tickle Nora's stomach. She almost spits out her orange juice.

"Geez Dad, it's about time you got here. I thought I was going to have to walk to school."

"Oh, come on kid, I'm not that slow."

"Honey, if you were any slower, it would be Christmas before you got here," my mom calls from the corner of the kitchen where she's making pancakes for all the guests.

Just like Nora, my mom, Suzanne, is obsessed with Christmas. Decorations cover every empty surface at the inn. Outdoor lights went up the day before Thanksgiving, and a huge Douglas Fir sits in the front picture window. It's overkill if you ask me.

The living room is off the entrance to the inn, and it's where the reception desk sits for check-in.

In the summer months, you can find the guests spending time on the huge front porch in the rocking chairs, but in the winter, there's another tree on the porch with Christmas decorations and twinkly lights.

I snag a chocolate-chip muffin from the reception desk and walk through the inn, passing the formal dining room and my mother's massive library on the way to the kitchen, ensuring everything is good before taking Nora to school.

"Nora-Bean, you ready?" I yell as I make my way into the kitchen.

It's a huge space where my mom cooks all of the meals for the guests and bakes most of the desserts.

"Dad please, I'm not a baby anymore," Nora says as she rolls her eyes. "Let me get my backpack and then I'm ready to go."

When did my little girl get so grown? Before I know it, she'll be bringing boys home. I'm going to have to sit on the porch with my shotgun to scare them away.

"Heeeellllooooo! Earth to Dad!"

"Sorry, sorry, let's go." Traffic might be bad this morning with the setup for the Winter Festival starting.

She puts her coat on, grabs her backpack, and kisses my mom on the cheek before we head to my truck.

As old as dirt, Betty the truck has been with me for years and is one of my most prized possessions. Sure, the exhaust stinks and she rumbles through town but it gives her character.

We drive down Blueberry Lane and turn right onto Main Street. No matter which direction you go, it's like Christmas threw up.

Wreaths hang on every lamp post. A gigantic Christmas tree sits in the middle of town. Blow-up characters line people's yards, and the old-fashioned Christmas carolers come to our doors all season long.

It's inescapable.

There are events happening almost every day during the season. I'm not joking.

From the Christmas Tree Lighting and the Christmas Log Parade to the Winter Festival and the Christmas Eve Ball, each day brings festive cheer and lots of traffic from visitors who come to take part in the madness.

Just as I suspected, the people on Main Street are moving slow as molasses this morning. Townsfolk are setting up rows of tables on the green surrounding the gazebo. Directly in the middle of town.

Our little town only has a few stoplights and the population hovers around four hundred. We have no big box stores or chain restaurants. In the morning, if you're out early enough, you'll catch the group of old men sitting with the paper and gossiping in Sally's Diner.

The owner, Sally, is around my age and opens early so the guys can get their morning cup of coffee in before the town wakes up.

As we pass Sally's Diner, I wave to Mrs. B, the crotchety old woman who's been alive since the dawn of time. She's practically a hundred years old and still yells at every kid who runs past her.

"Dad, why is Mrs. B always so annoyed?" Nora asks as my truck crawls by.

"I'm not sure, she's been like that since I was little."

"I wonder if she's lonely."

"You know, that might be it," I say as I pat her on the head, ruffling her hair and earning myself another eye roll.

Smirking, I turn back to the road and slam on my breaks. Traffic sits at a complete stop.

What's with these people? Did they forget that the gas pedal is the long one?

"Hey, Dad, what's going on up there?" Nora asks.

She's definitely going to be late for school now. I bang my hands on the steering wheel before unbuckling my seatbelt. If no one else is going to see what's up, I will.

"Stay buckled, I'm just going to go check it out," I say as I open my door.

"Be nice, Dad."

"Aren't I always?" I answer with a wink.

"Suuuuure." Nora chuckles into her hands and shakes her head.

I make my way past the line of cars in front of me, mumbling a greeting to each driver.

At the very front of the line, a white Porsche sits turned off in the middle of the road, blocking traffic.

"What the...?" I say as I approach the driver's side window and peer inside. A woman with brown hair pulled on top of her head, huge black sunglasses shading half of her face, and the fullest lips I've ever laid eyes on sits in the driver's seat.

"Are you okay?" I ask. When I notice the tears falling down her face, I hesitate. "Crap."

Tears from my daughter? Those I can do.

But tears from a random stranger? I'll pass.

Chapter Four

Penelope

Driving with no cell phone and no destination sounded like a good idea initially.

Now that I'm stuck in the middle of the road in the smallest town I've ever seen—in *Vermont*—it might be the dumbest thing I've ever done.

I was expecting to stop when I ran out of gas or when I got too tired to keep driving. What I didn't expect was to break down when I stopped at a red light. When was the last time I had the oil changed or the engine checked?

That would be never.

And how long have I been driving around with the service light on my dashboard? Probably over a year.

I live in Manhattan and have a driver. I barely even use my car!

So, here I sit, crying in my car while a line of cars backs up behind me because the street is so narrow that they can't get around me. Awesome.

Could this day get any worse?

After what feels like hours, but is really only a few minutes, a large man walks right up to my window.

"Are you okay?" he asks as he peers inside.

Embarrassed and completely panicked by his sudden appearance, I sneak a peek at him through my sunglasses and am taken aback by the sight of him. He has to be at least 6'3" with dark hair, bright blue eyes, a beard that most men would be jealous of, and a black hoodie that his massive chest is fighting to break out of.

He looks nothing like the men I meet on the red-carpet events, and for a moment I feel like my heart is going to beat right out of my chest.

"M-m-my car won't start again," I manage to choke out as the tears continue to run down my face.

I put my hand over my chest to try and slow my heartbeat. I take a few deep breaths while the handsome man continues to stare at me like I'm from another planet.

"I noticed. Do you know what happened?"

"I was just driving along, taking in the sights when I stopped at the red light and my car turned off," I explain. "It just stopped and now it won't turn back on and I'm holding up traffic and people are going to start beeping and getting angry and I don't know what to do!"

"Okay, calm down. No one is going to beep or get angry, that's not how folks are here. Except you *are* making me late to get my daughter to school, so if we could figure this out and get you moving that would be great." His eyebrows pinch together as if talking to me pains him.

Glancing at the line of cars behind me, he lets out the biggest sigh I've ever heard. "Let me get traffic moving and then we can see what we should do. Sound okay with you?"

"That sounds perfect."

"Be right back," he says.

As he makes his way towards the line of cars, I can't help but stare at him in my side mirror. My cheeks heat.

"Pull it together Penelope," I scold myself. "You just found out your fiancé was cheating on you. Plus, you don't even know this guy's name.

This is absolutely not happening, and you are *not* attracted to this man even if your hormones are telling you differently. The end."

I take a couple more deep breaths—my therapist taught me to focus on breathing when I'm feeling anxious—and watch as the handsome, but unfriendly, man starts to direct traffic past me. He takes complete control of the situation and all I'm doing is sitting here crying. Typical.

Oddly enough each driver waves to me as they pass. They tell me they hope I'm okay and not to worry about the traffic. I'm not even sure what to make of it.

If this was the city, I would've had middle fingers and curse words thrown at me. But here in this tiny town, no one seems mad except for McHottie back there. It's throwing me off.

As I sit here, waiting for my handsome hero, I take a minute to look around at possibly the cutest town I have ever seen. On both sides of the street are quaint little shops with names like Ye Olde Tea Shoppe, The Corner Stop, and Sally's Diner. There are more Christmas decorations than on 5th Avenue in NYC, which I didn't think was possible.

Now that traffic is moving again, I can breathe.

I take a peek in my rearview window to gauge what state my face is in and try to catch a glimpse of where this stranger is and catch him turning off a truck. I notice a little girl sitting in the passenger seat. I can't make out much except for her head of blonde curls that any adult would envy.

"So, McHottie is a dad. I didn't see a ring on his finger, I wonder if he's married," I say to myself in the mirror a minute later. I lift my sunglasses to swipe at the moisture on my cheeks.

"McHottie, huh? That's a new one," a deep voice comes from my open window, cutting into my thoughts. McHottie himself stands there scowling. I swear a little smirk tries to break free, but the way his eyebrows pinch together tells me I probably won't be seeing anything other than annoyance on his face today.

What else could possibly happen today?

"Oh um... I... um..." I try to speak but can't form words.

"It's okay, I've been called worse."

"If there's a hole that could open up and swallow me, I'd be very happy right about now."

"That makes two of us," he says. He shakes his head, rubbing his hand over his beard. "I don't have time to wait here with you for Ben, the mechanic, to come and check out your car. How about if you ride in my truck with us while I drop her off at school and then we can go to the auto body shop together and see about getting your car towed."

There's a flash of annoyance in his eyes, and it's gone so fast I'm not sure I actually saw it.

I hesitate. "I guess that works."

He's a complete stranger and I'm not sure this is a good idea.

"I mean, if that doesn't work for you, I could always leave you here and you could find Ben yourself. Up to you." He turns to walk away.

Wow. "I don't have another option at this point," I spit out. Who does he think he is, talking to me like this?

"Didn't think so," he says as he turns to walk away again.

I poke my head out the window, yelling at his retreating back. "Can I at least get your name before I get into your truck? You could be a serial killer or something."

"Seriously?" He mutters. He walks back to my car. "First of all, I'm not a serial killer. Second, I'm doing you a favor, which I don't have to do. Third, my name is Brent Harrison and the little one in my truck is Nora. Now, can we go?"

"Aren't you going to ask my name?"

"Eventually, yes. Right now I'd just like to get going."

"I'd like to tell you my name first before we leave," I say.

"Of course you would. Okay, what's your name then?" His blue eyes glare at me. I think Brent would definitely leave me here if he could, and to be honest, I'm surprised he doesn't.

"I thought you'd never ask. I'm Penelope Smith. Nice to meet you, Brent."

"You too. Now, let's go."

I want to tell him my real last name, but something holds me back. Maybe no one here will know who I am, and I can crumble in peace. No one has recognized me so far.

"Be right behind you. I just need to grab my purse and put up the windows," I say as I try to hide the blush creeping up my neck and onto my cheeks. Instantly, I'm nervous to get out of my car in case there are paparazzi standing on the sidewalk, waiting to snap my photo and make up some story about me.

I open my car door and take a look around, but I don't see anyone with a camera. I try to stop my racing heart before I step onto the street. I'm not used to being without my security team. It feels strange. Turning toward Brent, I can't stop myself from staring at him as he walks away.

I'm nursing a broken heart, which means I'm vulnerable and should *not* be checking out another man.

"I forgot to ask if you have any luggage or anything," he asks over his shoulder.

Oh man. Do I have luggage.

"Actually, there are a few things in my trunk," I say as confidently as possible.

"Figured." He grunts and jerks a thumb toward the trunk. "Open up." He reaches in and grabs my bags.

Wow, that's nice. I open the trunk and he grabs my very expensive bags out. It crosses my mind that I hope he's gentle with them before mentally slapping myself because this handsome man is literally saving my ass right now.

"Wow, did you pack a whole house?" He grumbles as he walks toward his truck.

I round to the passenger side of my car and grab my black purse that spilled onto the floor. Gathering up my things, I glance at myself in the mirror one more time before slowly putting my windows up.

I lock my car and head toward Brent's truck, so I don't continue to make Nora late for school. I don't care how small this town is, living in NYC for so long, I don't trust anyone.

As I approach Brent's truck, I see Nora whisper something into her dad's ear, and I feel like running back to Manhattan. Who needs a car anyway?

I open the door and I'm immediately hit with the smell of leather mixed with cologne and hairspray. Nora scoots to the middle of the seat, leaving room for me.

"Hi there," I whisper to Nora, who's looking at me like I have twenty-five different heads.

"Hi, I'm Nora. Dad said your name is Penelope, I like that. I'm seven years old and in second grade. I hope there's enough room next to me for you to sit. Dad said it would be fine but if you need me to I can move over more."

I blink a few times as I process everything she says.

"I think there's plenty of room, thank you for letting me ride with you and I'm sorry if I've made you late for school."

"That's okay, Dad always makes me late for school." She glares at him over her shoulder. Boy is he in trouble.

"Thanks, Nora," McHottie says. "Let's get going before I get another call from the principal."

"See," Nora whispers. "Told you he always makes me late."

"You do know I'm right here and can hear you right?" Brent says.

I can't help but laugh at the scene in front of me. It reminds me so much of how my dad and I used to talk to each other when I was Nora's age. A small ache forms in my chest

"Get ready for the worst smell ever when Dad starts driving. Not coming from him, but from the truck." She giggles in my ear. "So what happened to your car?"

"I'm not sure exactly. I was driving and I stopped at the red light, and it just turned off. Your dad is going to take me to the auto shop after we drop you off and hopefully, they can fix it."

"Ben can fix almost anything. He's nice but kind of smells sometimes."

"Nora, don't tell people that," Brent says as he tries to hide a laugh.

"Sorry, Dad but it's true."

Clearly trying to hold back a laugh, he just shakes his head and turns the car on. As soon as we pull out onto Main Street, the smell of the truck invades my nostrils, causing me to scrunch my nose.

"Yep," Nora says. "Told ya."

"Wow, that's some smell your truck has there," I say to Brent with a hint of amusement in my voice. "Maybe you should have Ben look at it while he checks mine out."

When all I get is a glare from Brent, I decide to shut my mouth and not provoke my knight in shining armor. Even if the smell really is bad.

What the hell *is* that?

The ride to the school is short. Brent and Nora chat about their Christmas plans and the events happening in town. Nora squirms in her seat as she talks, and Brent looks like he wants to throw up.

"Will you still be here when I get out of school?" Nora looks at me hopefully.

"I'm not sure. I don't even know what's wrong with my poor car."

"Well, I hope you will be. I like you." She reaches over and gives me a surprise hug.

"I like you too. Have a great day at school!"

She grabs her backpack and lunchbox from the footwell and hops out after Brent.

"Okay, little one, let's go," Brent says. "I'll be right back. I just have to walk her in."

"I'll be here."

The pair walk into the building, hand in hand, and a smile forms on my face as I watch them. Peeling my eyes away, I glance at the part of town we're in while I wait for him to come back to the car.

To the right, across the street, is a tree-lined street that looks like it has cute houses on either side and people walking with their pets and families even though it's freezing outside. Everything just seems so happy. Whenever you walk down the street in Manhattan, people are rushing, and if you get in their way, you'll hear about it. Not many people smile at you in the city, and as big as it is, it's easy to feel lonely.

Here, it's the complete opposite.

Farther down the street, on the same side as the school, are more little shops. Each of the shops has windows with twinkle lights, scenes painted on the glass and wreaths on the doors. Everything is festive.

I notice a small coffee shop that has tables outside for people to sit, and I immediately make a mental note to visit before I leave.

At the end of the road ahead, there's a large lake with a wooden pier that juts out into the water. Benches and adorable rocking chairs line the shore. With the lapping waves and the wind coming off the water, it's so peaceful.

Between the slow-paced cheer and lack of paparazzi hounding me, I already feel some of the stress from yesterday leaving my shoulders and I haven't even done anything yet. It feels so cozy and wholesome here.

I could get used to this, I think to myself as I spot McHottie coming out of the school, walking towards the truck.

Chapter Five

Brent

I'm a grown man for God's sake but one look from Principal Mc-Sweeney and I feel like a scared little kid again. With her severe gray bun, black-rimmed glasses, and a scowl visible from the next county over, she has to be a hundred years old by now.

"Don't be such a baby," I scold myself as I walk out of the school.

As expected, Mrs. McSweeney was pissed that Nora was late again. She pulled me into her office for a chat, and I couldn't decline. The woman doesn't accept no for an answer.

I bolt out the front door and breathe a sigh of relief that I made it out alive to enjoy another day.

As soon as the cold air hits my face, I catch a glimpse of Penelope in my truck and am struck again by how beautiful she is. When I first saw her car in the middle of the road, blocking traffic, I was so annoyed I couldn't even see straight. But when I got to her window and peeked inside, I was tongue-tied.

Which doesn't happen to me.

And to be honest, there hasn't been another female I've wanted to get to know since Michelle. But the moment I saw Penelope, she was someone I wanted to know.

Even with her big sunglasses on, I could tell that she'd been crying. I felt the urge to fix it for her. Whatever it may be. The instant connection was inexplicable, and the best thing I can do is ignore it. I have enough going on with Nora, my parents, the inn, and my law practice. I sure as hell don't need to add another complication on top of all that.

Shaking my head to dislodge the thoughts of her, I descend the concrete steps. As I make my way toward my truck, I greet the other parents who are also dropping off their kids. A few residents stroll past, waving hello. I'll never understand how people *enjoy* walking in the cold.

Mr. and Mrs. Thompson pass, walking their yappy dog who pees in everyone's yard, and Fred, a single dad like me, runs his son down the street toward school. At least I know Nora isn't the only student late today and Principal McSweeney will have another poor soul to chastise.

"Late again," Fred says as he rushes past me. "How was McSweeney today?"

"Same as always, unfortunately," I tell him. "Good luck."

I can't lie to the man. He's in for it.

As I reach my truck, Penelope's head quickly snaps to where I stand. Tears dampen her cheeks again. She plasters on a fake smile as I open the door and get into the driver's seat.

"Sorry about that. The principal here is... a little strict."

"That's okay. Did I see the sign correctly, the town is called Winterberry?"

"You don't even know where you are?"

I mean, who the hell is this woman? I pull my truck onto the road and head in the direction of Ben's Auto Shop. We need to figure out what to do with her car.

"Nope. Never heard of it before."

"To be fair, most people haven't heard of this town until the holidays. When Christmas rolls around, the whole town gets a little nutty and people travel to see all the holiday madness."

"Has the town always been this decked out for Christmas?" She says through a laugh.

"Oh yeah. This is a Winterberry tradition." I roll my eyes.

"Do you not like Christmas?"

"Um, not really. Nora loves it, and so does my mom, but I'm not a fan."

"I don't think I've ever met someone who doesn't like Christmas," she says as she looks at me, in a very judging way.

"Well, I've never met someone who didn't know where they were," I say, scoffing. "Didn't you look at the map on your phone?"

"I don't have a phone with me," she says with sass, crossing her arms.

"It's 2023, who doesn't have a phone on them?"

"Me."

"I don't even know what to say to that," I say. "Where do you live?"

"In the city."

"This is a riveting conversation. Reminds me of the answers I get from Nora when she gets home from school."

Out of nowhere, she lets out such a pure laugh that I find myself gripping the steering wheel tighter and glancing at her out of the corner of my eye. Does this woman have me under some kind of spell or something?

"Anyway, I'm taking you to Ben's Auto Shop so we can get that car of yours towed. Ben's great, you'll like him. Hopefully, he can figure out what happened and then you can be on your way back to the city and to your phone."

When the words are out of my mouth, she shivers and stares out the window, a million miles away.

The drive to the shop is pretty short and for the rest of the ride, we sit in silence. I keep stealing glances at her out of the corner of my eye but neither of us says anything, so I don't push it. I turn on the radio in my car, and Christmas music blares through the speakers. I flick through the stations to discover Christmas music infiltrating every channel. I punch the power button on my dashboard with a heavy sigh, and the car is once again filled with silence.

After a few minutes, we pull up outside of the auto shop. I put the truck in park and turn off the engine.

"We're here," I say as I unbuckle my seatbelt. "Let's see what he says."

She scrambles to keep up as we exit the truck, and I can't help but notice that her breathing has grown ragged, and she keeps looking back. My instincts kick in and I put my hand on her lower back and guide her into the shop. Heat transfers from her body to my hand, making me sweat. I hope she doesn't notice.

When I remove my hand to step aside and open the door for her, she shifts her sunglasses to the top of her head, and we lock eyes.

"Thank you," she whispers, holding my gaze.

The bell above the door jingles as it closes, breaking the spell.

"Brent, I thought that looked like you," Ben says from behind the counter. He sets his newspaper down and shifts his attention to us.

An older man with gray hair, a small mustache, and suspenders, Ben has lived in Winterberry since before I was born. He's a regular at Sally's Diner and enjoys his breakfast and paper every morning with the other old guys.

Tinsel hangs from the ceiling and a large tree sits in the corner, adorned with ornaments that represent the shop—tires, cars, trucks, and tools. An old school train rides on a track high above our heads and it's decorated for the season. Honestly, it's a sight to see, and surely his wife's doing.

"Hey Ben, the shop is all ready for Christmas I see."

"Like it, Mr. Scrooge?" he asks with the ghost of a smile on his lips.

"Very funny." I gesture toward the meek woman beside me. "Ben, meet Penelope. She needs help with her car."

"Ah, so you're the one who backed up Main Street. Nice to meet you, Penelope."

"Nice to meet you, too." She shakes Ben's hand. "How did you know about my car?"

"It's a small town, love, word travels fast," he says.

"Penelope here is from the city and would like to get home. Do you think you could take a look at her car?"

"Absolutely," Ben says. "It's quiet in here this morning so let's get the tow truck out and see what's going on."

"You're the best mechanic in this town, thanks for taking the time to help."

"I'm the only mechanic and it's my pleasure. How about I follow Brent's truck and we can bring your car back here, Miss Penelope."

"That's perfect," Penelope says. "Brent, is that okay with you? Or do you have somewhere you need to be?"

"Nope, good with me. I'll give my parents a call and let them know I won't be at the inn until later."

"I'll meet you two out front," Ben calls as he makes his way behind the counter and to the back of the shop. "Tell your folks I say hi!"

"You got it. And thanks again, Ben." We head to the front door and back out into the cold.

"Do you live with your parents?" Penelope asks me and I detect a small hint of curiosity mixed with judgment in her tone.

"Nora and I live on the grounds. I help them at their bed and breakfast. Is that a problem?"

"Oh not at all, I wasn't judging you," she says as her cheeks turn pink.

"Uh-huh. Let's go mystery woman."

When we reach my truck, I open the door for her. After she hops in, I round to my side and get behind the wheel. Ben's tow truck comes around the corner, and I start my truck, and he follows me to Main Street. The town is getting ready for the kick-off to the Christmas season and the first onslaught of visitors to our sleepy little town with the Winter Festival.

Soon, large, carnival-like booths will be set up along the perimeter of the gazebo and the walking paths through the grass will be filled with decorations, games, and so many people. Nora has been asking me for weeks now if we can go to the festival. Of course I'm going to take her.

I'll have to plaster on a fake smile to get through it, but I'll be there.

It's in a few days and I wonder if Penelope will still be here.

I shouldn't even care.

"What are they setting up?" Penelope asks, pulling me from my thoughts.

"My biggest nightmare," I say. She giggles, which makes me smile. "Winter Festival, the first event of the season. There are events from now until Christmas here and we get tons of visitors. It's awful."

"Sounds magical," she says with a wistful tone. Silence descends on the car, so I glance at her and catch her staring at me.

I feel like this is the first time she's really looked at me since I walked up to her car window, and I'm wondering what she sees. Insecurity creeps up like an old enemy. We reach her fancy car and thankfully, traffic is flowing. There isn't another jam awaiting us.

As soon as I park, we both get out and can hear Ben letting out a long, high-pitched whistle through his teeth as he slowly runs his hand over the hood. After a few minutes of admiring the luxury vehicle—something we definitely don't see often in Winterberry— he grabs his diagnostic tool from his truck and connects it to the Porsche.

"Well, I have good news and bad news," he says to Penelope after a few minutes of running the device. "Which one do you want first?"

She taps her chin, contemplating. "Give me the bad news first."

"Unfortunately, it's the transmission and I'm not sure if I have the parts it needs in my shop. Good news is you'll get to hang out in Winterberry for a little bit." He smiles, eyes twinkling.

Penelope turns around, glancing at me before responding. I exhale a long stream of air. She can't stay here.

"Well, that does present a problem. When do you think you will be able to have it ready to drive?" Penelope asks.

"Let me take it in, get a better idea of where I can get the parts from, and I'll give you a call to let you know what I'm thinking."

"There's only one problem with that plan. I don't have a cell phone on me. I left it in Manhattan."

"Well, I have to be honest with you, that's a new one. I haven't met someone your age in years who doesn't have those little devices attached to their hands."

"You can call my cell, Ben," I interject. "I'll take Penelope over to the diner for some food and I'll keep my cell on me. Give me a call when you know more, and we will sort out the details."

"That works for me," Ben says as he starts to walk away. "Oh, Penelope, get the chocolate chip pancakes from the diner, they're to die for!"

"Thanks for the suggestion, Ben, and for helping me with the car," she calls after him before heading back to my truck.

"Well, looks like you're stuck with me for the day," she says as we get ready to pull away from the curb.

Her personality is starting to come out little by little, and I want to see more.

"I guess it could be worse."

"Oh, wait a minute, does Mr. Grumpy Pants have a sense of humor now?"

"Did you just call me Mr. Grumpy Pants?"

"I sure did," Penelope says, nodding defiantly.

"You know, I think I liked you more when you were shy," I say. "Let's go get some food. I have a feeling you and Sally are going to hit it off."

We make the short drive to the diner, park in front, and go inside to order some of Sally's delicious food. As soon as Sally sees me, a big smile appears on her face. Her eyes dart to Penelope, who's at my side. Oh boy, here we go.

She's also single like I am, and half the town has been trying to set us up since I moved back. But I think she has her eyes set on Dominick, my best friend from high school who recently moved back to town. She hasn't told me that personally, but the way she looks at him says it all.

I haven't had a serious girlfriend since Michelle. Sure, I've gone on dates and even had random hookups, but I've never brought a woman to my house, and I've felt no attachment.

Not for lack of trying on the entire town's part.

"Brent! I didn't know you were coming in today," Sally says. She leads us to a table. A Santa hat covers most of her blonde bob, and combined with the green apron, she looks like an elf. Her signature red glasses tie the look together. "Thanks, Sal. This is Penelope. Penelope, this is Sally. She owns the diner and is one of my best friends."

"So nice to meet you," Penelope says as she reaches out to shake Sally's hand. "This place is so cute and I *love* your outfit."

"Oh honey, I'm a hugger," Sally says as she pulls Penelope in for a bear hug. "So, you're the one whose car broke down on Main Street. Glad to see you're okay and in good hands."

"Wow, news travels fast here doesn't it." Penelope laughs.

"That's small-town life for you. Come sit over here and I'll get your menus."

She takes us to my favorite booth. I sit in my usual place and Penelope slides in across from me. This is the first time since meeting her that we're face to face and all her beauty is on display. Her full lips and brown eyes are mesmerizing, and I find myself staring. I give myself a few seconds before snapping out of my daze.

Sally sets down menus, winking before leaving.

I grit my teeth. Can't a man take a beautiful woman for food without it being a thing?

"So, what's your favorite thing to eat here?" Penelope asks me.

"I'm partial to the chocolate chip pancakes with a side of bacon and a black coffee. But to be honest, everything is good here. Sally has a great spot."

"Are you guys old friends?"

"Yep I've known her since middle school when we were both really awkward with braces and pimples. Luckily I grew out of that stage, her not so much," I say loud enough for Sally to hear.

Sally sticks her tongue out at me across the diner and I can't help but laugh.

"It must be so great to have people you've known for so long still in your life."

"It has its advantages and disadvantages, but Sally is like a little sister to me, and I'd do anything for her. So, what are you going to order?"

Sitting here, the anticipation of more time together grows. And that's not going to happen. As soon as her car is fixed, I'm sure she'll be on the road back to Manhattan. Based on her designer brands and luxury car, she's clearly used to a fancier lifestyle than Winterberry can offer.

I stare at her across the table, reminding myself she's only here temporarily. No use getting to know someone who's only going to leave.

Chapter Six

Penelope

After checking out the menu, I order the same thing Brent does—chocolate chip pancakes with whipped cream and a side of bacon. When Sally takes our menus away, I don't know what to do with my hands and I sit there awkwardly. I don't even remember the last time I sat with someone who wasn't a costar, bodyguard, or Drew.

I mess with the strings of my sweatshirt as my face grows clammy. I'm in the public spotlight daily, so why am I getting nervous sitting at this diner with a man?

Brent appears just as uncomfortable, so I take a chance and break the silence.

"Are you taking Nora to the Winter Festival?" I ask.

"Unfortunately, she's obsessed with Christmas, just like this town, and she wants to go to every single event, so I'll be taking her," he says gruffly.

"When does it start? If I'm still here, I'd love to go."

"It's a few days from now actually. If you aren't back in the city yet, you're more than welcome to tag along with us. My parents usually go, too."

"That'd be fun. What other events are there?"

"Oh so many," he says. He shakes his head and starts ticking things off on his fingers as he speaks. "The Christmas Tree Lighting, Christmas Log Parade, the Winter Festival, and finishing off the season with the Christmas Eve Ball."

"That sounds amazing," I say.

Christmas in Manhattan is different. Yes, there are lots of decorations and events, like the Rockefeller Center Christmas Tree Lighting Ceremony, but sometimes it feels so lonely. I'm usually working my ass off during the season. Deep down, I hope the parts don't come in for my car so I can go to the festival.

Sitting in silence, I avert my gaze away from Brent. The diner's floor is checkered, perfectly matching the black booths. There's a large chalkboard behind the counter, listing the day's specials alongside a countdown to Christmas. I smile at that.

Inside the bakery display beneath the register are classic treats like red velvet cupcakes, snickerdoodles, and cheesecake. Desserts that remind me of Christmas. My mouth waters. Red-and-white decorations fill the space, various holiday trinkets on every surface.

As an actress, I've had to be strict with my diet. If I gain even a few pounds, my agent is on top of me to lose them. It's exhausting. But while I'm here, I'm not an actress, and I want to taste something sweet.

My broken heart still aches, and dessert might help the healing process.

Sally stands behind the counter, smiling as she takes orders. Every so often she'll help her waitresses serve meals. She's clearly comfortable in her element. Jealousy trickles through me. What must it be like to be so at ease and in your element?

The diner is so warm and inviting it's hard to believe it's freezing outside.

I glance at Brent. His eyes stare out into the diner and his chin rests on his steepled hands as he waits for our meals to arrive. Luckily, a few seconds later, Sally arrives with our food, breaking up some of the tension.

"Here you go, you two," Sally says. "Sorry it took so long, it's still the morning rush in here."

As soon as she places the plates on the table, I want to dig right in. Pancakes are definitely *not* on my approved food list. I haven't tasted one in a few years. I can't help myself and practically stab the pancakes with my fork as Sally pulls her hand away.

" Sowwy... haven't ha...pancake... in years," I struggle to say through a mouthful.

Brent and Sally look at each other and burst out laughing. Blushing, I quickly chew what's in my mouth and swallow. I've basically spent the entire day embarrassing myself.

"Wait, you haven't had a pancake in years?" Brent asks with a curious look on his face. "That should be illegal. Are you allergic to them or some shit?"

"No, I just always kept myself on a strict diet." It's not a full lie, and I'm not even sure why I say it, but it's out there before I can stop it. Honestly, the people of Winterberry probably won't even care if they know who I really am, but I'm so used to standing out, it feels nice to fit into the crowd.

"Well, that's ridiculous. Eat the pancakes."

"Aye aye sir," I say, saluting him.

"I hope you enjoy, Penelope," Sally says. "Okay, if you need anything just holler. Not for real though, Brent, that wasn't funny when you did that."

She heads toward the counter, but after a few steps she pauses. She turns, scrutinizing me, and I fear she recognizes me.

Shit.

"This might sound weird but, do I know you from somewhere?" she asks. "You look so familiar to me, but I can't place it."

"I don't think so. I've never been to Winterberry before. Maybe I just have one of those faces." Please, please, please, let her buy that.

"You're probably right. Enjoy!"

With that, Brent and I enjoy our delicious breakfast. Every few minutes someone new stops by our table to greet Brent and introduce themselves.

They ask how his parents are, how Nora is doing in school, how the law firm is going, and other personal things about his life. They genuinely care about what's happening in Brent's life. Many are curious about who I am and greet me cheerily. Brent introduces me and explains that my car is being fixed, and that he's keeping me busy until it's ready. Without fail, every person remarks that it's so nice to put a face to the woman they've heard so much about from the Main Street incident.

"Small town living." Brent shakes his head after the fifteenth person leaves the table. "It's the most exciting thing to happen in a while."

"Have you known all of these people since you were little?"

"Not everyone, but mostly, yep. Lots of people are born in Winterberry and never leave. Or, like me, leave but find their way back. I'm not sure what it is about this town, but it's like an ex that you just can't shake."

I laugh at his analogy. "We've all been there."

What he doesn't know is that I'm there right now. Yes, Drew cheated on me, and our relationship is over, but there's this small piece of me that wonders if it was taken out of context? Maybe the paparazzi contrived the photo to look like something it wasn't.

It's hard to let go of a relationship that I thought was my forever. But, since I have no phone and I can't contact him, I guess it's time to move on.

I would love to call Georgia and ask her opinion, but like most people in their late 20's, I don't have her number memorized.

I hope I didn't make a mistake coming here.

Brent and I continue eating and fielding guests at our table until every single delectable morsel is devoured. I'm tempted to lick the plate clean but think better of it. I've embarrassed myself enough for one day.

"You look like you're deep in thought over there," Brent says, frowning.

"Oh. Not at all. I was just contemplating how embarrassing it would be if I literally licked the plate clean and decided it wasn't worth the humiliation." I somehow manage to keep a straight face.

"Now *that* I would pay to see."

"Listen, don't tempt me. I've done worse and those pancakes were so good. I don't think I'll be going years between pancake inhaling again."

As soon as the statement is out of my mouth, his brows fly up and his eyes lock with mine. What am I even saying?

He stares at me for a beat before saying, "Good. No number on the scale is worth skipping the deliciousness of Sally's pancakes."

"You know, I may not have agreed with a lot you've said today, but *that* I totally am on board with. Pancakes for lunch will definitely be in my new rotation."

A small smile spreads across his lips and I find myself smiling right along with him.

"I'll get the check now. Feel like taking a little tour of Winterberry before I have to pick Nora up from school?"

"That sounds great!" I say a little too enthusiastically. "Let me know how much I owe you for lunch."

"That's okay, I've got this. Want to meet me at the truck?"

"Why thank you, kind sir," I say. "See you in a few."

After saying goodbye to Sally and thanking her for the magical pancakes, I wait at the truck for Brent. I can't even lie, I can't wait to see more of the town and take in all the Christmas spirit. In fact, I haven't been this excited in months.

When Brent makes his way to his truck, my heart starts beating faster. My breath catches in my throat.

I don't think I've ever felt this way with Drew. I never felt out of breath or flustered around him. Yes, I was attracted to him and loved him, but it was nothing like this.

"Earth to Penelope!" Brent says as he opens the passenger door for me. The annoyance on his face almost makes me laugh. How long was I lost in my thoughts?

"Sorry, I was a mile away there. Let's do this tour!"

Climbing into the old truck, I settle in my seat, and we begin driving down Main Street. I'm surprised when he leaves the Christmas music on this time. We drive past the town bookstore, the corner market, an antique shop, a music store, the gazebo, and an adorable bakery with a black-and-white awning above the door. The sidewalk is full of people carrying bags, walking with friends, and saying hi to each other as they pass.

"This is my law firm where I work when I have big cases that need my focus," Brent says as we pass a stout, red brick building with a huge sign out front that reads Harrison Law. "I fell in love with the old-time vibe the office has when I first saw it."

I frown when I notice his firm's windows sitting empty, without any stickers, lights, or tinsel like the neighboring shops.

"Why do you have the only windows in this entire town not decorated for Christmas?" I ask.

"Nora makes me decorate every inch of our house, but here I can get away with no Christmas cheer thankfully," he says stubbornly.

I sneak a peek at him and notice that his knuckles are practically white from gripping the steering wheel. His jaw is tight, and I decide not to push the matter any further. "How often do you work in the office?"

"It depends on what kind of case I'm working on. I try to work from home as often as I can and help Mom and Dad with whatever they need at the inn. What about you? Where do you work in the city?"

I hesitate while I decide if I should tell him the truth. I don't know him at all, and yes he's been so kind and patient while I take up most of his day, but I have a habit of not opening up easily. This is no exception.

"I do freelance work," I say vaguely. "I get to travel a lot, so I'm lucky."

He quickly looks over at me before turning his head back to the road. "That sounds interesting. Were you on your way somewhere for work when you broke down?"

Oh God.

I try not to fidget under his gaze. "Yeah, that's a long story I don't think we have the time for."

"I'm assuming your phone is also a long story?" he asks with a small smirk that disappears much too quickly.

"You'd be right about that."

"Fair enough," he says, sounding resigned.

He checks his watch, continuing down the road and it hits me that we have been driving around the town for hours now. I've been enjoying this ride so much, I completely lost track of time.

"Time to get the rugrat from school. Let's call Ben and see what's going on with your car. Hopefully you can be on your way back home to that long story."

He hits the buttons on the dashboard and Ben's gravelly voice fills the truck before the phone can even ring.

"I wish I had good news for you Brent," Ben says. "Is Penelope with you?"

"She's here in the truck, Ben. I have you on speaker."

"Hi Ben," I chime in. "Lay it on me, I can take it."

"I'm sorry to tell you this but your transmission is completely shot and definitely needs to be rebuilt. I don't have the parts I need in the shop so I'm going to have to order them which could be a few days. Do you have anywhere you can stay while you wait?"

Silence fills the truck as my palms start to sweat. This was a mistake, and it just keeps getting worse.

"She can stay at the inn," Brent says, cutting through the awkward silence. "I'm sure Mom and Dad will have a room available for her. How long do you think it will take?"

Brent doesn't glance my way once.

"At least a few days. There's a snowstorm rolling in and I'm being told it's going to hold up deliveries. I'll do whatever I can to have the car fixed soon for you, Penelope. I'm sorry about this."

"Not your fault at all. Thank you for all you're doing, Ben, I really appreciate it," I whisper.

I feel like I'm intruding on Brent's life and I'm not sure what to say. He doesn't even know my real name and I'm going to stay at his parent's inn? I feel so guilty. But I still don't feel comfortable enough to open up.

"I'll keep you updated," Ben says. "Brent, can I call you or the inn to reach Penelope?"

Damn it, for the millionth time today I wish I hadn't left my phone in the penthouse. What an idiot.

"You can call either," Brent tells him. "Don't worry, Ben, she'll be fine. Talk to you soon I hope."

He hangs up and we silently pull up in front of the school. Honestly, I should be freaking out right now but a big part of me is excited at the opportunity to stay in this little town for another few days. When was the last time I enjoyed the Christmas season surrounded by kind people?

"Be right back. I'll grab Nora and then we can head to the inn," Brent says as he leaves the truck. Walking up to the front of the building and standing with all the other parents, Brent waves at his daughter. Nora's face lights up when her eyes find her dad, and she jumps into his arms. He sets her down, ruffling her hair, and they head back to the truck.

I scoot to the center of the seat so Nora can get in the passenger side. Brent climbs in the driver's seat, and the heat radiating off his thigh makes me shiver. We're so close I can hear him breathing. I flush.

On the drive to the inn, I sneak a peek at him and catch him looking back at me. I'm completely tongue-tied and attracted to this semi-stranger. His daughter is also beside me, chatting away about taking me to the Winter Festival.

The way Brent is with Nora fills me with such warmth I consider trusting him. A man who treats his daughter the way he does must be a good man.

Before I know it, we pull up to a charming inn and I suck in a breath. Fir trees with lights and ornaments line the driveway. Garland decorates the wraparound porch, from one end to the other, and each window hosts a candle.

It looks like something out of a movie, and I find myself staring.

"Home sweet home," Brent says, cutting through my thoughts. "Welcome to the Butterfly Inn. I'll grab your extremely heavy bags and we then can go in to meet my parents," he says with a teasing tone.

Nora exits the truck and darts to the front porch, calling for her grandparents. I slide out, pausing to take in the scenery. Just as I'm about to take a step, a small snowflake lands on my cheek and I can't help but smile.

Chapter Seven

Brent

"You've got to be kidding me," I mutter as snow begins to fall. I hate snow. This is the third time it's snowed this year, and it's only the first week in December.

As I round the truck, I immediately stop in my tracks when I see Penelope frozen there with the biggest smile plastered on her face. She faces the sky as the snow falls, collecting on her eyelashes. It's a beautiful scene. Another snow lover at the inn.

"Oh my god, I'm so embarrassed," she says with red cheeks when she notices me standing there. "I haven't seen snow in forever."

"Does it not snow in Manhattan?" I tease.

"It does, but since I travel a lot for work, I'm not usually there for the holidays. In fact, I haven't even had a tree in my apartment the past two Christmases," she says sheepishly.

"What do you usually do on Christmas Day then?"

"Sometimes I go out to dinner, or I'll sleep in and get takeout."

"That's so different from the chaotic Christmas I have here. Do you spend it with your family?"

"I don't have any family," she says quietly, and I feel bad for asking. "It's just me so I don't do much. It winds up just being a normal day of the week for me and then back to work on the 26th."

"I'm sorry to hear that." And I mean it. "No one should be alone on Christmas."

"It's fine, I'm used to it," she mumbles as she turns her face back to the sky.

I have the urge to ask her more questions, but I don't want to come across as pushy.

"I realize you're enjoying this terrible snow, but why don't we go inside and meet the family where there's heat and hot coffee."

"Don't tell me you don't like the snow? Geez, first Christmas, now snow. What *do* you like?"

"Eh there are a few things I like but that conversation is better for a different day," I tell her as her cheeks redden again. I realize I'm probably wasting my time, but I still find myself flirting with her. Yes, she's way out of my league and will be on her way back to her life in the city as soon as her car is ready, but I can't help it.

"Shall we?" I gesture for her to walk up to the inn. I hope she's ready for the holiday craziness that waits to greet her.

Christmas music rings out as we approach the front door. The bells chime as I push it open.

Here we go.

Penelope follows me in, and I gesture for her to go ahead of me. In the foyer, she pauses, taking in the Christmas spectacle before us. Her eyes dart from one end of the space to the other. It's a lot to take in.

"Hey Mom, are you here?" I call as we round the corner into the kitchen.

"Hi honey," she says as she turns down the Christmas tunes. She stands in front of the oven with her favorite elf apron on. It jingles when she walks. My heart swells at the sight of her. I'm a proud Mama's boy.

"Mom, meet Penelope. Penelope, meet Mom," I say. I give my mom a kiss on the cheek, then ruffle Nora's hair—which I know pisses her off.

"Hi Penelope, you can call me Suzanne. It's so nice to meet you! Are you hungry? I just made some scones."

"It's so nice to meet you, too, I've heard so much about you," Penelope says. "They smell amazing, but I'm still stuffed from the pancakes at the diner but thank you."

"Where's Dad?" I ask Mom. He can usually be found in his reading chair by the window or out in the woodshed.

"He's outside in the shed."

"I'll introduce them when he comes in. Did you see it started snowing?"

"Nora told me, how exciting! Just in time for the festival. Will you still be here to come with us, Penelope?" I roll my eyes and Mom playfully smacks me on the arm.

"Mom, she's leaving when her car is fixed," I say quickly so Penelope doesn't feel obligated to respond.

"To be honest, between you and me, I'm hoping it isn't ready yet so I can stay. I've never been to a small-town festival before," she says, surprising me. I look at her with wide eyes and she giggles at my reaction.

"Well, you are more than welcome to stay as long as you'd like," my mom says. "I have a room for you to stay in. Where is your luggage?"

"I put them at the front door," I say.

"That was nice of you to carry them inside," she says as she winks. I know that look and it means she's up to no good. "Did Brent tell you about the festival?"

"Only that it was hell," Penelope says. She glances at me, stifling a laugh with her palm.

"Of course he would say that. Don't listen to my grumpy son, he gets it from his father," Mom mutters.

"I heard that, Mom."

"I don't know what you're talking about honey," she says before turning back to Penelope. "It's the first event of the season and everyone will be there. There's so much to do, you'll love it."

Penelope's eyes light up at my mom's words, and I have a feeling she's going to be just as enamored with the festival as everyone else in town. Nora turns from where she's sitting on a stool at the large island in the middle of the kitchen, and her words spill out a million miles a minute, telling Penelope what she can expect.

Nora begins ticking things off on her fingers. "Hot cocoa. Games. Reindeer—"

"As you can tell, there's lots to do," I say. My kid could go on for hours about Christmas and her favorite is the festival.

"Dad, I wasn't done. Don't you know it's not nice to interrupt someone?" She grumbles as she takes her attitude into the other room.

"Brent, honey, why don't you take Penelope upstairs and let her get settled in. The Monarch Room isn't booked, so she can stay in there. Don't feel like you have to come down for dinner, Penelope. Just get comfortable."

Is this the same mom I've had all my life? Don't come downstairs for dinner? I must be dreaming. The woman still makes me come in from my house some nights to eat with them.

"I'll show you to your room. This way," I say to Penelope.

She follows me down the hall, passing the expansive dining room, and I stop at the front desk to grab the key to her room. I hand her the key before grabbing her luggage and making our way to the dark wooden staircase that leads to the rooms. I put my hand on her lower back as we ascend the stairs, and it feels so natural.

"Your room is right down the hall. It's one of my mom's favorite rooms, so I'm not surprised she told you to stay in there. She usually keeps it open for family or anyone who is visiting," I ramble as I show her to the room.

We stop outside the Monarch Room and her eyes widen as she takes in all the Christmas madness around her. On the door to the room is a huge wreath filled with lights, butterflies, and a huge bow.

"Your mom really knows how to do Christmas, doesn't she?" Penelope puts the key with the huge butterfly on it into the door.

"Oh just you wait."

She opens the door and sucks in a breath at what she sees inside. There isn't an inch of this room that isn't decorated, just as in every room at the inn. From the red-and-green quilt and lights around the ceiling to the literal Christmas tree in the corner, and garland on every surface, Mom puts her heart and soul into the holiday at the inn. It doesn't go unnoticed.

"This is incredible, I can't believe I get to stay here," Penelope says. "I'm used to five-star hotels and let me tell you, nothing has come close to the way this place feels."

She turns around in front of the four-poster bed and her face looks like Nora's on Christmas morning—when she first sees the pile of gifts under the tree.

It's the face of pure joy.

I stride to the window and throw open the curtains. Then, I make sure the bathroom is stocked with toilet paper and towels for her. When I re-enter the room, Penelope has taken the sunglasses off her head. Pieces of her brown hair fall haphazardly into her face. Before I can stop myself, I cross the length of the room and stop in front of her. I reach up and move a strand of hair out of her eyes, tucking it behind her ear as we lock eyes.

Her chest rises and falls rapidly while my hand remains frozen at her ear. The tension in the room is palpable, and the way her breath hitches in her throat tells me she feels it too.

Unable to break eye contact, we stand there as the seconds tick by. She shifts her weight and that small movement brings me back to reality. She could have someone waiting for her in the city for all I know.

I yank my hand away like it's on fire and take a step back.

"Penelope, I'm so sorry. I shouldn't have done that," I say too quickly.

"Why are you apologizing? It's not like I stopped you."

She stares at me with those gorgeous eyes as confusion crosses her face, and it feels like all of the air has been sucked out of the room.

Clearing my throat, I try to speak again.

"Anyway, there's a phone downstairs in the kitchen if you want to call anyone to let them know you're safe and sound. I'll be in my house if you need anything, and my parents are just downstairs. Their bedroom is just off the formal living room. I'll grab your bags really quick before I go home."

Now it's her turn to take an abrupt step back.

"Okay great thanks Brent. I really appreciate it." She folds her arms in front of her. "What time do you guys usually have dinner?"

"Usually around 5:00 p.m. Mom and Dad go to bed early most nights."

"Great. Maybe I'll see you down there," she says too quickly before turning toward the bed and going through her purse. Looks like this conversation is over.

I leave the room without saying or doing anything else I'll regret. Closing the door behind me, I stop in the hallway. Balling my fists at my sides, I rest the back of my head against the wall.

It's been a long day and I'm starting to feel the weight of the Christmas season upon us. That coupled with the day spent with Penelope and the snow that won't stop falling has me all out of sorts.

Taking a deep breath, I push off the wall and make my way downstairs, my mind spinning. I just need to make it through the next couple days, and then Penelope will head back to her life and I can forget all about her.

Forget about the way her eyes look at me... the way her floral perfume smells...

At least, that's what I am telling myself.

Chapter Eight

Penelope

What just happened?

Standing with my ear to the door, I listen to Brent's footsteps as he pads down the hall and out of earshot. I exhale heavily.

My pulse pounds in my temples. I lick my lips, trying to moisten them. Less than five minutes ago, Brent looked like he wanted to bend down and kiss me. And if I'm being honest with myself, I would've let him.

Of course, I was attracted to Drew, or I wouldn't have said yes to marrying him, but, did he ever make my pulse quicken or my lips go dry just by moving hair out of my eyes? Nope.

Coming out of my thoughts, I step further into the room and am still in awe. This isn't The Plaza or The Ritz, and I can't believe I am saying this, but I like it even better here. The coziness of the room floods the space, and it feels like home.

There are no fluffy white robes or room service but there's beautiful Christmas decor, a small wood fireplace against the wall, snow falling outside and a sense of peace.

No Instagram notifications, interviews to do, or phone calls to make.

Sometimes, I find myself so caught up in my life and the appointments on my calendar that I forget to breathe and take a look around me.

And it isn't until this moment that I realize I haven't been at peace in more years than I can count.

The slam of a car door pulls me out of my thoughts and into the present. Back to a world where Drew has cheated on me and I'm in a small town in Vermont, hiding out and pretending to be someone I'm not.

And out of nowhere, it's like the dam breaks.

The tears begin to slide down my cheeks. I can't hold them back any longer, so I let them out. Picturing the tabloid again in my head brings a fresh wave of pain.

After a few minutes, I'm able to gather myself enough to grab my Louis Vuitton bags, hoisting them onto the bed so I can find my silk pajama set. I'll change into them after I take a much-needed shower.

I can't believe it's only been a few days since I saw that tabloid with Drew's picture on the front. I feel like I am in some alternate universe.

Unzipping the suitcase, I reach to the bottom and freeze before pulling out my pajamas. Maybe I *will* go down to dinner before I get ready for bed. I may not be hungry, but I'll be ravenous in the morning if I don't eat now.

Feeling nervous, I wipe my hands on my pants and take one more look at myself in the mirror and open my door. The smell of pasta and garlic bread immediately fills my nose and my mouth starts salivating.

I make my way down the steps and stop when I hear chatter and laughter filtering out of the dining room. A longing spreads through my chest at the sound of family, and I slowly descend the rest of the steps.

Each step creaks under my weight, and I swear everyone can hear the beat of my heart.

As soon as I round the corner, I spot Nora's gorgeous curls and the back of Brent's head. The long oak table spans the length of the room and is big enough for guests to also sit and eat. In the center of the table is a huge centerpiece with sprigs of holly and cinnamon pinecones.

Tonight, it looks like I'm not the only guest joining, as I count four other people already eating.

The conversation stops and every head swivels as I enter the room. Under the weight of Brent's stare, I feel exposed, worried that at any second someone will realize who I am, and the paparazzi will appear. It's what always happens.

"Penelope! You came!" Nora jumps up from her chair, racing over to me.

"I'm sorry, am I late for dinner?" My cheeks grow warm.

"Not at all." Suzanne smiles, getting up from the table and heading to the kitchen as Nora grabs my hand and leads me to the table.

"Here, you can sit next to me. Right, Dad?"

"Right," Brent says without breaking our eye contact. I take the seat next to Nora and try not to glance across the table where Brent is sitting.

Suzanne comes back into the room with a plate full of food, setting it in front of me with silverware and a glass.

"I hope you like pasta and garlic bread." She smiles.

"Oh, I do."

Taking my first bite, I let out a contented sigh. When was the last time I had a bite of pasta? Probably around the same time I had pancakes.

"That good, huh?" Brent eyes me from his seat, a small smirk playing across his mouth.

Instantly, my cheeks grow hot and a sweat forms on my upper lip. On a normal day, I walk red carpets at award shows, have conversations with high-powered celebrities, and have fake stories shared about me in tabloids.

But here? I feel like a completely different person. I'm fumbling over my words and getting embarrassed way too easily. Pushing my thoughts aside,

I use the skills I learned in my improv classes, faking confidence I don't currently possess, and stare back at Brent.

"*So* good." Take that.

"I'm so glad you like it. How do you like your room?" At Suzanne's voice, I tear my gaze away from Brent.

"It's beautiful! I love it. Thank you for letting me stay here. Hopefully Ben has my car ready soon, so I don't impose for too long." I already feel bad for taking up a room at the inn. I'm paying for it, but still.

"You can stay as long as you want." She winks before turning to talk to the other guests.

For the rest of dinner, the conversation flows. I comment here and there, but for the most part, I simply enjoy the warmth that fills the room. It has nothing to do with the food or the crackling fireplace in the other room, it's the cozy feeling of sitting down, with no phones or TV on, enjoying each other's company.

I find myself sneaking peeks of Brent across the table, noticing the way his seemingly permanent scowl lifts whenever he's talking to Nora.

Time seems to pass faster than usual, and before I know it, plates are being cleared and the other guests are headed to their rooms for the night. I take my dishes to the kitchen then head back to the dining room to say goodnight.

"Suzanne, do you need help doing the dishes?"

"That's so sweet of you but you're a guest here and you've had a long day. I hope you sleep well."

"Thank you and thank you for dinner, it was delicious."

As Brent collects their dishes and heads for the kitchen, he tells Nora to get her shoes on. I turn to the little girl. "Goodnight Nora, maybe I'll see you tomorrow?"

"You betcha!" She bounces on her feet before walking over and hugging my middle. Totally caught off guard by her affection, I pause for a beat before hugging her back. She stares up at me with her big eyes.

My skin prickles ever so slightly as I realize that Brent has come back from the kitchen. He's standing there, almost frozen in place, and his eyes are fixed on me and Nora. I can see the wheels turning in his brain, but he stays silent.

"Goodnight," Nora says as we pull apart. I give her a little wave as she runs to the door.

"I'll call Ben in the morning and see if he has any news." Brent eyes me. "Night."

He turns on his heel to follow his little girl. I watch them for a second. He tenderly helps her with her boots, puts her jacket over her shoulders, and ushers her out the door, stopping to kiss his mom on the cheek.

Before he pulls the door fully closed, our eyes meet. Heat surges through me but then he's gone.

Making my way up the steps, I have a little bounce in my step after such a comforting night. When I reach my room, I grab a pair of fuzzy socks and slippers from my suitcase.

I also open the smaller bag I packed and get all of my skin care products out. I need to shower this day off. I may be in a tiny town, but I still need to keep up with my skin regimen. Who knows what kind of water they have here.

With my arms full of products, I leave the pajamas on the bed and head to the bathroom. Turning on the light and the shower, I let the steam fill the bathroom before stepping into the water.

Letting the heat hit my body, I stand there for several minutes before grabbing my body wash and washing the past few days off my skin.

I stay in there awhile longer before begrudgingly turning off the water and getting a towel so I can dry off and head back into the bedroom to get comfy.

My eyelids are heavy, and the bed calls my name.

I secure the towel around my body before walking to the window. It's pitch-black outside, but with all of the lights filling the yard, I notice the snow steadily falling and the entire ground is covered in white. It's so beautiful that it takes everything in me to peel my gaze away from the sight so I can get dressed.

I take my time putting my pajamas on and getting ready for bed. Snagging the book I was reading before I left the city, I snuggle up under the covers.

It takes only a few minutes before my eyes grow tired and I'm fighting to keep them open. A few more pages in and I turn off the lamp, succumbing to sleep.

The last thought before I drift off is wondering what Brent is doing right now. Is he thinking of me, too?

Chapter Nine

Brent

I should have immediately left the inn to go to my house after that incredibly awkward moment with Penelope, but Nora wanted to have dinner with my parents, so we stayed for a little while. I could feel her enter the room before I heard her voice, and I was hyperaware of her all through dinner.

The entire time we were at the table, I forced myself not to stare at her. The stress of the day was on her face, apparent in her swollen eyes and blotchy skin, and I could tell she's holding the weight of the world on her shoulders.

But when she finally settled into her seat and relaxed, she fit right in. She might drive an expensive car and carry designer luggage, but at dinner? She was as down-to-earth as the rest of us.

And Nora loves her.

My little girl, the sweetest soul I know, sees something in Penelope.

Me and Nora trudge across the snowy yard, and she grabs snow every few feet. We enter our house, stomp off the snow, and get ready for our nighttime routine.

Michelle came up with the routine when Nora was little. It consists of a bath, pj's, hair brushing, teeth brushing, singing, and tucking Nora under the covers—snug as a mummy.

This time of the year, Nora always picks a Christmas song for us to sing. And although my voice is terrible and she makes fun of me, I sing with her every night without fail.

Tonight, since dinner was a little later due to the arrival of our newest guest, we skip the bath and go right to pj's and hair brushing.

Before long, we're singing "Rudolph the Red-Nosed Reindeer" and laughing at how awful we sound. Nora definitely got her singing voice from me, poor kid.

Once the song is over, it's mummy time and then sleep for my little rugrat. Sometimes, I still can't believe she's growing so quickly. When I look at her, I still see her at two years old.

"Okay, now that you look exactly like a mummy, time for you to sleep," I whisper as I kiss her forehead. "Have sweet dreams and I'll see you in the morning."

"Daddy?" she says when I'm almost out the door. "Do you think Penelope will be here for the festival?"

I don't say what I actually feel—that I hope she'll be. "I'm not sure honey. I bet she'll want to get home as soon as she can," I say instead. "We will see what happens. For now, go to sleep. I love you."

"Love you too, Daddy."

I leave her room and head into the kitchen, where I crack open a beer.

Today has been a day. I didn't know when I woke up this morning that I'd be meeting a beautiful woman who I can't stop thinking about. She's only steps away, at the inn. I may need something stronger than a beer to keep my thoughts off her, but this will do for now.

After a few minutes, I'm restless and unable to sit still so I grab my flannel jacket and head out into the cold. Snowflakes continue to fall quietly around me, and as much as I hate it, it's undeniably peaceful when the town is bathed in white.

To be honest, I didn't always loathe this time of year. In fact, when Michelle was alive, snowy nights were my favorite. We would bundle up on the couch with blankets, hot cocoa, a lit fire, and let the world outside fade away.

I haven't watched snow fall the same since I lost her. But tonight, the snow beckons to me.

Snowflakes melt in my hair and my breath escapes in white puffs. Closing my eyes, I can almost picture Michelle next to me, snow dotting her blonde curls and catching on her dark eyelashes.

Usually, these memories physically hurt. But tonight, I find peace in remembering what it was like when Michelle was here.

My mind is filled with the day's events, and I feel like my whole world has shifted on its axis. The thing is, I like my life the way it is. I've worked hard to make it as normal as possible for Nora, and anything that disrupts that? I'm not interested.

The Christmas lights glow through the inn's living room window. Almost all the other lights are out, which means Mom and Dad and the other guests are probably in bed, winding down for the night. Out of the corner of my eye, I notice that one light is still on in an upstairs room, and I quickly realize that it's the Monarch Room.

Where Penelope is staying.

I'm wondering what she's doing when I catch her figure in the window. She stops to look down at the yard below. As soon as I spot her, I quickly turn around and face my house, feeling like a kid who got caught doing something naughty. I highly doubt she can see me out here in the dark, but it still feels wrong to watch her through the window.

Adjusting my jacket, I head back inside and into the warmth. This has been the strangest day in a long time.

I chug the rest of my beer before crumpling the can and tossing it in the recycling bin. I take off my jacket, slip out of my boots, and turn off all the lights in the living room and kitchen. The morning is going to come way too fast, and Nora will kill me if we're late to school again.

Quietly making my way down the narrow hallway, I peek into Nora's room to make sure she's sleeping. When I confirm she's asleep, I head to my room and shut the door behind me.

My bones are still frozen, so I take a shower to warm up and calm my racing thoughts.

The instant attraction to Penelope twists my stomach into knots. It almost makes me feel like I'm cheating on Michelle.

I know that's ridiculous, and Michelle would want me to be happy, but in my heart, I can't help but feel guilty. She's the only woman I've ever been in love with. One-night stands or isolated dates are one thing, but with Penelope, it feels different.

I *want* to get closer to her.

And that scares me. I'm afraid that if I give in, if I get closer to her and keep spending time with her, I'll fall.

Or worse, Nora will.

And the only woman I ever intended to feel that way about—or have in Nora's life— was Michelle.

The next morning, I wake to Nora's face hovering over mine as she chastises me for sleeping through my alarm. We run around getting ready for school and somehow manage to make it out of the house without seeing anyone, particularly the newest guest at the inn.

After dropping Nora off at school—on time, thank you very much—I drive to Ben's shop to inquire about Penelope's car.

The bell above the door announces my arrival at the shop.

"Ben!" I call out. The shop just opened for the day, so I'm sure I'll find Ben in the back with his cup of coffee.

"Brent! Nice seeing you so early in the morning. What's up?" He rounds the counter, coffee mug in hand, just like I expected.

"I wanted to check on Penelope's car," I say as nonchalantly as possible. "She's probably itching to get back to the city, so I wanted to see if there was any update."

"Unfortunately not." He shakes his head. "With the snow, everything is backed up. The earliest I'll have the parts will be a few days from now. I hope you don't mind her staying at the inn."

"When you say a few days, do you mean... a few days?" I clear my throat. My mouth dries out.

"Yep at least four or five days. Don't worry, I'll keep you updated and will call when I find out more information."

"Okay... great. Thanks, Ben, I appreciate it." I let it sink in that she'll be here for a little while. "I'll let you get to work. Have a great day and I look forward to hearing an update when you have it."

"You got it. Will we see you at the Winter Festival tomorrow?"

"Oh, you know it. Nora wouldn't let me miss it if I tried."

With that, I make my way back out in the cold and drive to my office. Today was supposed to be my day to work from home, but I can't spend all day in my house knowing *she* is so close by.

This is going to be a long few days.

Chapter Ten

Penelope

The sun seeps through the curtains, waking me up. Stretching, I sit up and swing my legs over the side of the bed. I slide my feet into my slippers before crossing the room and opening the curtains.

I gasp at the sight.

The snow continued through the night, covering every surface in a thick white blanket. It's truly a winter wonderland.

I glance at Brent and Nora's house but notice his truck isn't in the driveway. Probably for the best.

Dying to get out into the snow, I quickly throw on skinny jeans, an ivory sweater, UGG boots, and grab a coat and scarf. Running a brush through my hair, I slap on some light makeup before rushing down the stairs like a kid seeing snow for the first time.

As soon as my feet hit the landing at the bottom of the stairs, the smell of brewed coffee overwhelms me. I follow the scent into the kitchen.

"Good morning Mrs. Harrison," I say as I locate Brent's Mom.

She's sitting at the table with the paper spread out in front of her. Next to her is Brent's dad, reading the paper with the same scowl on his face that Brent wears. "Penelope, so good to see you. How did you sleep last night?"

"I haven't slept that well in so long," I say honestly. "I feel so refreshed today."

"So nice to see you again, Mr. Harrison."

When he grumbles something in response, I can't help but laugh. He and Brent are so much alike.

"Please, call us Tom and Suzanne. We aren't formal around here," Suzanne says with a laugh.

"Sounds good. Thank you so much again for the room."

"Our pleasure! Would you like a cup of coffee?"

"Actually, as amazing as it smells, I can't wait to get out into the snow. It's been a really long time since I've seen snow this beautiful. Is Sally's Diner a close enough walk from here?"

"Oh honey, no. You could walk there but it would take you forever in this snow. You can borrow my car if you'd like. I have lots to do around here today and don't plan on going anywhere."

"I don't want to impose," I say. She has to be the sweetest woman I've ever met.

"Not at all. I just got new tires for the winter, so you'll be safe to drive in this. Keys are by the front door, with the S on the keychain. Keep it as long as you need it today!"

"Thank you so much Suzanne. I promise I'll drive carefully. Could you tell me how to get to the diner?"

After she gives me directions, I thank her, put my coat on, and grab the keys. As soon as I close the front door behind me, I take a deep breath and let the smell of fireplaces and the frigid air fill my nose. Carefully, I step down from the front porch onto the walkway that leads to the driveway.

Like a little kid, I can't help myself. I bend down and take a handful of snow, molding it into a ball, and throwing it across the yard. I feel like I've stepped into somewhere magical, and I am wrapped in the gorgeous white of the snow.

Despite the freezing temperature, I take my time walking across the yard before approaching the car, unlocking the door, and climbing behind the wheel. As soon as I turn the key in the ignition to turn it on, the sounds of Christmas music fill the car and I make my way down the driveway.

Pulling out into the road, I take it slow since it's been so long since I've driven in snow like this. I follow Suzanne's directions closely, and within a few minutes, Sally's Diner appears. I can almost smell those pancakes of hers as I enter through the front door.

The smell of grease and the clang of silverware greet me and I quickly spot Sally. I cross the length of the diner, quietly saying hi to the people I pass.

"Penelope! Hi!" Sally comes out from behind the counter to hug me as soon as she notices me there. I can't help but shift uncomfortably as I hug her back. I'm not used to this kind of affection from a new friend.

"I came back for those pancakes of yours," I say.

"Is your car not fixed yet?" She leans closer. "I was secretly hoping you would still be here today."

"To be honest, me too!" I laugh. "Ben is having a hard time getting the parts that my car needs and this snow has slowed it all down. Looks like I'll be here for the festival in a few days after all."

"Oh good! Are you going with Brent and his family?"

"I'm not sure. I haven't seen him today. He was gone before I left. I'll definitely be there though. I've never been to a Winter Festival before."

"Perfect! Come this way and I'll get you seated. Same thing as yesterday?"

"Yes please! Those pancakes are delicious."

Sally seats me at a table then brings me a cup of coffee. Without a phone, I'm not really sure what to do with myself while I wait for my food. I don't usually sit alone—someone from my security team is usually with me.

After a few minutes of feeling awkward as hell, familiar faces start stopping at my table to say hi and ask how I'm liking Winterberry. It seems like everyone here knows about my car troubles and wants to make me feel welcome.

Before I know it, Sally brings me her magical pancakes. I spend the next half hour eating and talking in between bites. And here I thought I was going to be sitting alone with no one to pass the time with.

Not in Winterberry.

"Want more coffee?" Sally asks when she sees that my cup is completely empty. "I'm so sorry I haven't had a chance to sit and chat, today has been so busy and one of my employees called out for the day, go figure."

"Oh no!"

I know what it's like to have a busy day waiting tables with no help. During my time as a waitress, I took every single shift I could to grow my savings account. And for some of those, I was alone.

It was a small restaurant, but every Friday night in the fall kids from the local high school would fill every single seat. I'd run around fulfilling orders. Sitting here now, watching Sally do the same, I'm transported back to that time.

"Do you need help?" I ask before thinking. It's been many years since I've waited, but it's probably like riding a bike. Muscle memory will take over and I'll be fine. At least, I hope so. I really like Sally and want to help her.

There's something about her that makes me feel like we'd be friends if I lived here. I don't know if she'd get along with Georgia, who's even more high-maintenance than me and wouldn't be caught dead waiting tables again, but I like her laid-back demeanor.

"Really? You would do that?"

"Of course! Only if you promise to be patient with me because it's been a long time since I've waited tables."

"You got it, sister. Once the breakfast and lunch rush are over I should be okay. Does that work?"

"Whatever you need!"

Grabbing my purse and coat from the booth, I put them behind the counter. Sally briefs me on the table numbers, gives me an apron and pad of paper to write down orders, and I get to work.

The next few hours pass in a blur, and I work until my feet ache. These boots are warm, but they don't have the proper support to be on my feet for hours.

Each time the door to the diner opens, I silently hope that it's Brent coming in to eat. But he never does.

When lunch is over, Sally finds me to let me know it'll be slow until closing.

"You saved me today, Penelope!" she says "I don't even know how I can thank you enough."

"I enjoyed myself! I got to meet so many people and everyone was so nice. This town is something else."

"You can say that again. Have time for a cup of coffee?"

"I do! I have to get the car back to the inn soon, but Suzanne said she'll be busy all day so no rush."

"Great! Don't you just love Suzanne?" she asks as she makes us coffee. "She's like a mother figure to so many people in this town."

I sit at the booth closest to the counter and wait for her to join me.

"She is so sweet. I love staying at the inn, it's the coziest place I've ever been."

"It's so beautiful there. That's why the Christmas Eve Ball is held there every year. There's no place better." She slides into the seat across from me. "So, tell me, what brought you to Winterberry?"

I blow on my coffee and take a sip to delay. "It's a long story but I'll give you the abbreviated version. I found out my fiancé was cheating on me, so

I decided to drive until I wanted to stop or ran out of gas. Little did I know, my car would break down. Now, here I am." I laugh because I realize just how crazy it is.

"Wow. I'm so sorry Penelope. Does your family know where you are?"

"Actually, I don't have any family. It's just me. And, believe it or not, I left my phone at home."

"No way," she says, shaking her head. "Well, I for one am glad you broke down here. And I think Brent feels the same way." Her grin turns mischievous.

"Um, I have to disagree with you there," I say. "That man has done nothing but scowl at me since he found me on Main Street."

"I wouldn't be so sure. I've known him for a long time, and since his late wife Michelle, I haven't seen him eye any other woman."

Wow, so Brent is a widower. I wanted to ask him earlier but didn't want to push my luck.

Now I know.

"If by *eye* you mean shoot daggers, then that I believe," I tease. The thought of Brent being attracted to me makes my pulse quicken in the best way possible. And I am in no place to meet a man.

I'm supposed to be nursing a heartbreak.

"Do you have to get back home soon for work?" she asks, expertly changing the subject.

"I, um, work freelance so my work is flexible luckily because I don't know when Ben will have my car ready." The lie rolls off my tongue faster than I'm proud of.

It's getting way too easy to keep this up.

"Oh good! Ben is the best, I'm sure he will have it ready as soon as he can. Until then, I'm happy you're here. We should do this again." She reaches across the table and covers my hand with hers.

For the next hour, we chat about anything and everything as we sip our coffee. I want more than anything to tell her who I am. What I really do for a living, but I can't. It would change everything, and right now, I'm content. After a while, our coffee turns cold, and we both look at the time.

"I should get the car back to the inn in case Suzanne needs it. Thank you for the coffee and the girl talk. Promise we'll do it again before I leave?"

"We better."

Standing, I give her a hug before heading for the door. During the short walk to the car, I'm greeted by people who wave and smile as they pass.

As soon as I climb into the car, Christmas tunes pump through the speakers. I find myself singing along, so I take my time getting back to the inn.

When I pull into the driveway thirty minutes later, I peer eagerly out the windshield and notice that Brent's truck still isn't in the driveway. My shoulders slump and my frown deepens. As soon as I step inside the inn, the smell of cinnamon hits my nose. I take a deep breath, letting it fill my nostrils.

"Hi Suzanne, here are the keys to your car!" I call as I stroll through the inn. "Thank you so much for letting me borrow it."

"Oh anytime! Did you get a chance to explore our little town while you were out?"

"I didn't unfortunately. Actually, I helped Sally out at the diner and waited tables for her. One of her employees called out and she was running around like a chicken with her head cut off. We sat and had coffee after, but my feet are still killing me."

"That is so nice of you! I bet she was grateful. Why don't you sit by the fire for a little and rest your feet?"

"I think I'll do just that."

Going upstairs to my room, I put my coat and purse down on the bed, peel off my boots, and grab the book I was reading last night. Heading back downstairs, I notice that the chair by the fire is unoccupied. It's the perfect reading spot, so I sit down, curl up, and spend the next two hours completely immersed in the story.

I read until dinnertime, then I help Suzanne and Tom set the table for dinner. The same few guests from last night join us, but there's no sign of Brent.

"Will Brent and Nora be joining us?" I ask as nonchalantly as I can.

"Actually, he texted me earlier that they wouldn't be coming over tonight. Something about a friend from school."

"Oh. Okay." I try to keep the disappointment out of my voice as I finish setting the table and sit down to eat with everyone.

If Suzanne notices the change in my demeanor, she doesn't let on. The conversation flows throughout the meal.

Afterward, I jump in and help Suzanne clean up. Side by side, we wash the dishes and clean the kitchen.

"Thank you for the help, Penelope." She pulls me in for a side hug before releasing me. "You know, I could get used to you here." She smiles. "Time for us to turn in. I'll see you tomorrow."

"Me too."

She makes her way out of the room. It scares me how much I could get used to this after only being here for one full day.

Back in my room, I take a shower and my thoughts spiral. Has anyone tried to contact me? How long can I hide out in Winterberry before I have to go back to my life in the city?

Is Brent avoiding me? Maybe he feels uncomfortable after that heated moment between us last night. The one I can't stop thinking about. It was only one innocent touch, but it's played on repeat in my mind.

I read to distract myself, finishing the book before drifting to sleep.

The next four days go by in the blink of an eye, and I spend them the same way— drinking coffee, helping Suzanne around the inn, walking in the snow, reading, and trying to keep myself from knocking on Brent's door and asking if he's avoiding me.

Sally and I have met for coffee two more times at the little coffeehouse near Nora's school. Our chats have become something I look forward to.

I love everything about this place, except for the one thing I can't get out of my mind... or I should say, the one person.

In fact, I've only seen him once since my first night in Winterberry, when he stopped by to help his dad shovel. He stayed outside, only coming in to get coffee, and barely looked my way. It's driving me insane, but I'm focusing on my excitement for the festival tonight.

I've heard so much about it, and since it's the start of the Christmas festivities here in Winterberry, I can't wait to see what it's all about. Ben has called the inn each day to let me know there's no update on my car. But there's also no snow in the forecast for the next few days, so he's confident I'll be on my way soon.

As much as I don't want to leave, I'm aware that filming for my next movie starts soon. It's not easy getting a starring role in a film, and one wrong move could blacklist me.

I'm going to have to get in touch with William, my agent, but not today. I've been trying to keep my mind busy today because the anticipation for tonight is threatening to spill over.

"Penelope, do you want to come with us to the festival?" Suzanne asks, pulling my attention from the book I'm devouring.

"Yes please! When do you want to leave?"

"How does half an hour sound?"

"Perfect. I'll go get ready."

Practically running upstairs, I get out my luggage and pick out an outfit. I decide to go for an off-the-shoulder cream sweater, skinny jeans, over the knee leather boots, and a cute headband. I haven't worn my normal makeup since I've been here, so I take my time applying a full face, complete with a perfect winged liner that I'm proud of.

If only Marco, my makeup artist, could see what I've created.

After staring at myself in the mirror, I head downstairs to meet Tom and Suzanne.

"You look gorgeous!" Suzanne says when she sees me.

My cheeks heat and I can't help the smile that stretches to my ears. "Thank you so much. I'm excited for this!"

It takes a few minutes to find parking at the festival, so we have a bit of a walk to get to the event gazebo. When I see the festival, it takes my breath away. The entire town has come out for food, games, Christmas decorations, music, shopping, and more.

I'm in heaven.

Making our way through the crowd, I stay close to Brent's parents as they stop every few seconds to say hi to people they know. Many of the residents I met during my short stint as waitress at Sally's Diner, or on my daily walks around town, but they introduce me to anyone I haven't met.

I'm a lot less on edge in the crowd than I'd normally be. Yes, the possibility that someone could recognize me is still at the front of my mind, but I'm starting to feel comfortable here. I'm no longer looking over my shoulder for a paparazzi hiding in the grass and...it feels good.

As we walk further onto the snow-covered park in the middle of town, I hear a voice that I immediately recognize. "Hey, we've been looking for you guys."

Nora comes running up and throwing herself at her grandparents, while Brent takes his time approaching us.

I want to ask him why he hasn't been to dinner at the inn, why he's been avoiding me, but I hold my tongue and decide to be civil instead. That should be easy, right?

Chapter Eleven

Brent

I notice her before she sees me, and my breath catches in my throat. She looks gorgeous with her makeup done and she's at ease with my parents. The complete opposite of when I first met her a few days ago. Her smile looks so genuine. She's laughing at something my mom said as they walk, with no hint of slumped shoulders or red-rimmed eyes like she had that first night.

I've done everything I can to avoid seeing her, even missing dinners with my mom and dad, and working at the office instead of home. The other day, I was driving into town and saw her and Sally sitting outside at the coffee shop. It took everything in me to keep driving and not stop to say hi.

Why? Because my pulse quickens when I'm around her. She makes me anxious. I'd rather avoid her than try and hide how many times I think about her each day. But now, here she is, with her arms around my daughter, right at home at the festival.

I'm pretty sure this town has doubled the amount of Christmas cheer that's at the festival, and Nora is so excited about it. Me, on the other hand? I could do without it.

"Dad, Dad, look!" Nora screams from beside my parents. "It's Grandma, Pop and Penelope! She's here Dad, she's here for the festival!"

"I see that," I say, cautiously making my way across the snow. "Penelope, welcome to the start of the worst season here in Winterberry—I mean the Winter Festival."

"Hi honey," Mom says, "we've missed you at dinner. Has work been keeping you busy?"

"Yeah, working on a big case. I've been working from the office to get everything done before the Christmas season picks up and Nora here has me running all over town doing seasonal things. How's everything at the inn?"

I try not to look at Penelope as I catch up with Mom.

"It's great. Penelope has been helping me in the kitchen and she even waited tables at Sally's Diner the other day."

I already knew this of course—*hello small town*—but I pretend I'm hearing it for the first time.

"That's nice. I didn't take you for a waitress." I glance in her direction and lock eyes with her.

Her cheeks turn pink, and I can't help but hope that it's me affecting her the same way she affects me.

"Sally was running around like crazy. I liked doing it, I met so many people."

"Oh I bet you did. Almost everyone in town goes to Sally's." Normally I can talk to people just fine, but when I'm in front of Penelope, my tongue sticks to the top of my mouth.

"There's my new favorite person!" I hear Sally before I see her.

She comes running up and wraps her arms around Penelope like they've been friends forever. I knew they'd get along, and a part of me is glad to see I was right. The other part wishes they hated each other so it would make Penelope leaving easier.

"Hey Sal, nice to see you too," I say to her back. Pulling apart from Penelope, she spins around and pins me with a glare.

"Well, *you* used to be my favorite person. You haven't even come in for your morning coffee lately. Where have you been?"

What's with the third degree from everyone?

Penelope stares at me and I hope she doesn't realize my avoidance is because of her.

"I'm working on a big case, but I promise I'll stop in to see you soon."

"Poor Dad," Nora adds. "He's been so stressed and more grumpy than usual."

Thanks kid. "I have not!" I say as I flick her in the arm and mess up her hair, which I know she hates but it makes her laugh.

"Daaaad." She rolls her eyes and fixes her curls.

I love this kid. And she's right. I've been stressed and low on patience, but it isn't for the reason Nora thinks. In fact, there isn't even a big case—only my thoughts of Penelope making me lose the little bit of patience I normally have.

"Well, I'm off. I have a booth over there selling some pastries and hot cocoa. Stop by before you guys leave." Sally jets off to her booth.

A few inches of snow cover the ground and our breath is visible. The smell of chestnuts roasting fills the air. The sound of Christmas music blares from huge speakers and can be heard throughout the entire town.

"Grandma, Pop, can you take me to get some hot cocoa?" Nora asks.

"I can take you," I tell her quickly. I don't want to be alone with Penelope.

"That's okay, we've got it," Mom says with a wink. "Why don't you take Penelope and show her some of the booths and games."

Evil, evil woman.

With that, they're off and I'm left standing on the walkway with Penelope. This is exactly what I *didn't* want to happen, and by the look on her face, I have a feeling she's thinking the same thing.

Both of us stand there, like middle schoolers at their first dance, saying nothing.

"Which way do you want to go?" She nudges me with her shoulder, breaking the awkward silence. "You know where everything is better than I do."

"Are you hungry? We could go grab some roasted chestnuts from over there and then visit all the booths."

"Actually I am. Would you believe I've never had roasted chestnuts before?"

"Really? Don't you live in Manhattan where they roast chestnuts on every street corner?"

"Yep. I've smelled but never tasted them."

"Definitely time to fix that. Let's go get some."

Putting my hand on the small of her back, I guide her through the crowd, locating the booth with chestnuts. As we approach, she sniffs the air and smiles. I try not to stare but the way her eyes dance around makes my heart go wild.

"Hi Nancy. This is Penelope and she's never had roasted chestnuts before. We're here to change that."

"Oh my! Here ya go honey. I hope you like them," Nancy says as she hands Penelope a bag and then hands one to me.

We both watch as Penelope takes her first bite of the Christmas staple, waiting in anticipation to see what she thinks of them.

"These are so good!" She laughs. "I can see why everyone talks about them and why they are in a song" Then she looks directly at me. "Thank you, Brent."

"You're welcome," I whisper as we make our way to more booths.

It seems like every single person in town has come out for the festival, yet the only person I see is Penelope. I love watching her light up at the different vendors. She wears a smile on her face even as she loses miserably at a game of Christmas Candy Cane Toss.

"Wow, you're really bad at that," I say as she finishes the game. I try not to laugh. She wasn't even close to landing the candy canes on the ledge like she was supposed to.

"Oh yeah, like you are any better."

"Sweetheart, I'm the master at this game. Stand back and prepare to be jealous of my skills."

Paying for another round, I receive five plastic candy canes, and within thirty seconds I successfully toss them all onto the highest ledge. "Told ya."

"Okay, I'm a little impressed. But only a little. I bet you've played this game a million times over the years," she teases.

"Maybe, maybe not. I guess you'll never know." I wink.

As the night progresses, we fall into an easy banter. Luckily, teasing and flirting replace the earlier awkwardness. And it's not one-sided.

We continue walking through the festival, stopping at all the booths and playing each game.

Penelope's excitement is palpable, and it fills the space around us.

"So, I have a question for you," she says as we walk, sipping the hot cocoa we got from Sally. "Why have you been avoiding me?"

I was hoping she hadn't noticed. "What do you mean?" A cop-out, I know, but hopefully it'll buy me time to think of a good answer.

"Come on Brent, I'm not stupid. All of a sudden, you have a big case and can't come to dinner with your parents? Or stop by and see Sally? Did I do something?"

I want to tell her the truth, that I can't be in the same room as her without wanting to be near her, but I can't.

"I haven't been avoiding you," I lie. Right through my teeth. "Trust me, you did nothing wrong." That part is true.

It's not her, it's me.

She eyes me suspiciously and I hold my breath in anticipation for what she'll say.

"If you say so. You can tell me though if I did or if me being at the inn is bothering you."

"Nah, no reason to think that. This time of year is always busy. I was actually planning to come to dinner tomorrow night, if you'll be there." Lies, so many lies. I had no intention of going there for dinner until she was safe and sound back in the city.

"Yep, I'll be there in all my glory." She laughs at herself, and I can't help but smile.

"So, since you asked me a question, now I get to ask you one," I say. I've been dying to hear her story since I found her on Main Street.

"Dad! Look what I got!" Nora interrupts. She comes running from the other side of the park, with my parents in tow, shattering the moment. "Isn't she pretty?" She holds up a stuffed pink unicorn for me to see.

My girl and all things pink.

"I love it. She'll go perfectly on your bed with your other stuffed animals." There's a lot of them. I pat her head. "Are you having fun, munchkin?"

"So much fun." She stifles a yawn with the back of her hand. Her eyelids droop.

Guess I won't be able to ask Penelope that question after all.

"Maybe a little too much fun?" I wrap my arm around her and kiss the top of her head. "Time to get you home and into bed, little one."

"But Dad, I didn't get to play all the games yet." She sticks out her bottom lip trying to make me feel bad. It never works but I don't tell her that because she looks so cute when she does it.

"Actually, we were planning on heading home too," Mom says. "Why don't we take Nora with us so you two can enjoy the rest of the festival?"

She's smooth, I'll give her that.

"That's okay, Mom, I'm sure Penelope is tired too." I peek at Penelope's face out of the corner of my eye, trying to gauge her reaction. Would she want to stay with me? "What do you think Penelope?"

A few beats pass before she responds. "Actually, I'd love to finish seeing the festival. If that's okay with you, Brent."

Oh boy. "That works for me." I turn to my mom. "Do you mind tucking her in at my place and staying there until I get back?"

"Of course, sweetheart. You two enjoy." My mom stands on her tiptoes to kiss me on the cheek before turning and briefly embracing Penelope. "Come on Nora, maybe Pop can carry you so your little legs can rest."

Dad grumbles under his breath as he bends down and picks Nora up. He may be grumpy most of the time, but he'd do anything for that little girl. I watch them walk away, and my heart constricts in my chest. I can't tell if it's anxiety about being alone with Penelope again, or just the overwhelming love I have for my family.

"All right, where to next?" I ask Penelope. "You're lucky. I don't stay longer at this festival for just anyone."

"Wow, you sure know how to make a woman feel special." She playfully nudges me with her shoulder.

We walk around in silence for a while, and I periodically glance over to make sure she's enjoying herself. By the huge grin and wistful look in her eyes, I'd say she is. We stop at a vendor, where I buy a new ornament for Mom and Dad's tree, then I purchase a soft pretzel to share with Penelope. We continue weaving through the crowd, making our way to Sally's booth for more hot cocoa.

"This town really does love Christmas. Has it always been like this?" Her voice is barely audible over the loud music.

"It has actually. I grew up here and the town has always gone big for Christmas. What about you? Where did you grow up?"

"I grew up in Pennsylvania before moving to New Jersey with Gran after my parents died. I don't have any siblings, so it was just me. Gran tried but it wasn't the same for me after they passed."

"I'm so sorry you went through that. When did you move to the city?"

"I started working in the city and then when Gran died, I stayed in her house since it was paid off until I could move into the city. I didn't get much from the sale of her house, but it helped me pay rent and I had roommates. Have you always lived in Winterberry?"

"I did grow up here in Winterberry but then my late wife, Michelle, and I moved to a beach town on the Jersey Shore after we got married. I moved back after she died because I needed help with Nora and my parents needed help with the inn when they bought it."

"Oh Brent, I'm sorry. If you don't mind me asking, what happened?"

Pausing, I take a few deep breaths. It's not something I talk about often. "She died of cancer. We thought we would have more time but unfortunately it took her faster than we expected. Nora is so young, and I'm scared she'll forget her, so we talk about her a lot. She was an amazing mom."

"Looks like we've both been through heartbreaking loss in our lives," Penelope whispers, almost to herself.

A question lingers on the tip of my tongue. I probably shouldn't ask it, but I need to know.

"Do you have someone at home waiting for you? He's probably so worried since you have no phone with you."

"I did have someone... I was engaged actually. But he cheated on me and I found out recently. So no, no one is waiting for me or missing me," she says sadly. "Although I *do* have a best friend named Georgia who's my rock. I haven't talked to her since I've been here though."

"You can always use the phone at the inn if you want to. Mom and Dad won't mind, and I'm sure Georgia would love to hear that you're okay."

"Would you judge me if I told you that I don't have her number memorized?" She winces as the words leave her mouth.

"No judgment here. To be honest, the only number I have memorized is for the inn," I reassure her. "They do have a desktop in the office at the inn if you know her email."

Her face brightens. "I actually do. That would be so great if I could just let her know I am good. Thanks Brent, I'll ask your mom about it tomorrow."

"Sounds good. Hey, there's Ben. Let's see if he has an update on your car parts." I gesture to where he's standing, munching on funnel cake. We make our way over. "Hey man, enjoying the festival?"

"Hey guys, I sure am. This funnel cake is my favorite thing every year," he says through a mouthful of the sweet treat. "I was going to call you earlier, but I lost track of time. Still no parts for your car Penelope. I'm so sorry. I'm sure you want to get home and I'm working on it. Seeing if anyone closer can get them for me."

"Thanks for the update, Ben," she says. "I know you're working hard, and I appreciate it."

"Maybe I'll see you at the Christmas Tree Lighting this weekend," he says before turning back to his funnel cake.

You've got to be kidding me.

I don't think I'll survive a few more days with her in town. I need her to go home, like yesterday.

"Well, there's that." I try not to sound rude but I'm suffocating with all these people around.

Penelope lets out a huge yawn. I take that as my cue it's time to go. I've stayed at the festival longer than I have in years, and I've had my fill.

"All right, let's go. I need to let mom and dad get back to the inn."

"Thank you for staying here with me, even though I know this isn't your favorite place to be. It means a lot."

"That's an understatement." I laugh. "But I didn't mind."

I place my hand on the small of her back and guide her through the crowd to my truck. As soon as we're out of the madness, I can breathe again. I help Penelope enter the truck before hopping behind the wheel. It's a quick ride back to the inn, and when I sneak glances at her out of the corner of my eye, I notice her eyelids are growing heavier with every street we pass.

I park in the driveway when we arrive a few minutes later. I make sure Penelope's awake before opening the door for her and walking her to the entrance of the inn.

The porch is illuminated by twinkle lights, allowing us to see our way to the door.

"Goodnight, Penelope. I'll see you tomorrow at dinner." I give her a small wave as she opens the door and disappears behind it.

I stand there for a minute after she leaves, processing the night. With a heavy sigh, I head across the snowy lawn to my house.

This has been a long night and I'm ready for it to be over.

Chapter Twelve

♥

Penelope

I practically crawl my way up the stairs and into bed.

The Winter Festival was everything I could've hoped it would be. There were decorations as far as the eye could see, delicious food that was definitely not a part of my diet, and everyone from town. Seeing so many people milling around and getting into the Christmas spirit was so beautiful.

Literally, every surface had something Christmassy covering it, and I adored every second. Too often, I found myself reaching for my phone to take a photo for social media. I can't even remember the last time I did something, even just sitting on the couch with Georgia, that I didn't post about. And as weird as it was to not be able to share the beauty around me, it was nice to experience the festival without that distraction.

I was exhausted, but when it was time to go, I cried a little inside and felt the overwhelming urge to stay wrapped up in the Christmas bubble for as long as possible.

It was nice having some time with Brent. I enjoyed learning more about him. I definitely wasn't anticipating opening up about Drew, but it felt good to get that off my chest.

Lying in bed, a wave of contentment washes over my body. I'm happy to be here in Winterberry, at the Butterfly Inn. It feels like a dream, and I never want to wake up.

The next night, I get dressed and ensure my makeup looks natural, so no one notices I put on as many products as I did.

I felt like myself last night at the festival, in my makeup and cute outfits, and I want to feel that way again.

I head downstairs to help Suzanne get ready for dinner. If I'm being honest, I need something to keep my mind off Brent.

I enter the kitchen where Suzanne is putting the final touches on dinner.

"Penelope, you look beautiful! You don't need to help me, go make yourself comfortable," she says. "Actually, Brent mentioned to me last night when I talked to him that you wanted to use the computer to email your friend. Why don't you go do that now before this is all ready."

"That would be amazing. Are you sure you don't need help? I won't be long."

"Take your time sweetheart, I've got this."

As I enter the office, I'm taken aback at how cozy the room is. There's floor to ceiling bookcases that hold all kinds of paperbacks and hardcover books, a rustic fireplace with a gorgeous mantle, and a large mahogany desk sitting by the window.

In the corner is a huge Christmas tree completely decorated with home-made ornaments and white lights, creating a soft glow in the room.

Making my way over to the desk, I sit down in the leather chair and swivel around to face the computer. It lights up when I move the mouse. I hesitate, not sure if I should really open myself up to this or if it's better to stay in ignorant bliss.

To be honest, I used to laugh when people said they hated social media. But since I've been here in Winterberry, I haven't missed living on Instagram at all.

Well, time to rip the Band-Aid off.

I open Google, take a deep breath, and type in my name. The number of articles that come up when I hit enter makes my head spin.

"Has Penelope Maxwell Left Town?"

"Where Has Penelope Maxwell Gone?"

"When Will Penelope Maxwell Post on Instagram?"

I can't believe the amount of articles there are talking about me skipping town. The paparazzi must be looking for me, dying to get the first photo of me. No one here in Winterberry knows my real name, and now, I *really* don't want them to know. I want to stay in this bliss as long as I possibly can, even though I know it won't last forever.

I take a few minutes to scroll through the articles, clicking on a few. They all incorrectly speculate my whereabouts.

Leaning back in the chair, I open a new tab in the browser and log into my Instagram account.

Wow.

I have *thousands* of messages and even more notifications. This would take me days to get through. Clicking on my messages, I notice most people are asking where I am or if I'm okay. Scrolling down, my heart jumps when I spot Drew's name.

I click the thread. Dozens of new messages pop up. All sent after news of his affair broke.

They start out calm and worried, but quickly morph into anger. He's practically yelling at me, accusing me of embarrassing him.

Wait a second...

I'm embarrassing *him*?

You've got to be kidding me.

How dare he say anything to me other than an apology for what he's done and the pain he's caused me?

My blood boils and my face heats. I block him before he can contact me again. I'm so glad I never have to look that man in the face again.

I'm so mad I can't see straight. I need to take a walk and cool down, but I don't want to leave until I reach out to Georgia and let her know I'm okay. It's been days. Surely my best friend is worried about me.

Walking over to the window, I breathe deep into my stomach and try to calm my nerves. I didn't think I'd ever have this type of reaction to the man who I thought would be my husband.

I can't believe I wasted time on him. What an idiot. The worst part is that I was getting ready to marry him. I was truly planning to spend the rest of my life with him.

Meanwhile he was cheating on me and making me look like a fool.

All those years wasted.

But you can't go back in time, right? It's time to put my big girl panties on and face it head on. At least I can choose pretty lace panties.

I crack my knuckles and stretch my arms then sit back down to get this over with. Now or never. I continue scrolling through my messages until I land on the word "engaged". I stop to see what it says.

Did Drew tell the tabloids we're still getting married?

Clicking the article is a mistake. A photo of Drew pops up. His arm is around the same woman he was caught cheating on me with.

The title reads "Drew Henry Engaged Again!"

I can't be seeing this right. Something has to be wrong with my eyes. I rub them with my fists to make sure they're working.

There's no way my ex-fiancé is already engaged to the woman he was having an affair with. Nope, not possible. I have to be dreaming. It's only been a week since I found out he was cheating on me, and now he's engaged to her?

How long has he been seeing her? How can he be *marrying* her?

I pinch myself to see if I'm awake. "Ouch!" I am.

This is real life.

What a slap in the face. First, he betrays me by breaking my trust and letting it play out for the world to see, now he's put a ring on her finger.

The only person I want to talk to right now is Georgia, so I exit Instagram and open my email. My inbox is so full there's no way I'll be able to read through everything. And I don't even want to.

Clicking on the compose button, I start a new email to Georgia to let her know that I'm fine. For some reason, I leave out the details of Winterberry and the inn, but I lay everything else out and tell her exactly how I'm feeling. She's my best friend after all, if I can't do that with her, who can I lay my soul bare to?

As I'm writing, memories of our friendship flood my head. For so many years, Georgia was all I had. We were both trying to make something of ourselves and were living off Ramen noodles and hot dogs. With no family members, she became the family I didn't have.

When I moved to New York City, I had to share a spider-infested apartment with four other girls. We'd met them during acting class, and we all had the same goals. So, the four of us rented a two-bedroom apartment. Georgia and I slept in the same room. It was so small we could barely fit our twin sized beds and a single dresser. We hung a threadbare sheet from the ceiling, between our beds, to give ourselves some privacy.

We shopped at secondhand shops and shared our beauty products because we couldn't afford our own.

For holidays, I would either go home to Georgia's parents' house and spend the day with them, or we would hide out in our shitty apartment and eat Chinese food.

She means the world to me, and the only thing I want to do right now is hug her. I want her to tell me it'll be okay.

I quickly send off the email then close it out. I slip out of the office, hoping that no one notices me as I head outside. As much as I like Suzanne and Tom, I need to sort through my feelings. Alone.

I stand on the front porch and try to calm my rapid pulse. I was hurt when I found out Drew cheated on me, but this pain is on a whole new level.

As I look around, I see the Christmas decorations lighting up every inch of the inn and hate that this is happening during what's supposed to be the most beautiful time of the year.

How will I come back from this?

Chapter Thirteen

Brent

Usually, as soon as my head hits the pillow, I knock out. But tonight, I can't fall asleep. I've spent the past hour tossing and turning. So many thoughts whirl in my mind.

I give up after a few more restless minutes. Tiptoeing out of my bedroom, I make my way down the hall and peek into Nora's room. She's sprawled out on her back, blonde curls surrounding her head like a halo, with her arms tight at her side under her blanket. The sight warms my chest. It takes everything in me not to go kiss her little head.

I miss Michelle every single day, but when I look at Nora and see the zest for life that she got from her mom, I'm happy. It's taken a long time to get to this point.

I pad down the hall, sidestepping all the creaky floorboards so I don't wake my little angel.

There are no lights on, so I feel my way into the kitchen, trying not to bump into anything. I don't turn any lights on, because if I do, it'll awaken the FOMO in my little rascal.

Maybe I just need to drink something.

I grab a bottle of water from the fridge, and after chugging the whole thing, I still feel like shit. Rather than sit around overthinking, I grab my flannel coat, put my boots on, and quietly open the door. The cold air smacks me in the face and I immediately regret my decision.

I'm about to retreat into the house when I see someone walking around in circles on the front lawn. I'm in no mood to talk to anyone tonight but I venture over in case it's a guest to the inn and they need help.

The snow is no longer falling, but the wind has picked up. It gnaws at my face as I make my way across the lawn. Pulling my coat tighter, I try to bury myself in the collar so I can save some of the skin on my face from the bitter cold.

I approach the pacing figure as I would a lost animal, quietly and cautiously so I don't startle them.

"Hello?" I say. "Everything okay over here?" The person pauses and slowly turns around. I blink, making out the familiar face. "Penelope? Is that you?"

Tears stream down her face. The tip of her nose is red and raw.

"Yep, it's me," she mutters. She stands still, stuffing her hands into her armpits, likely trying to keep them warm.

"We have to stop meeting like this," I say lightheartedly, trying to crack a joke. She doesn't laugh. "Why don't you have a coat on? It's freezing out here."

I approach her, shrugging out of my coat so I can wrap it around her. Her shoulders slump and she appears small and fragile with my coat swallowing her.

Instinctually, I begin rubbing her arms in an effort to warm her up faster.

"I kind of ran outside and forgot to put my shoes or coat on. And, well, here I am."

"Let's get you inside and by the fire. You don't need to stay out here in the snow." She hesitates, and it's much too cold out here, so I put my hand on the small of her back and guide her up the porch steps.

We get inside. I close the door and shut out the world beyond the inn.

The warmth immediately embraces us. It's a stark contrast to the bone-chilling cold outside. Penelope sits on the couch without removing my coat. I sit next to her.

Silence stretches on around us.

The tension unsettles me, and I clear my throat to break the silence.

"So, are you going to tell me why you are out here in the freezing cold in the middle of the night?" I ask, leaving out the part about her crying.

"I don't even know where to begin."

"You don't have to tell me if you don't want to."

I don't want her to feel like she *has* to share, but I want her to know that I'm here for her.

"I used your parents' computer to check my emails and social media. I found something I wasn't expecting."

I glance at her as another stray tear falls from her lashes. I wait patiently, giving her the chance to share if she wants to.

Another few minutes goes by before she speaks.

"Remember how I told you the other night that my fiancé had cheated on me?"

How could I have forgotten that piece of information? That guy is up there on my list—right next to whoever first created the Winter Festival. Instead of saying anything, I nod.

"Well, when I went on my Instagram, I saw that a bunch of people had tagged me in posts, so I looked to see what they were." She stops to clear her throat and take a deep breath. "There were dozens of pictures of my ex-fiancé with his arms around the woman who he cheated on me with. They're engaged."

Are you kidding?

I don't say anything and let her continue.

"It's been only a week since I even found out that he was cheating on me and now, he's already put a ring on her finger. This is the man who I thought *I* was going to spend the rest of my life with."

Tears stream down her face, her body shakes from the force of her sobs.

I don't even know what to say.

I don't do crying.

But the sight of a broken Penelope crushes me.

Wrapping my arm around her shoulders, I pull her against my chest to soothe her. She drenches my shirt with her tears and snot.

"You don't deserve that, Penelope. I've only known you for a few days and I already know you're a good person. My mom and Sally might be starting to like you more than me." That gets a small chuckle out of her. "Some people just suck. Plain and simple. But no one deserves to be betrayed by the person they love. I'm so sorry this has happened to you."

I can't say anything that will fix it, so instead of trying, I let her cry it out. I just hold her. We sit like this for a while, with her head on my chest and my arm wrapped around her.

Once her sobs slow down and her breathing levels out, a thought pops into my head. Something that might take her mind off this.

"Hey," I say into the top of her head. "Want to come to my house and watch a Christmas movie?"

Her head pops up and she looks at me with red-rimmed eyes. Her cheeks are blotchy. And at that moment, I would burn the world down to make her feel better.

"Really?" she asks.

"Sure. I usually only watch Christmas movies when Nora makes me but I'm willing to sit through one if it will cheer you up."

"Wow, you really know how to sell something. You missed your calling in life."

"What can I say, it's a gift," I say as I rise from the couch and bow exaggeratedly. This makes her laugh.

I offer a hand to help her up. She stands, shrugs out of my coat, and hands it back. I stride to the front door and grab a blanket from mom's basket. She keeps throw blankets for the guests. I hand it to Penelope, and she wraps it around her shoulders like a cape.

"Don't tell me you're coming over looking like that," I say, holding back a laugh. "I don't know if I can be seen with someone in a cape."

She punches me in the arm, and I pretend to be injured. "Ow! Now I have to cancel because my arm is broken, good job."

"You don't need your arm to watch a movie, idiot. And yes, I'm wearing this blanket because it's cold out there, duh."

"You're the one who thought it was a good idea to come out front without a jacket or real shoes on. You don't need to tell me it's cold."

I love when she smiles.

"Okay, give me a few minutes to make sure Nora is all good and you can ditch the blanket if you want, I have other ones at my house if you are still cold."

Laughing, she leads me to the front door and tells me she'll see me soon. I make my way across the yard to the guesthouse and quietly slip inside.

With the Christmas tree all lit up and the decorations Nora and I put out, it hits me how much I love this little home of ours. It definitely isn't much. I have a feeling, based on the luggage she carries and the smell of her perfume, that Penelope is used to luxury, but *this* is home. I wonder what she'll think of the place. If she'll find it as cozy as I do.

Picking up a few stray pieces of clothing on the way to the bedroom, I stop at Nora's door and check that she's still asleep. I gently pull her door closed so we don't wake her, throw the dirty clothes in my room, and make my way back to the kitchen.

Grabbing my kettle, I begin boiling water for hot cocoa.

A soft knock sounds at the front door.

She's here.

Chapter Fourteen

Penelope

W hy am I so nervous?

It's just a Christmas movie... Sure, it's with a man who's so hot I'm breathless at the mere sight of him, but it's an innocent movie.

I mean, I've gone on dates with some of the hottest celebrities before settling down with Drew. But I've never been *this* nervous.

Once Brent leaves, I run upstairs to get ready. I know for a fact I look like a hot mess. Looking in my bathroom mirror confirms this. I groan at my reflection.

Wow, it's worse than I thought.

Quickly, I splash my face with water, put on some tinted moisturizer, a coat of mascara, and lip balm. I don't want him to think I'm trying to impress him, which I'm not by the way, I just don't want to look like a mess.

I shake my hair out of the bun and braid it, letting it hang over my shoulder. Casual but cute.

Brent seemed embarrassed by my blanket cape, so I put it back on. It's fun to mess with him.

Drew and I definitely didn't have a playful relationship. He wanted me to look a certain way, act a certain way, and would even pick my outfits when we went out together. He often called the paparazzi to take photos of us. It felt like I was an accessory to him. Something to be paraded around and admired.

At the time, I'd thought it was sweet he cared about me looking my best. But now, I'm realizing it wasn't about me—it was about how *he* looked.

Spending time with Brent makes me feel valuable for who I am, not how I look. He didn't even bat an eye at my appearance while I sobbed. The only thing he cared about was helping me feel better.

Drew would've been appalled by my crying face.

That feeling of having to be perfect for Drew, even when I was going to bed or going to the gym, was stressful.

Being here in Winterberry, I haven't felt that pressure even once.

Shaking the thoughts away, I wrap the blanket around my shoulders, take one more look at myself in the mirror, grab my room key, and head out the door.

If these butterflies in my stomach could knock it off for a few minutes, that would be awesome.

Opening the front door of the inn, I shiver at the icy shards that fill my lungs. The town smells like a mix of fireplaces, evergreen trees, and snow. It's a scent I've never experienced before, and it evokes a new feeling inside me.

Peace.

Wrapping the blanket tighter around me, I quickly cross the lawn and stop at the two steps that lead to Brent's front porch. I haven't ventured back here since I arrived, and I'm struck by how cute it is. Definitely *not* what I'm used to in Manhattan, but it's so homey that it makes me smile.

For someone who isn't into Christmas, Brent's house is decorated beautifully. There's a swing, similar to the one at the inn, and a small Christmas tree lights up the corner of the porch. The trim around the windows has white lights, and there's a huge wreath on the door.

I knock lightly. I know Nora is asleep and I don't want to wake her up. As much as I love that little girl, I'm looking forward to spending time alone with Brent. After a few seconds, Brent opens the door and the little smirk on his face makes wearing this blanket even more satisfying.

"You just couldn't help yourself with that blanket cape, could you?" He opens the door wider so I can enter.

"It's just so cozy and I know how much you loved the look, so I just had to," I say as I make my way into his living room. I stop, taking it all in, and am completely surprised by what I see. Sure, Brent is a single dad, but his home doesn't reflect that at all.

There's a huge Christmas tree in the corner of the room, a beige couch, a wood fireplace with stockings hung on the mantle, photos on the walls, and a huge TV. A perfect spot for movie nights.

"You're allowed to come in, you know," he says, voice rumbling. Brent has let some of his grumpy wall down, and I like what I've seen behind it.

Maybe a little too much.

"Why thank you, grumpy pants. I love your home."

"You sound kind of surprised by that. Did you expect something else?"

"I'm not sure what I was expecting but it feels so homey here. I love your couch. I want one for my apartment when I get home."

"Well hopefully Ben will have your car fixed soon and you can get back home. I don't know what's taking so long with these parts."

"Are you trying to get rid of me?" I tease, secretly hoping that he isn't.

"I didn't say that. Just surprised at how long this is taking, that's all."

The trill of a teapot fills the air and cuts the tension.

Saved by the teapot.

"Ahhh," he whisper-yells. He bolts across the room to the kitchen, almost tripping over one of the island stools as he goes, and I suppress a laugh behind my hands.

As soon as he reaches the stove, he quickly turns it off and removes the kettle. He snatches mugs from a cabinet and assembles two hot chocolates complete with mini marshmallows.

While I wait for Brent to finish, I glance around the room. There are photos from when his late wife was alive, memories of Nora as a baby, pictures with his parents, and a wedding photo.

What a gorgeous woman Michelle was. Nora definitely gets her spunk from her dad, but her looks? They're clearly from her mom.

Brent startles me out of my thoughts when he asks if I like coffee creamer in my hot cocoa.

"I thought I was the only person who drank their hot chocolate that way." I eye him warily. "I never drink it without it."

"I almost didn't ask you because I thought you'd think I was weird."

We both laugh as he takes the peppermint mocha creamer out of the fridge and adds it to the mugs.

"To be honest, before the festival, I hadn't had a cup of hot cocoa in years. I'm definitely getting my fill now."

"Wait, what? Why?" His brow scrunches in confusion.

"I have to be so conscious of the way that I look for work, and much like the pancakes, hot chocolate was definitely not part of my approved diet."

"Well, that's insane, you're beautiful."

I flush and my pulse quickens. Do I hear that a lot? Yes, from strange men who want to be seen with a celebrity, or from paparazzi who want the right shot. But from someone who doesn't want anything from me? That doesn't happen often.

"Thank you. I don't always feel beautiful. I have to watch what I eat and work out seven days a week so I can fit into certain clothes and make everyone around me happy." I pause, mulling over my words. "But being here in Winterberry has made me question if I have forgotten about my own happiness in the process."

"So, what makes Penelope Smith happy?" he asks.

I take a few minutes before I answer. "Christmas trees, dinners with family, taking walks in the snow, sitting down to read a book. All those things have made me so happy this past week. Oh, and the pancakes at Sally's Diner. They've definitely made me happy."

"I'm glad Winterberry has brought some happiness to you—it does have that effect on people."

"People, but not *you*, right?"

"It's complicated. And I don't want to get into those deep feelings right now, over a cup of hot cocoa. That's more of a conversation over a shot of whiskey."

"Is there even a bar close by here?"

"There's one in town that everyone goes to, which sometimes is not a good thing because you run into people you were trying to avoid, but that's been my spot since I was old enough to drink."

"I love that. Maybe one day before I leave you can take me there."

"We might be able to work that out," he says as he finishes stirring the creamer into the mugs.

He hands me a pink princess one that I'm assuming is Nora's. He holds a blue superhero one in his hand as he makes his way to the couch where I'm sitting.

"Brent, are you sure I can drink my hot cocoa on this couch? It's beige and looks expensive."

"Are you going to spill?"

"I mean, I'm not going to try and spill but what if I do? I'll ruin it."

"That's what stain remover is for. Do you know how many things Nora has spilled on this couch? More than I can count. Relax."

I'm still unsure about sitting on the couch with hot cocoa. Flashes of Drew scolding me for eating or drinking on my couch fill my head.

Brent grabs a dinner tray from next to the couch and sets it up.

"There, put your mug on there. That way when you don't have it in your hands, you can set it on the tray. Better?"

"Thank you. Sorry I'm such a pain. My ex was very particular about the way things should be and never allowed drinks on the couch."

"What if you had a movie night or something?"

Well, this is embarrassing. "Um, we didn't really do that. We went out most nights and when we were home, he was usually busy doing work or creating content for social media."

"Wow. Okay, well, here at my house, you can have drinks on the couch, we love movie nights, and I don't even have social media so no creating content," he teases.

Before that fateful day, when I saw the tabloid cover, I always thought of myself as confident and high-maintenance. I judged people by their clothing labels, never left my penthouse without a full face of makeup, and wouldn't be caught dead in a town like this. But, somehow, I fit in perfectly into this little town.

"Okay, now that we have the hot chocolate debacle fixed, what movie should we watch?" he asks, glancing my way.

"Do you have a favorite?"

"How about *Elf*? Nora and I love that movie. Have you seen it?"

"I love *Elf*! I watch it every year."

As soon as Brent says *Elf*, I can't help but smile. It's my favorite Christmas movie. I mean who doesn't love Will Ferrell dressed in an elf costume? It's one I watch every year.

But I've never had someone to watch it with.

"Did your fiancé... I mean *ex*-fiancé... watch it with you?" he asks.

"Nah I watched it by myself. I liked it that way." That's a lie, but I'm not going to tell him that.

"If you say so." He eyes me suspiciously but doesn't press the issue. "Do you want some popcorn before I start?"

"Sure, popcorn sounds delicious. That's so nice of you Brent."

"It's my pleasure," he says, getting up from the couch and taking a fake bow before heading to the kitchen.

I can't help but stare at him as he walks into the kitchen in his gray sweatpants. He clearly works out and it shows. Honestly, if it were up to me, Gray Sweatpants Day would be a national holiday starring Brent Harrison.

As soon as the popping begins, he turns around and his gaze finds mine. We lock eyes and stay that way for a minute too long, and I can feel the heat in that stare before I look away and break the moment.

Beep beep beep.

He puts the popcorn in a bowl and when he sits back down, so close his thigh rests against mine. And I like it.

No, I take that back, I *love* it.

"Okay, let's do this." he says, pressing play.

I try to focus on the screen and not on the way his leg feels up against mine.

The room has such a vibe. There are no lights on, just the roaring fireplace, TV, and the Christmas tree. I'm feeling much more relaxed and so cozy, two things I definitely expect after seeing Drew with his new fiancée.

"Can you pause it really quick? I need to use the bathroom," I say. My nerves are starting to get the best of me, and I need a minute.

"Down the hall on the left is the bathroom. Do you mind popping your head into Nora's room and just to make sure she is still asleep?"

"No problem. Be right back."

I make my way down the hall and find the bathroom. Closing the door behind me, I lean against it and take a deep breath.

I stride to the mirror and give myself a pep talk.

"What is wrong with you, Penelope? You're a successful actress. You've been in the same room with gorgeous men before. You can do this. Focus on the movie and ignore everything else."

Taking more deep breaths, I flush the toilet, so it seems like I used it, and wash my hands. "I've got this."

On the way back, I find Nora's room and check on her. She's such a beautiful little girl.

I've never had the urge to become a mom. It was off the table with Drew because he didn't want kids, and I was okay with that. I guess I've never seen myself as maternal.

My career has always been my baby. I've spent so long nurturing it, letting it consume me, and that's been fine for me.

But seeing Brent with Nora over the past few days, it makes me rethink things. Maybe I *do* want to be a mom one day. Maybe it would be nice to slow down, move out of the city, and make a real life for myself. Somewhere where people know me, not for brands I wear or the people I date, but for who I truly am at my core. And honestly, I'm not even sure I know who that is.

Strip away the makeup, glamor, and money, and who *is* Penelope Maxwell?

That's a question I've never asked myself.

However, something about Winterberry, Brent and Nora, the inn, and this Christmas has me thinking about the answer for the first time.

Sneaking out of Nora's room so I don't wake her, I head back down the hall to the living room and find Brent throwing popcorn in the air, catching the pieces in his mouth.

"You've got skills, Mr. Harrison." I laugh as I take my seat back on the couch. "Nora is sound asleep with all of her stuffed animals."

"Those stuffed animals will be the death of me. She has to have them in a certain spot every night and I have to kiss each one good night. If she wasn't so cute, I'd say not a chance."

"You'd do anything for that little girl."

"I would. She has me wrapped around her little finger. When her mom died, it was really hard for her, and before we moved her, it was just us. I tried to make up for that loss as much as I could." His chest rises and falls rapidly with the admission. I want to put my hand on his arm, something to let him know that I'm here, but I don't want to interrupt him.

"Eventually I realized I couldn't take that place and instead we began to create our own routines and memories. When we moved back here, it was the best decision I could've made. My parents love her more than life and it's filled a huge hole for her."

"Was it a hard decision to move back here?" I ask hesitantly. I don't want to say the wrong thing and have him shut down.

"Yes and no. We loved our little Jersey Shore beach town, but I knew Nora needed her family and the people of this town. They may drive me crazy but they're really good people. Everyone looks out for each other, and you don't find that everywhere."

"You definitely don't. I never experienced that until I arrived here. I was a stranger to everyone just a little while ago and I've been welcomed with open arms."

"Yeah, I'm not sure what you have done but everyone loves you. I think they're going to miss you when you leave."

Just the mention of me leaving Winterberry makes my stomach constrict, and a profound sadness settles over my heart. In such a short time, I've become attached to this town.

I know I need to go back to my real life, but I'm going to be sad to go.

I don't want to ruin the night, so I drop it before the mood shifts.

"Shall we get back to Buddy the Elf?" I ask, trying hard to sound cheerier than I feel.

I can't help but stare at the dark stubble on his jaw, those blue piercing eyes, and those kissable lips. The way his chest bulges beneath his black t-shirt is enticing.

He's a perfect specimen of a man.

In Hollywood, so many men have their eyebrows waxed and foreheads Botoxed. They wear designer everything and care excessively about their appearance. It takes a *lot* to be the prettier one in the relationship.

I went through it with Drew.

But Brent? He's all man.

And I'm here for it.

Pulling the blanket up around me, I turn my attention back to the TV. I need to stop wondering what it would be like to run my fingers through Brent's dark hair or grab ahold of his biceps.

Venturing a little bit closer to him, I spend the rest of the movie stealing glances in his direction and trying to ignore the rush of heat running through my veins.

"Nora's going to be so mad I watched this without her," Brent says once the movie ends. "Let's keep this our little secret."

"Is this her favorite, too?"

"She can't get enough. She would watch it every single day from Thanksgiving to Christmas Day if I let her."

"My kind of girl," I say, winking at him. "Your secret is safe with me."

I offer my little finger for a pinky promise. When he reaches over and wraps his finger around mine, I feel a tingle down to my toes.

Neither of us make a move to pull apart. We sit there with our fingers intertwined, gazing at one another. There's nothing I want more than to lean over and kiss those lips of his.

The energy in the room is charged with so much lust and want, it's impossible to ignore.

And Brent seems to feel the same.

With our fingers still wrapped, his thumb starts rubbing my palm slowly in circles. After a few seconds, he takes his left hand and moves a piece of hair out of my face. His hand rests on my cheek and the gesture is so intimate, so sweet, that I find myself turning my head, letting his massive hand cup my cheek.

The calluses on his palm are rough against my skin. The need to feel his hands on my body becomes almost too much to bear.

Removing his hand from my cheek, he swipes his thumb over my lower lip. His gaze heats and his tongue darts out to wet his lips. Slowly, he leans forward until I can feel his breath on mine. My pulse jackhammers.

His lips finally find mine, grazing softly before pressing firmly and giving into the kiss.

He smells of citrus and cedar, and tastes of chocolate.

Wow, he tastes so good. Somehow, I knew he would.

"Penelope," he murmurs. "I've been daydreaming about kissing you for days."

I smile against his lips. "Oh yeah? Makes me feel better that I'm not the only one."

I did *not* expect grumpy Brent to be as attracted to me as I am to him. This night keeps on surprising me.

Brent reaches over to turn off the TV, so the only light comes from the Christmas tree.

Shifting to deepen the kiss, a small voice cuts into the silence.

"Daddy? I can't sleep…"

Chapter Fifteen

Brent

"Crap!" I whisper as Penelope and I jump to opposite sides of the couch, putting as much space between us as possible.

I can hardly catch my breath. The taste of hot cocoa mixed with the salty popcorn lingers on my lips. Nora's little footsteps slap down the hallway as she makes her way toward us. Her favorite teddy bear dangles from her left hand while she uses her free hand to rub her eyes.

"Daddy?" She squints to locate me in the dim room.

"I'm right here baby, it's okay."

I climb off the couch and scoop my little girl up, letting her rest her head on my shoulder as I rub her back. She doesn't wake up in the middle of the night often, so I know she must've had a bad dream.

"Penelope?" Nora perks up. "Hi! What are you doing here?"

Ugh, I was hoping she wouldn't notice her. I don't want Nora to wake fully so I can quickly put her back to sleep and I can pick up where I left off with Penelope.

"Hi Nora, your dad and I were just hanging out," Penelope whispers. I peer over Nora's curls to try and read Penelope's expression.

"Daddy, can Penelope take me back to bed? I want *her* to tuck me in."

"I'm sure Penelope needs to get going sweetheart, but I can do it."

"No Daddy, I really want her to. Pleeeease?"

I can tell she's still in that space in between sleep and wake. When she's like this, she gets stubborn and emotional, which means she could be on the verge of a complete breakdown.

"I can do that, Nora," Penelope says.

"You don't have to, Penelope, I can take her."

"I don't mind, really," she says.

A moment later I feel her presence behind me. As soon as Nora notices, she reaches for her. To my surprise, Penelope lets Nora climb into her arms.

"Be right back," she whispers as she gently places her hand on the back of Nora's soft curls.

"Goodnight Daddy. *Mwah*."

"Goodnight baby, go right to sleep, okay?"

I watch them go as they head toward Nora's room, and my heart feels like it's going to burst out of my chest. No other woman, besides my mom and Sally, have put Nora to bed since Michelle died. I'm not sure if it terrifies me or if it warms my heart to see them together.

I guess I didn't realize how much Nora enjoyed having Penelope around. Between the dinners at the inn and the festival, Nora has gotten to know Penelope and clearly really likes her.

Unfortunately, that makes two of us.

I'm not looking for a relationship now. And maybe I'll never be looking for one, but, Penelope is not the type of woman you hook up with one night and forget the next. She's intoxicating. She's someone worth committing to and spending all your time with.

The complete opposite of what I want in my life.

It's not that I don't get lonely, because I do, but when I exchanged vows with Michelle all those years ago, I meant every word of them. I truly felt like she was the love of my life—my soulmate. No one could ever take her place, and I'd never want them to.

The problem is that I could see Penelope fitting nicely into my life, in her own way.

Would she like staying in this small town? I'm not sure. She's enjoying it now because of all the Christmas festivities, but how would she feel making this her home for good? She's used to New York City which is a far cry from Winterberry.

Why am I even thinking about this?

Her lips have sent me spiraling.

Grabbing the empty cocoa mugs, I take them to the kitchen to clean them, so I can attempt to silence my mind. I need a distraction from how I'm feeling.

I hear footsteps coming quietly down the hall a few minutes later, and I turn to see Penelope entering the kitchen.

She's out of this world beautiful. Way out of my league.

She's still flushed, lips swollen from my kisses. The shy smile on her face tells me she might be feeling what I am.

"Your little cutie is asleep," she says as she reaches me. "She asked me to rub her back, and within a few minutes, she passed out. You honestly have the sweetest child in the world, Brent. You're doing a great job with her."

"Thank you. Some days I feel like a complete failure as a parent. I never expected to be a single dad."

"All you have to do is look at her and see that you are definitely not a failure. She's something else."

"She also has perfect timing," I tease.

A small smile creeps across her face, and she moves to tuck that errant piece of hair behind her ear. I'm learning that it's a nervous tic of hers.

"That she does. Brent..."

"It's okay, we don't need to talk about it," I say. "We were both caught up in the moment. I'd be lying if I said I didn't like it, but I get that you're leaving as soon as you can." As soon as the words come out of my mouth, her body language changes.

She wraps her arms around her midsection. Did I say something wrong? Was this more to her than just a kiss?

"Yeah, you're right. I should get going, it's later than I realized," she says too quickly.

Even though the walk back to the inn is short, I don't want her getting cold. I stride to the couch where she left her blanket, pick it up, and wrap it around her shoulders. I'm tempted to lean down and kiss her again, but instead, I graze my lips across her cheek.

"I'll watch from the door to make sure you get back to the inn okay. Your blanket cape will keep you warm."

"Thank you for tonight, I had a great time."

"Me too. I don't get much adult company other than my parents, and they don't count." I pause. "Are you going to the Tree Lighting Ceremony tomorrow? That is, if Ben doesn't have your car ready?"

"I was planning on it. Will I see you there?"

"Yep, Nora won't let me miss it. She's all about that Christmas spirit," I say with a laugh.

"Goodnight, Brent, see you tomorrow."

She gives me a tiny wave before wrapping the blanket across her chest, heading out the door, and making her way across the lawn.

I stand there, watching her leave with a heaviness in my chest. I stay rooted in place, long after she disappears from sight, until I can breathe again. I shut and lock the door for the night.

Navigating the living room, I put out the fireplace and unplug the Christmas tree.

When darkness fills the room, my thoughts swirl.

What have I done?

Chapter Sixteen

Penelope

When Brent kissed me, it felt like the world stopped. The only two people that existed were me and him. Nothing outside that room mattered. It was the best kiss I've ever had, and I never wanted it to end.

But based on the way he reacted, I don't think he feels the same. I'm such an idiot.

I was expecting to put Nora back to bed then pick up where we left off. Boy was I wrong. I'm not sure how I'm going to look at him and pretend that I didn't feel anything.

Because I did.

But he was just caught up in the moment.

Taking another deep breath, I sneak through the inn's front door. The glow from the twinkly lights makes me feel at home.

But this place isn't my home, I need to remind myself of that.

I ascend the stairs as quietly as possible. It's silent save for my own breathing, and I don't want to wake anyone up.

I slip into my room, close the door behind me, then lean against it. I slide to the ground and hug my knees to my chest. My mind continues to replay my night with Brent.

Did I read that kiss all wrong?

After who knows how long, I push myself up and head into the bathroom to get ready for bed.

Tomorrow is the Winterberry Christmas Tree Lighting Ceremony, and even though I'm completely mortified to see Brent, I'm looking forward to the event.

The blanket I wore to Brent's house still smells like him, so I snuggle up to it and rest my cheek on it. Trying to quiet my thoughts about seeing Brent tomorrow, I close my eyes and drift off to sleep.

Before I know it, light streams through the sheer curtains, waking me. My dreams were filled with Brent, the feel of his lips on mine, and the smell of him surrounding me. Not good.

Stretching my arms above my head, I glance at the window and think about the day ahead of me. Will it be awkward when I see Brent? Will I be able to pretend like nothing happened?

Good thing I basically play pretend for a living.

I'll treat it like I would an acting role. Playing his friend, and nothing else, for the remainder of my stay in Winterberry.

The big question is, why does that make me so sad?

Looking over at the old school alarm clock on the nightstand, I see that it's just after eight a.m. which means Brent should be out of the house already. Maybe I won't have to see him until tonight.

Once I'm dressed, with light makeup on and my hair in a bun, I head downstairs. The smell of French toast greets me.

"Good morning, Penelope," Suzanne says from the dining room where she's setting the table. "You're just in time for breakfast. I hope you're hungry!"

"Morning," I say. "It smells amazing in here. French toast sounds perfect. Can I help you set the table?"

Entering the kitchen, I notice she also has chocolate chip cookie dough on the counter, ready to go in the oven for tonight's dessert, and the crockpot is on in the corner.

This woman is going to put ten pounds on me before Christmas.

"That's okay honey, you sit down, I'm bringing the food to the table now."

Suzanne is the mother I wished I had when I was growing up. Gran did her best but she was too busy working to cook. I often ate by myself. I didn't mind, I knew it was a lot on her shoulders, but damn if I didn't wish it could've been different.

With her warm smile and signature apron tied around her waist, Suzanne brings a huge plate to the table. It's filled with pieces of French toast coated in powdered sugar and maple syrup. When she sets it down before me, I waste no time digging in.

"Would you like coffee to go with that?" Suzanne asks.

"I can get some myself, thank you though," I say in between bites.

"Nonsense, I'm getting myself a cup too so I'll pour you one. Cream in it, like you usually take?"

She knows how I take my coffee. For some reason, this makes my heart squeeze, and I smile. "Yes please."

After a few minutes, she reenters the dining room with two piping hot mugs of coffee and joins me. None of the other guests are up yet, so it's just us.

"What are your plans for today?" She asks as we eat. "You're coming to the Christmas Tree Lighting, right?"

"I am! I can't wait. I think I'm going to take a walk after breakfast then stop in and see Sally for lunch. I finished the book you left in my room, and I know you have so many here but I'm going to walk to the bookstore and see if I find any that pique my interest."

"That sounds like a great day sweetheart. Have you heard anything else about your car?"

"Not yet. I may stop into Ben's shop if I have time to check in. I'm sure the parts will be in soon and I'll be out of your hair," I joke.

"I've loved having you here. Nora has loved it too. She keeps talking about you."

"She sure is a special little girl," I say, my cheeks reddening as I remember last night at Brent's house.

For the next few minutes, we eat in silence before we're joined by guests who undoubtedly smelled the delicious breakfast and followed their noses downstairs. I don't blame them.

"Here, I'll take your plate, you sit and enjoy your coffee," I tell Suzanne when we're done eating.

In the kitchen, I load the dishwasher, wipe down the counters, and put away the breakfast ingredients.

The oven dings and Suzanne enters the kitchen, putting the cookie dough in to bake. I throw on my jacket before heading out into the cold. Since arriving in Winterberry, I've taken a daily walk, and it's something I really enjoy.

In the city, you can get to so many places by walking, but I never did. I always had my driver take me, even if it was only a few blocks away.

But here, I wake up in the morning and look forward to walking. Even when it rained the other day, I took an umbrella, put my hood up, and explored the streets.

Today, the sun is shining but it's cold. I zip my coat up before stepping off the porch. Without my phone to distract me, and no pressure to update social media, I'm truly present in the moment.

I've found myself noticing it all. From the smallest details—like the way the air smells or the way the trees look in the cold—to the larger things like the gorgeous Christmas decorations that cover the town, I don't think I'll ever forget.

There are so many people out today, probably because of the gorgeous sun, and most say hi as they pass. I'm starting to recognize faces, and a few people even stop to ask if my car is fixed or if I'll be at the Tree Lighting tonight.

In the city, people stopped me when I went places, but it was always to take my picture or get an autograph. They didn't care about *me*. Not really. They were just excited to get a photo for their Instagram feed.

After a few blocks, I arrive at the lake and stroll down the pier. Benches surround the water, with people sitting and taking in the view. It's so peaceful. I find an empty bench and take a seat.

Small waves lap at the shore, and there's a smell I can't describe in the air. It's a combination of the trees, the water, and the promise of snow.

It smells like hope.

And it feels like home.

Shivering against the cold, I stay on the bench for as long as I can, sharing small moments with passersby.

An hour later, my stomach rumbles and I realize it's nearing lunchtime. I make my way over to Sally's Diner.

When I enter the diner, I see Sally behind the counter in her usual spot, and wave.

"Penelope! Hi! Just one second and I'll get your favorite table ready for you."

"Thanks Sally!"

With her signature smile and eclectic taste in fashion, she interacts with each patron like they're her best friend. She knows everyone's names, their favorite dishes, and who their family members are.

I love seeing her in her element, being the amazing owner—and friend—that she is.

While I wait, I take in the framed photos on the walls, and I'm drawn to a picture of Brent and Nora. They're smiling, with their arms around each other, and Nora can't be older than a year or two.

A small smile appears on my face and my cheeks heat. Will I ever be able to look at even a picture of Brent again and not think about that kiss?

"Here you go, your table awaits my lady," Sally says, interrupting my thoughts.

"Yay thank you." I follow her to the table I always sit at when I come in. It's right next to the window, with a lovely view of Main Street. Sally sat me there once, and now it's my favorite spot. Sally tries to keep it open for me when she can.

I love her.

"How are you? Are you coming to the lighting tonight? Have you heard from Ben about your car?" She fires questions at me at warp speed, without pausing to take a breath.

"I'm good. I wouldn't miss the lighting. No word from Ben, I'm going over there after this to see if there's any news."

"Let me guess, you'd like a BLT with curly fries?" She's getting to know me too well.

"You're good, my friend, you're good."

"I try. Have you seen Brent lately? I feel like he hasn't been here in days."

"Ummm actually we watched a movie last night at his house. *Elf.* And we had some hot chocolate. He kind of found me outside in the snow, pacing, and cheered me up."

"A movie night huh?"

"Yeah. It was nothing, really." I'm really hoping my face doesn't give me away.

"Was Nora home?"

"She was actually, she woke up and wanted me to put her back to bed. She's just too cute."

"Wait, Brent had you over while she was there? And you put her back to bed?"

"Yep." Something tells me this is going to be a thing. "Is that surprising?"

"Um yeah. The only other women who have been inside while Nora is home, since Michelle died, have been me and his mom."

"Really? What about dates?" Well, now I am intrigued.

"He's gone on some dates but has never brought anyone home, at least not while his little girl is there. Don't repeat any of this, he will have my head." She groans.

"My lips are sealed." I mime locking my lips and throwing away the key.

She's right. If Brent knew she was sharing this information with me, he probably wouldn't be happy. I decide to change the subject. "Want to meet and go to the Christmas Tree Lighting together tonight?"

"Yes please! I think Dominick is going to go too. Have you met him yet?"

"I haven't, but I've heard much about him."

Brent has told me that Dominick is his best friend here in Winterberry and Nora calls him Uncle D. I'm surprised I haven't run into him yet or seen him at the inn but I'm excited to meet him tonight. "I'm excited to meet him."

"Yeah, an interesting one. I'll go put your order in."

While I wait, I people-watch out the window. I love seeing what people are wearing, what they're doing, and what's going on in town.

From my position by the window, I can see the big gazebo in the center of the park, and there are a few residents setting it up for tonight's event.

It's being adorned with strings of lights, a large gold star, and decorative presents.

It is going to look beautiful all lit up.

After a few minutes, Sally brings me my lunch. I eat leisurely while I chat with diners and watch the park get decorated.

"Sally, that was so delicious," I tell her as she comes back to clear my plate. "I don't know what you put in that sandwich, but I can't get enough. You may need to roll me out of here. I'm going to head over to Ben's to check on my car baby. I'll see you tonight!"

"I'm so glad you came in. See you tonight!"

Afterward, I head toward Ben's shop. Luckily, it isn't a far walk so I make it there before I'm completely frozen. December in Vermont is no joke.

I open the door to the shop, and the smell of oil and grease hits me in the face.

I hear his gruff voice before I see him, singing to Jingle Bell Rock behind the counter.

"Hi Ben!" I say. "You have the voice of an angel."

"Oh why thank you." He takes a bow. "I'm guessing you aren't here to hear me sing."

"As much as I adore your singing voice, I was at Sally's for lunch and thought I would stop in while I was out and check on my baby."

"Actually, I was hoping I would run into you at the Christmas Tree Lighting. I should have everything I need in the next few days and as soon as I do, I will get it fixed so you can get home. I'm so sorry it has taken so long. This nonstop snow has been slowing everything down."

As soon as the words are out of his mouth, my stomach drops. "Oh great... That's great news, Ben." I fake excitement.

I know I need to get home and get ready to film my next movie, but I'm not ready.

My feelings for Brent keep growing, and saying goodbye to Nora is going to be so hard. Not to mention leaving Sally, Suzanne, and everyone else who's made me feel welcome here.

"I knew you'd be happy with the update. Will I see you at the Tree Lighting?"

If he can tell I'm faking it, he doesn't let on, and for that I'm grateful. I don't want to sort out my feelings alone, let alone with someone else.

"You've been amazing, Ben. Thank you! I will be there!"

We chat for a few more minutes, and as soon as we're done, I head back outside into the fresh air. So many thoughts fill my head—from my life and career in Manhattan to Brent and Nora here in Winterberry. I struggle to calm my racing heart.

I look up and notice that gray clouds are starting to roll in, promising more snow. I stand there for a minute longer before letting out a silent prayer that my car won't be fixed until I can sort through my feelings. Slowly, I put one foot in front of the other and head back to the inn.

I have a special night to get ready for.

Chapter Seventeen

Brent

"Daaad. Daaad, hurry up, we're going to be late to the Christmas Tree Lighting," Nora calls from the living room.

I'm in my room taking my time getting ready and stalling the inevitable night that awaits me. And Nora is worried we're going to miss the lighting.

Not that missing it would be the worst thing ever, if I'm being honest.

"I'm coming Nora, we won't be late, don't worry," I yell. "We're meeting Grandma and Pop in front of the inn and going over with them."

I settle on my favorite black hoodie, dark blue jeans, work boots, and black beanie.

I'm not looking forward to seeing Penelope and trying to hide the way last night made me feel. But Nora won't let me out of this.

Here we go.

"Okay, okay, I'm here, let's go."

"Finally, geez, Dad, what were you doing in there?" she says, narrowing her eyes at me.

We head out the front door to meet my parents.

"Grandma! Pop! We're here, we're here! Dad almost made us late," Nora yells when we see my parents outside.

She turns around, sticking out her tongue at me. If she wasn't so cute, she'd be in trouble a lot more.

Turning back toward my parents, she runs and jumps into my mom's arms, wrapping herself around her body.

"That's okay sweetheart, we have plenty of time to get there," my mom says into her hair.

Now, it's my turn to stick my tongue out back at Nora. "See, I told you."

"Really, Brent?" My mom shakes her head.

Grabbing Nora's hand after my mom has put her down, I can't help but laugh as we start walking toward the center of town. Along the way, we run into tons of our neighbors, all on their way to the same place.

I hear the event before I see it, the sound of Christmas music filling the air, children laughing, and animal noises from the North Pole Petting Zoo that's been temporarily set up. I look down at Nora and notice that she can hear it too.

"Dad, can we hurry please? I want to see the reindeer before the tree lights up!" She drags me along.

"Sure, let's go munchkin."

We pick up our pace and I can't help but search for Penelope. I wasn't sure if she'd walk over with us, since she came to the festival with my parents, but so far there hasn't been a sign of her.

As soon as we hit the center of town, my senses are overloaded by all things Christmas. Seriously. Each year there's even more crap.

Nora heads straight for the makeshift petting zoo, where there are goats, donkeys, and domesticated deer wearing antlers. Reindeer, I suppose.

I follow my daughter closely, so I don't lose her. She could get easily lost in the crowd.

"Dad, do you think Santa needs his reindeer before Christmas? Like don't they need to practice flying or something?"

My daughter, the thinker.

"I think he's okay without them for just tonight, then they probably do need to practice," I say as I ruffle her hair.

I wonder how much longer she'll believe in Santa. I'm trying to hold on as long as possible.

"Penelope!" My daughter's loud yell pulls me from my thoughts.

I turn just in time to see Penelope walking over with Sally. Those two have become good friends since she got here, Sally doesn't shut up about her.

"Hi Nora! Omigosh are these Santa's reindeer?" Penelope says as she gives Nora a big hug. Her eyes connect with mine.

"They sure are. Dad says Santa is okay without them for tonight but that they have to go back to practice for Christmas."

"Your dad is probably right. Hey," she says quietly, blushing.

"Hey yourself." I can't help it, my eyes flicker to her lips, drawn there by the memory of our kiss. I have to look away.

"Hey Sal," I say looking at Sally instead.

Her eyes dart between me and Penelope. Damn, of course she noticed something's going on. She knows me too well.

"Hey, stranger." Sally waves at me with a smirk. Awesome. "How's work? Been busy on another case?"

"Yeah, this one's a monster. I promise I'll come in soon for breakfast or lunch. Did you guys come together?"

"We did," Penelope answers. "I went in for lunch today and we decided to walk over together. Sally promised to show me everything there is to see here at the lighting."

"I can show you too!" Nora tells her, jumping up and down like she has springs on her feet. "Dad, can we show Penelope all the fun things too?"

Of course she wants to.

"As long as they don't mind us tagging along,"I say, giving her an out. If she doesn't want to spend tonight with me, she can decline.

"I'd love that." She glances up at me through her eyelashes.

She has some makeup on, and her brown hair is curled, falling below her shoulders. She looks beautiful.

"Let's do it. What shall we see first, Nora?" I grab my daughter's hand.

It's going to be a long night.

Chapter Eighteen

Penelope

Wow, Brent looks *good* tonight.

He even has gel in his hair and cologne on. It's a delicious mix of citrus and cedar that I can't get enough of. Yesterday, I could've sworn I smelled it when I was walking to the diner, and I looked around for way too long, thinking he was nearby.

Pathetic, I know.

Now, here he is, and there's something about seeing him with Nora that makes my heart melt.

To be honest, I've never seen anything like this Christmas Tree Lighting Ceremony. Not even the Rockefeller Christmas Tree Lighting in the city comes close. Sure, there are celebrities and awesome music in the city, but this is something else. From the small-town vibe to the impressive tree size, I'm in awe.

As soon as we got here, I spotted Brent and Nora petting a reindeer, and my heart instantly skyrocketed. It took everything in me not to kiss him right there.

It seems like all 400 residents of Winterberry are here at the event, and I'm in Christmas heaven. I never knew how much I loved this season until coming to Winterberry.

Yes, I enjoyed holiday movies and putting on Christmas music, but here the experience is immersive. I'll never be able to do Christmas the way I used to.

I was thrilled Sally came with me to the lighting. I was nervous to come by myself. Now, here we are following Nora to the food vendors, and I'm trying really hard not to reach out and touch Brent.

"Look at all the *food*!" Nora yells. I never considered myself a foodie, but everything here looks and smells ah-*mazing*. From pulled pork and funnel cakes to hot dogs and roasted chestnuts, the smells lure us in. I don't know what to choose.

"Whoa! How is anyone supposed to choose what they're going to eat," I say as I clasp a hand to my chest.

Sally threads her arm through mine with a laugh.

"Girl, we don't have to choose. Let's get one of each and share," she says as she leads us to the first tent. The white topped tents are lined up, with tables underneath them filled with goodies, and decorations covering every surface.

"Excuse me, Penelope and Sally, can I share too?" Nora asks, turning around. Looking down into her beautiful eyes, how can anyone say no.

"Of course you can, gorgeous girl."

One by one, we walk to each tent and buy more food than we could possibly eat while Brent walks behind us chuckling. We keep handing him our food, and eventually he finds a spot on a curb so we can all sit together and chow down.

I find myself seated beside him, our knees touching. Heat spreads throughout my body, telling me that our kiss meant more to me than just two sets of lips touching. Stealing a glance at Brent, I notice he looks back at me briefly. We both look away before anyone else notices.

"You guys, this is the best thing *ever*!" Nora exclaims in between bites.

"Right? I'm so content right now, even though I feel like I may burst out of my pants," I say laughing.

"Who saved room for hot cocoa?" Sally asks. "We can't watch the tree be lit without hot chocolate in our hands."

"I definitely didn't but I'm totally down to try," I say, putting my hands over my stomach. I'm *so* full but she's right.

"Hey guys, what are you doing on the curb?" A deep, unfamiliar voice says from behind us.

When I turn around, I look up and notice a handsome man in an impeccably tailored suit, with a huge smile on his face.

"Uncle D!" Nora screams. "I just knew we would see you here. Why haven't you visited me?" She jumps up and throws her arms around his neck.

Oh, so *this* is Dominick, Brent's best friend.

"I'm sorry, Nora, I've been so busy. But here I am. Hey, Brent." Dominick hugs Brent, patting him on the back.

"Long time no see, D."

"And who is this fine creature?" he asks, looking right at me. Next to me, Sally sucks in a sharp breath, and when I look at Brent, I notice his fists balled at his sides like he could punch a wall.

"Dominick, meet Penelope," Brent says. "She's been in town for about two weeks, after her car broke down, and she's staying at the inn until it's fixed."

"I've heard a lot about you, Dominick," I say. "It's nice to put a face to the name."

I stand and offer him a hand to shake in greeting. He looks similar to Brent, but shorter and with blonde hair. His blue eyes peer out from underneath the shag of his hair. He keeps glancing at Sally, even when he's talking to me.

"Nice to meet you, Penelope. I hope you're enjoying our little town," he says. "Hi Sally, I feel like I haven't seen you in forever."

"That's because you haven't, Dominick," she replies icily. Well, this is a side of Sally I haven't seen since meeting her. "How long are you in town for?"

"Actually, I'm staying this time. I bought a little house on Dragonfly Street just yesterday. Did Brent not tell you? He was my lawyer during the sale."

When Sally looks at Brent, no words are needed. Her narrowed eyes scream at him. "Oh really? Nope, he didn't tell me." Her eyes stay glued to Brent's face, and she presses her lips firmly together.

Well, if looks could kill.

"Yep, I'm excited about it," Dominick says. "I'm sick of all the traveling and staying in hotels. I need somewhere to call home and what better place to do that than Winterberry."

Bang, bang, bang.

"Is this thing on?" Someone's voice blares into the loudspeaker. Everyone turns, and I notice the mayor standing on the steps of the gazebo. In front of him is a podium with lots of wires coming out of it, a microphone, and a huge red button.

"Oh boy, who gave that man a mic," Dominick mutters, elbowing Brent in the side. The two chuckle.

"Residents of Winterberry, who's ready to light this Christmas tree?"

The crowd cheers around me. Everyone seems to move at once, making their way closer to the gazebo in anticipation of the ceremony. The elementary school chorus belts out Christmas tunes from where they stand to the right of the gazebo.

"Shall we?" Brent asks as he throws our trash in the garbage can, grabs Nora's hand, and puts his hand on the small of my back as we walk through the crowd. It strikes me how natural this interaction is and I'm instantly filled with joy.

Glancing behind me, I catch Dominick trying to steer Sally through the throngs of people. She slaps his hand away and I shake my head.

She's honestly one of my favorite people.

"Dad, Dad, can we get close so I can see?" Nora tugs on Brent's hand.

"Hold on, my love, we're going to get as close as we can."

As we approach the gazebo, I stop and take in the scene around me. I'm speechless at the Christmas spirit that this tiny town has.

Brent notices me stop and bends down to whisper in my ear. "Are you okay?"

"Sorry, just taking it all in," I say, as a wave of emotion washes over me and threatens to pull me under.

"It's a lot, I know. If it's too much, we can leave."

"No, I love it. Yeah, it's definitely a lot." I pause. "But I love it."

I can't stop the smile from spreading across my face, and when I glance at Brent, he's also smiling. It isn't often this man smiles, he's normally stoic or frowning, but tonight, even amongst all this Christmas cheer and people, he seems happy.

"And a partridge in a pear tree..."

The chorus sings their last song, and everyone erupts in cheers. The students take a bow and then one by one, step down from the steps to find their parents.

"Thank you to the Winterberry Elementary School chorus for the beautiful song," Mayor Young says to the crowd. "And thank you, to each and every one of you for coming out tonight, braving the cold, and celebrating this joyous season together as a town. Tonight, we come together to light the Christmas tree which will stay lit on the green until after the new year. It's a symbol of not only this holiday, but of the beauty of our town. Now, without further ado, can we all count down from 10 so we can see this gorgeous tree all lit up?"

"Yay! It's almost time, Dad! You *better* count," Nora says to her dad, pointing at him with a very serious look on her face. I try as hard as I can to hold back a laugh.

"I promise, cross my heart, I will count," Brent says.

"Yeah, you said that last year but I caught you, Dad."

"Can I count, too?" I ask, breaking the moment between dad and daughter.

"Yes! Let's all count," Nora says. "Sally, Uncle D, Grandma, and Pop, you too!"

I am so entranced by the crowd that I don't even notice Brent's parents coming up behind us, holding hands with Suzanne's empty hand wrapped around Tom's arm. They're relationship goals. "We're ready to count Nora!"

"Ready? 10... 9... 8... 7..." Everyone in the park counts together, our voices ringing out in unison. "6... 5... 4... 3... 2... 1!"

When we get to one, Mayor Young presses the big red button on the podium, and the most brilliant colors light up the entire town square. Every single inch of the massive tree has lights on it, and the star on top is a beautiful golden color. It takes my breath away.

As I'm staring at the tree and taking in the joy on everyone's faces around me, something brushes against my hand. Looking down, I see Brent's pinkie finger grazing mine, slowly moving in circles against my skin.

Not wanting to make a big deal out of it, I gently rub his finger back. I glance up at his face and catch him peering down at me with a hunger in his eyes. The same hunger I saw last night.

Nora's voice cuts through the air and the moment comes to an abrupt halt. Brent moves his hand to Nora's curls, and she looks up at him with such affection that it brings tears to my eyes.

All around us, families laugh and smile, singing along to the Christmas music blaring over the speakers. Nora spots some friends from school and asks her dad if she can say hi.

"Only for a few minutes, we need to get going soon so you can get to bed."

Once she's gone, I'm alone with Brent.

"Well, what did you think of that craziness?" he asks.

"Ha ha. I didn't find it crazy," I say. "Where's your Christmas spirit, Mr. Grump?"

"Yeah yeah, Christmas spirit. Nora has enough for all of us," he jokes. "I'm glad you liked it. Next up is the Christmas Log Parade. I wonder if you'll still be here."

"I guess we'll have to see," I say as nonchalantly as I can.

"Hey, I have an idea, if Mom and Dad can watch Nora one night this week, would you want to go to that bar I was telling you about? Now that Dom is back in town, I thought maybe the four of us could go out. I need adult time."

My heart picks up its pace and my palms grow sweaty.

"That sounds fun." I work to keep my voice steady, so it doesn't betray my nervousness. I'm especially thankful for all those acting classes right now.

"Awesome. I'll let you know what night they're free. Time to round up Nora and get her to bed. Are you walking back with Sally?"

"Yep, I'm going to go find her now. Have a good night, Brent." I put my hand on his arm and squeeze.

Before I think better of it, I reach up and kiss his cheek.

"Goodnight Penelope."

I watch him walk away and can't help but stare. A night out with him can't come soon enough.

Chapter Nineteen

Brent

"Mom?" I whisper-yell as I slowly open the back door to the inn and peek my head inside the next day.

I saw Penelope leaving a little bit ago, all bundled up for her daily walk, so I know the coast is clear.

But still, I'm not taking any chances.

Yes, I'm being a child, but I'm okay with myself.

"Mom? Are you in there?" I creep further into the inn and go straight into the kitchen, where I can usually find her.

"Brent? Is that you?" She calls from the exact spot I expect her to be. "Hi honey, I was hoping you'd come by today."

To be honest, since that kiss with Penelope, I've been avoiding the inn when she's around. Which means I've also been neglecting the projects that need to get done for my parents.

I've found myself thinking about her nonstop, and when I invited her for a night out, I half-expected her to say no. Now, I'm not so sure going is a good idea.

"Sorry, I've been so busy at the office. What do you have on the to-do list for today?" I ask as I put my arms around her. I tower over her, but her hugs are the best thing ever.

They always have been.

"The bathroom in the Sleepy Orange room needs the toilet fixed and the closet door in the Painted Lady Room isn't closing right. Do you think you could look at those for me while I start tonight's dinner?"

"You got it." I release her shoulders and turn to head outside for the tools, then I pause. "Hey, Mom?"

"Yes dear?"

"Could you and Dad keep Nora overnight this week? I was thinking of going to the bar with Sally, Dominick, and Penelope on Friday."

"That sounds fun, of course we can keep her. We love having that little ball of energy here."

"Thanks, Mom. I have to check with everyone to see if they're free. Do you know when Penelope will be back?"

"She said she was going for her walk and then to the diner for lunch with Sally. So, maybe later this afternoon?"

"Perfect. I'm going to go get the tools from the shed and then get to work. I took the day off, so I can help with whatever you need."

"Does that mean you'll be here for dinner too?"

"Yep, Nora and I are going to come over if you have enough food for us."

"Hmm, let me think about it." She pauses, giving me a teasing smile. "I think we can swing it."

"We'll be here then," I tell her with a chuckle.

As soon as I open the back door, the cold wind whips around my face, and the smell of snow hits my nose. "You can't be serious, not snow again."

I head to the shed in the backyard and slowly open the door, taking in the scent of sawdust, cigars, and my dad's cologne. This is his favorite spot at the inn and where he spends most of his time.

He makes things out of wood, really beautiful pieces. When we moved back to Winterberry, he handcrafted Nora's headboard, footboard, and bed frame. He's insanely talented and could sell his work for thousands, but he refuses. He only does it because he loves it.

He's also a meticulous organizer and all his tools hang on the wall in a specific order, grouped by type and size.

I grab what I need, then I linger a little longer to check out his newest project—a new sleigh for Santa that will go in front of the inn. It's beautiful. I run my hand down the side, noticing how smooth the wood is. He hasn't painted it yet, but I can picture what the final project will look like.

Wrapping my arms around myself to ward off the cold, I close the door tightly behind me and make my way back to the inn. I know my mom has other things that need to get done, so I'm hoping I can work quickly and get much of it done before I have to get Nora from school.

The first room I visit is the Painted Lady Room to fix the closet door. The guests who are staying in this room are out for the day, which is why Mom is having me fix it now, but I knock anyway before entering.

I love the rooms here. Each one is named after a species of butterfly—Mom's favorites— and they all have individual fireplaces, en suite bathrooms, and flat screen TVs. But there are subtle differences in each room, too. Like the colors of the comforter or the type of furniture. In this room, the furniture is all white and the bedding is a pale orange. The bathroom has black and white tiles on the floor and in the shower, along with white cabinets and a granite countertop.

It's really a beautiful combination.

The closet doesn't take long to fix, and I make my way to the Sleepy Orange room, where all the furnishings are dark wood and the accents are pale orange colors, matching the butterfly it's named after.

The toilet is a quick fix, but some of the parts need to be replaced, so I go back to the shed to get the parts before finishing.

My mom gives me another few projects off her list, and by early afternoon I've completed everything. It feels good to help out, especially since I've been slacking.

I have just enough time to shower before leaving to get my little girl. Hopping in my truck, I make my way down Main Street, past the town Christmas tree, and park on the street in front of her school. It's freezing out, but I exit my truck to wait for her on the sidewalk.

"Hi Dad!" Nora yells as she comes running out of the building.

Her curls bounce as she skips down the steps and jumps into my arms, wrapping her little arms around my neck and giving me a squeeze. She still gets so excited when she sees me, and I hope that never changes. Everyone tells me it will one day but I'm crossing my fingers they're wrong.

"Hey little love bug!" I say, smooching her cheek. "How was your day?"

"Booooooring. School is so boring," she whines.

She's never enjoyed school much, but it got worse after Michelle died.

"That's okay, honey, you know Christmas break is right around the corner and then I get you all to myself for days and days."

"I can't wait!"

Christmas break is in under two weeks away, and Nora has been excitedly counting down.

She squeals as I carry her to my truck, opening the door and setting her on the seat.

"Let's get home, we're going to have dinner with Grandma and Pop tonight at the inn, how does that sound?"

"That sounds great. What about Penelope? Will she be there too?"

My palms start sweating and my heart beats harder at just the sound of her name. If she *is* there, I'm going to ask her about the bar.

"You know what, I didn't ask Grandma when I was there today. I guess it'll be a surprise."

"I *love* surprises!"

"Oh, I know you do, peanut."

Any other time of the year, you won't catch someone who doesn't live in Winterberry roaming around. But during the Christmas season, visitors take day trips to town to get into the holiday spirit.

More and more people have been coming to town to see the tree, walk around Main Street, and go shopping in the specialty stores. It's funny to see out-of-state license plates in our little town.

Today, luckily, there aren't too many cars on the road. Some days, it's hard to find a parking spot downtown.

"Do you have any homework, little one?" I ask Nora as we park in the driveway.

"Ugh yes," she says as she rolls her eyes. "My math teacher gave us two pages to do tonight. Can I do them when we get home from dinner?"

"You know the rules." I grab her backpack from her, slinging it over my shoulder. "Homework before anything else. I'll make you a small snack to eat while you work, how does that sound?"

"Can the snack be popcorn? Pleeeeease?"

"Sure, I can pop a bag. Let's get inside, it's cold out here."

"I think it smells like snow," she says, taking a huge whiff of the air on our way up the front steps of the house. "I hope it snows!"

"Ugh, snow."

"Don't be a party pooper, Dad. Snow is fun!"

As soon as we get inside, Nora hangs up her coat, throws her shoes into the corner by the front door, and curls up on a chair at the table. I hand her backpack to her so she can do her homework. Sometimes I look at her and can't believe she's mine.

I make a bag of popcorn and bring her a small bowl. It's her favorite snack.

She only needs help with one of her questions, which is good because I suck at math, and before I know it, it's time for dinner.

I throw on my black hoodie and my best jeans, for no particular reason, and we both bundle up to make the tiny trek across the lawn. It feels like my heart is going to beat out of my chest as we open the back door, and I'm immediately greeted by Penelope's laugh.

I love the sound of her laughing.

"Grandma, Pop, we're here!" Nora screams. She bounds through the inn and straight into my mom's arms. "Penelope, I just *knew* you were going to be here."

I take a deep breath, filling my lungs, and trying to calm my racing heart, before walking into the dining room. My gaze finds Penelope right as she's bending down to give Nora a hug. She picks her up and seeing the two of them together warms my otherwise cold heart.

"Hey, Brent," Penelope says as she places my little girl back on the ground. We lock eyes. Her cheeks flush and it makes me smile.

"Hey there. Nora was convinced you'd be here tonight. Are you staying for dinner?"

"Yep, I helped your mom get everything going. We're having pulled pork sandwiches and vegetables."

"Yummy! That sounds deeeelicious!" Nora squeals.

"Dinner is ready," Mom yells.

I wait to see where Penelope sits, but when she doesn't grab a seat, I wonder if she's doing the same thing.

"Come on Daddy, sit down, dinner is ready, didn't you hear Grandma?"

Out of the corner of my eye, Penelope covers her mouth with her hand, presumably to hide a laugh.

"Yes I did, bossy," I say, taking a seat next to Nora.

Penelope sits down across from me. I don't know how I'm going to focus on my dinner when I have her eyes right there.

Great.

Once the food is on the table, everyone digs in. Comfortable conversations flow around the table. Three of the guests at the inn have also joined us, and Nora is telling them all about Christmas in Winterberry.

The way she talks, it makes this place seem magical. And at this moment, as much as I was hesitant to move back here when we did, I couldn't be happier to be here.

Nora's eyes light up when she talks about the snow, the reindeer at the Christmas Tree Lighting, the Christmas Eve Ball, and all the decorations around town.

I take my eyes off of her and catch Penelope appearing completely entranced by Nora and her infectious happiness. I can't help the smile that tugs at my lips.

As everyone continues to eat, there's a lull in conversation, and I take the opportunity to ask Penelope about going to the bar. My hands start sweating, *again*, and my stomach starts churning.

"Hey Penelope," I say, barely above a whisper.

She looks up from her plate, and for a second, I'm not sure I can speak. My tongue feels ten times too big for my mouth and my lips won't seem to work. Clearing my throat, I wipe my sweaty palms on my jeans.

"Mom said she could watch Nora on Friday night after the parade so me, you, Sally, and Dominick can go to the bar I was telling you about. Does that sound good to you? If you... don't have other plans. Or if your car... isn't ready yet."

What the hell? Why can't I speak a full sentence?

My mom stares at me awkwardly and my dad tries not to laugh as he pretends to wipe his face with a napkin.

After a few seconds of silence that seems to stretch on, she finally says, "That sounds great!"

"Awesome, we can share an Uber. If that's okay with you."

"Yep, that's perfect. I haven't been to a small-town bar in so many years."

"Oh, this one is an experience," I tell her, starting to feel more confident. See, this is no big deal. I've got this. "You're in for a *real* treat."

Her flush deepens, and I'm beginning to think it happens when she's nervous or excited. I try not to read into it.

Ring... ring... ring...

The phone at the front desk rings, and I curse under my breath.

"I'll get it!" Mom says as she gets up and rushes to the front. Guests call that number to book their rooms, and she's usually the one to answer it. "Sure, one second, Ben," she says into the phone.

Why is Ben calling the inn during dinner time? His shop is closed by now, like every other store and restaurant in town.

"Penelope, it's Ben for you," Mom calls. "He has news about your car."

I suck in a breath, trying to hide the disappointment that is surely written on my face. Penelope glances up, locking eyes with me, before she makes her way to the phone.

Chapter Twenty

Penelope

I can feel Brent's eyes on me as I get up from the table. I head to where Suzanne stands with the phone, near the inn's entrance. My emotions are at war with themselves in my chest.

"Fingers crossed," she whispers.

She reaches out to pat my shoulder before returning to the table to give me privacy.

So much goes through my mind. It'll be great if my car is ready. I can go home and get back to work, resuming my life as Penelope Maxwell.

So why am I feeling shattered? It's just a town, and I always knew I'd leave at some point.

Breathing deep, I put the phone to my ear.

"Hey Ben, do you have news about my car?"

"Penelope, hey. I'm sorry to bother you during dinner, but I wanted to call as soon as I got the news. I found a shop not too far from here that has the parts I need to fix your four-wheeled baby." He laughs to himself.

"That is great news, Ben!" I say, trying to muster up enthusiasm. "When do you think it'll be ready?"

"As soon as the parts come in, I'll get started. Probably be ready for you to head back to the city by the weekend."

"Amazing! Thank you for calling me, Ben, you're the best. You've been a lifesaver with my car." A part of me means it and is relieved at the idea of being home in a few days. On the other hand, I'll miss everything, and everyone, in Winterberry.

I can hear his smile through the phone, and it makes my entire day.

"Aww thank you, Ms. Penelope, I'm doing what I can. I'm sure you want to be home for Christmas."

Christmas.

The thought of being in my empty apartment without a tree or anyone to eat dinner with makes my stomach hurt.

"Absolutely." My voice shakes. "Have a great night."

I hang up. Quietly walking toward the dining room, I pause and listen to the chatter around the table. Nora's little voice cuts through the air and my heart swells. Smoothing down my clothes and running my hands over my hair, I stall for a minute.

The thought of leaving sucks the air from my lungs.

Heading back to the table, I realize I could get used to this and that scares the shit out of me.

"What did he say?" Suzanne says as soon as I come around the corner.

I glance in Brent's direction but let my eyes find Suzanne before he can look back. "He found a local shop that has the parts he needs to fix the car. He said I should be good to go back to the city, Manhattan, by the weekend."

"That's great news honey!"

"It is. I'll be back home by Christmas." I force a smile before sitting down to finish dinner.

"Nooooooo! You'll miss the Christmas Eve Ball," Nora says. Her fierce frown strangles my heart. "You can't miss the ball. It's the fanciest."

"Nora, Penelope has a home and being home for Christmas is what makes people happy." Brent says. "And we want Penelope to be happy right?"

"But she's happy here." Nora pouts.

"I am happy here, Nora. But Brent is right, my home is in Manhattan. I want to enjoy the time here in Winterberry though. Want to go to the Christmas Log Parade together?"

"Yes, yes, Daddy can we, can we?" She bounces in her seat.

"Sure, that sounds fun. Maybe Grandma and Pop can come too."

"And Aunt Sally and Uncle D?"

"Definitely," Brent says as he ruffles Nora's hair, to which he's awarded an epic eye roll.

Though the food is delicious, I can barely taste it as I shovel it down. There's a lump in my throat and I'm trying to hold back tears, but I'm attempting to appear normal, so I keep talking to everyone at the table.

But I'm far from it, actually.

Could I stay here? No.

If I want to continue my successful career, then I *need* to get back to where the opportunities are, where I'm seen.

Here, I'm Penelope Smith. But that's not who I really am. Is it? I'm not even sure anymore.

The past few days have gone by in a blur. Friday came much too quickly, and now I'm getting ready for the Christmas Log Parade followed by a night out at the bar.

With Brent.

A night out with Brent.

That is, if I can pick something to wear and get myself out of this room in time.

Sifting through my wardrobe, I settle on a pair of black jeans, an off-the-shoulder red Chanel sweater, leopard belt, and black boots. At the last second, I put on a lacy black bra and matching panties. Butterflies erupt in my stomach, threatening to burst out.

Whenever I wear a matching set, I always feel sexy, and I want to feel like that tonight.

Once I'm dressed, I head into the bathroom to do my hair and makeup. I put on a full face, complete with foundation, bronzer, a perfectly winged eyeliner, mascara, and red lips. I curl my hair in big, bouncy waves.

Finishing off the look, I throw on leopard earrings and my gold watch. I feel good, better than I've felt since getting stuck here in Winterberry. In fact, I think this is the first time I've done a full face of makeup since arriving.

Damn, it feels good to be in my armor.

I give myself a once-over in the mirror and like what I see. I'm bringing my A game tonight.

Satisfied with how I look, I grab my coat and head out the door.

Standing in the hallway, I fill my lungs and quiet my beating heart by resting my hand on my chest. Reminding myself that it's just a night out with friends, I keep walking down the stairs, following the voices I hear into the kitchen.

As soon as I round the corner, I see Brent, Nora, Suzanne, and Tom standing around talking. I take a minute to appreciate the sight of Brent in his jeans and the long-sleeved thermal shirt his biceps threaten to break out of.

He must feel my attention on him because he turns in my direction before anyone else notices me.

The heat from his gaze is almost too much to bear. His eyes slowly roam my body, starting from the top of my head and moving all the way down to my feet, then back up, stopping at my chest before landing on my lips.

My cheeks heat under his stare. What is this man doing to me?

"Penelope!" Nora squeals when she spots me. She comes running across the room and right into my arms. Instinctively, I wrap my arms around her middle and take in her scent. She always smells like strawberries, and it's a smell I've come to adore.

"Hey sweet girl, are you ready for the parade?" I say into her hair before setting her down and turning to face Brent.

His eyes are still on me, and if we weren't in the kitchen of his parents' house with his family in the same room, I would stride over and embrace him.

"SO ready! Let's go, let's go," Nora says as she takes my hand and pulls me toward the door.

"I guess we're going." Suzanne laughs as we all follow Nora outside. "You look beautiful honey," she whispers into my ear so no one else can hear.

My cheeks burn at her compliment.

"Thank you." I push my hair behind my ears and pull my coat collar up to my ears to fight off the frigid air.

Winterberry isn't far from Manhattan, but it's much colder.

If someone had asked me two weeks ago what snow smelled like, I would've looked at them like they were crazy. But now? I'd tell them that it smells almost crisp, like there's a sweetness in the air. The air turns so sharp that it pierces through your clothes, no matter how many layers you may have on.

If I could bottle up that scent, I would.

Together, the five of us walk the few blocks to Main Street, where the parade will pass by. Honestly, I'm not even sure what this parade is, but the excitement in the air is infectious.

"I forgot to ask, what *is* the Christmas Log Parade?" I ask the group.

"Oh, just you wait and see," Brent teases.

We find a spot along the sidewalk, where Nora can sit on the side of the road with a front row seat. Both sides of the street fill up fast, but we leave enough space for Sally and Dominick to join us.

I lean over to ask Brent, "Are Sally and Dominick going to make it to the parade?"

"Yeah, Sally is closing the diner first and then Dom is coming from work, which means he's coming from home. That isn't too far from here."

As people pass by, they stop and say hi, talking about their upcoming plans for Christmas and sharing excitement for the parade. Christmas is less than two weeks away, and you can tell the little ones are ready.

Not for the first time since coming here, I wonder what people would think if they knew who I really was. That my last name wasn't Smith. Would they still like me if they knew I lied? I've gotten so comfortable these last few days that I haven't even thought about someone recognizing me.

"Hey guys! Who's ready for the parade?" Sally asks as she walks over to us, ripping me out of my thoughts.

"Me! Me! Me!" Nora yells with her arm up in the air and a big smile.

This girl is so full of excitement—the complete opposite of her dad, whose features are pinched. There's a blank stare in his eyes, and each time someone comes up to us, he waves but doesn't say much. I'm starting to realize that he's not only grumpy, but socially awkward, too.

"Having fun?" I whisper as I slide up next to him. Our arms brush, sending warmth through my body.

"Oh yes, a blast," he says, glancing around. "I'll be happy when we're at the bar. This isn't my scene."

"Is it the people? Or the Christmas?" I ask, hoping I don't regret that decision.

"It's both," he says curtly, signaling the end of this short-lived conversation. Yep, regret it. "Hey Sal, did you see Dom when you were walking over here?"

"I didn't. Don't worry, you'll be able to smell him a million miles away when he gets here. That man bathes in cologne I swear," she says, rolling her eyes.

I wonder what the story is between those two.

"Leave him alone, Sal." Brent laughs. It doesn't happen often, but when it does, it's a beautiful sound.

"It's starting, it's starting!" Nora screams in delight. "Dad, where's Uncle D?"

"I'm not sure sweetheart. He'll be here, he probably got stuck on a meeting or something. Don't worry, he won't miss it."

"I wouldn't miss it for the world," a deep voice says from behind us.

I spin around to see Dominick.

"Uncle D! There you are. Phew, I thought you were going to miss the parade and that made me sad." Nora bolts over to hug his leg before scurrying back to her spot on the curb.

"Yeahhhhh, we wouldn't want that," Sally mutters. Only I'm close enough to catch it.

Before I get the chance to ask her why she hates him so much, the sounds of Christmas music and excited, child-like screeching fill the air, indicating the start of the parade.

Brent is talking to his parents, and Nora yells at him to hush. She definitely gets her bossy side from her dad. She's going to be a force of nature when she gets older.

"Sorry, sorry, I'm hushing," Brent says, sticking his tongue out at his little girl.

I hear the sound of a marching band coming down the street before I see them. Followed by a banner that reads "Winterberry High School Marching Band" are rows of kids with instruments, playing all of the classics. Tunes including White Christmas, We Wish You A Merry Christmas, and Rudolph The Red Nosed Reindeer fill the air and I find myself singing along.

I glance over at Brent who's watching the parade and silently tapping his leg along to the songs. I don't think he wants anyone to notice, so I pretend like I don't see it.

Behind the band comes cheerleaders with their pom-poms, fire trucks with their sirens blaring, police cars with their lights on, and even more Christmas music.

There's a small lull in the parade, and I still don't get the point of the "Christmas Log Parade" name, but before I can ask Brent, I see a group of kids coming down the street, and the crowd's cheering picks up.

Nora jumps to her feet, bouncing excitedly as the kids approach. I notice one of them pulls a red wagon behind them. Other kids surround the wagon as they walk, and it isn't until they're almost in front of us that I can see what's being toted inside.

It's a huge log.

The log sits on a bed of red-and-green velvet blankets, with pieces of holly and red berries attached. As the wagon goes by, the entire crowd rises, vigorously clapping their hands and hollering.

I don't really understand what's happening, but I'm in awe of all the shared excitement around me. As soon as the group passes, I tap on Brent's shoulder.

"What in the world was that?" I ask once the excitement simmers down.

The crowd begins moving at once, toward the gazebo in the center of town, and I don't know if I should follow or stay where I am.

Brent leans down and whispers in my ear, sending a chill down my spine. "Come follow and see for yourself. I may not be a Christmas fan, nor am I someone who loves crowds, but this part I think you'll love as much as I do."

As we start walking, following along with the crowd, he puts his hand on the small of my back and stays close.

"By the way," he whispers. "You look beautiful."

I glance up at him and smile, unsure of what to say. I continue walking instead of responding.

The closer we get to the center of town, the more the excitement grows. The band is set up to one side of the gazebo, and the kids surround the wagon on the other side.

The crowd spreads around— covering every inch of the snowy grass and spilling into the street. The band plays festive songs before Mayor Young ascends the gazebo steps to the podium and everyone quiets down.

For the first time, I notice a stone fireplace set up on the sidewalk in front of the gazebo. This must've been set up today because I haven't seen it before.

Mayor Young says a few words into the microphone before the little girl who was pulling the wagon takes the log out and stands in front of the fireplace.

The whole crowd is silent, watching with rapt attention as the little girl puts the log into the fireplace. The mayor strikes a match and throws it into the fireplace and the logs erupt in flames.

As the logs crackle and pop, the comforting aroma of burning wood and smoke fills the air, the entire crowd goes wild, cheering, clapping, and singing along to "Have Yourself A Merry Little Christmas," with the band.

I glance around at the residents of Winterberry, all together celebrating this moment, together in song, and a small tear escapes my eye.

I've seen a lot of things in my life, from the Eiffel Tower lit up to lions roaming in Africa, but there's something about the homey atmosphere of Winterberry and its residents that sticks out to me. It's the most beautiful thing I've ever experienced.

Slowly, more tears fall, and I'm defenseless against them.

The moment I take the sleeve of my coat to wipe them, Brent turns to face me, using the sleeve of his shirt instead to catch my tears.

We lock eyes and I shake my head, pulling myself together.

"Are you okay?" he asks, voice laced with concern. He probably thinks I'm a crazy woman for crying over a log.

"Sorry. I don't know what came over me." I take a deep breath. "I've never seen anything like this before."

"Yeah, this is a Winterberry tradition. It started when the town was formed, as a way to keep warm during the winter months. Then, at some point, it became a Christmas tradition," he explains. "The fireplace stays lit through Christmas Day, and then that night the town comes together again for it to be put out. It doesn't make much sense but it's a thing."

"I love it," I say, and I mean it. I'm not sure why something as simple as a fireplace is making me emotional, but it is. The realization that I never want to leave hits me square in the chest. "If Ben was right about my car, I'm sad I won't be here to see it."

"Yeah, that's true..." he says quietly. Immediately, he shuts down and turns back to the crowd toward Nora and his parents, leaving me standing by myself.

"Penelope, you look amazing," Sally says as she fights her way through the crowd to reach me. "Are you ready for the bar tonight?"

"I am." I half-smile. "I've never seen anything like this before. Brent was explaining it to me and I'm literally in awe."

"Yeah, this is something special here in our town. I look forward to it every year. It's something so simple but so beautiful. I probably sound corny." She laughs.

"Nope, not corny at all. I completely agree."

"Do you have an ornament to put on the tree?" she asks.

"What do you mean?"

"The tree! It's empty right now, but from now until Christmas, people bring homemade ornaments and decorate it. Wait until you see it in a few days, it'll be overflowing."

"I love that!" And I mean it. "Maybe Nora and I can make ornaments to hang on there."

"She would love that. You can do it before you leave, then your ornament will be here as a reminder of your time in our tiny town," she says as she loops her arm through mine. "Okay, let's go find the boys and go to the bar. I need a night out. I could do without a night out with Dominick, but it'll still be fun."

"What is the story with you two?" I ask her.

"We dated in high school, I thought we were in love, he didn't, the end."

"It doesn't sound like the end to me," I say bluntly.

"Please, I can't stand that man," she says, giggling. "Let's go get the boys."

We join the group, approaching Brent and Dominick.

"Okay, are we ready for a night on the town?" Sally asks. "Small town, but still a town."

"Definitely ready," Brent says. I can tell he's itching to get out of here. "Our Uber will be here in a minute. I'm gonna say goodnight to Nora and then we can go."

As he walks away, I can't stop myself from staring. He looks otherworldly in those jeans. This man is like a Greek God and I'm under his spell.

I watch him as he embraces his little girl and kisses her forehead, hugs his mom goodbye, and waves to the other residents around him. He may not be a big people person, but damn is he loved here in Winterberry.

"All right, our chariot awaits," he says once he gets back to where we're waiting. "Let's go."

The four of us make our way to the Uber.

Here goes nothing.

Chapter Twenty-One

Brent

As soon as we get to the Uber, Dom climbs up front. Sally grabs the seat behind the driver. I open the back passenger door for Penelope, and she looks up at me before sliding into the middle seat.

The back seat is small, and when I get in, the three of us are squished together. Our legs are touching, and Penelope's nearness sends heat rushing through me.

I'm not sure where to put my hands, so I lay one on my left thigh and prop my head up with my right hand. Penelope puts both of her hands on her thighs, and I'm tempted to reach out and interlace our fingers.

The desire is almost out of my control, but I don't know how she would react if I did. I don't want to make her uncomfortable.

"All right, ready for a night at The Anchor Pub?" the Uber driver asks.

He's a young guy who can't be any older than twenty-five. He turns on the radio and blasts Christmas music. Dom starts singing along in the worst voice ever and Penelope giggles next to me.

She and Sally have been talking nonstop since we stepped into the car while I sit quietly. For some reason, I feel awkward, even though we're with *my* best friends.

The two of them stop chatting and Sally looks out the window while Dominick continues to belt out tunes. I sneak a peek next to me and immediately lock eyes with Penelope. Through her lashes, I can see her big eyes clearly, and my gaze travels to her red lips.

They look extra plump in that lipstick color. The memory of her taste comes back to me so vividly, it's like my mouth is locked on hers again.

I notice her chest quickly rising and falling, like she's trying to catch her breath, and I force myself to look away. Instead, I focus on the town going by out the window. The bar isn't far, but it's definitely too cold to walk.

"So, what can I expect at this bar?" Penelope asks me, breaking the silence.

"Well, there's beer, beer, greasy bar food, and more beer," I tell her.

This probably isn't the type of place she's used to, and I'm not sure how she's going to feel. With the way she looks tonight, guys are going to be all over her. Just the thought of this happening has me balling my fists on my lap.

"Here we are," the driver says, turning down the music.

As we pull up, familiarity swells in my chest at the comfort this bar brings. I've been coming here since I could drink, maybe even a little before that, so I know the place well.

In fact, the owner is one of my friends from high school. He bought the bar from his folks a few years ago and has been running it ever since.

As soon as we park, we all jump out, and I can't help but touch Penelope's shoulder as she makes her way out of the car. We're freezing, so we hurry inside to get out of the cold.

When we open the door, the music takes over. The people are loud and unfiltered, and Penelope shifts almost uncomfortably. She stops for a second, taking it all in, before I put my hand on her back. She immediately relaxes under my touch.

As we walk further into the bar, everyone turns to look at us. No—they're looking at *her*. All eyes are on the beautiful woman next to me and I think she can tell.

"It's okay, stick with me," I whisper in her ear.

I take a second to let her scent fill my nose before pulling away. I don't know why I feel protective of her, but I do.

Dom and Sally are already making their rounds, saying hi to everyone they know.

Tables and leather booths sit against the walls, with a large, open space in the middle of the room for people to dance. There's a small stage set up in the corner where bands sometimes play, or people sing karaoke. Christmas tunes, which I can't seem to escape, blast from the speakers, and white twinkle lights hang all over the place. A tiny Christmas tree sits on the bar near the register. The bartenders are in full swing, making drinks and serving what seems like the entire county.

Penelope and I make our way through the crowd to a booth near the bar where Dominick and Sally are sitting. This is our favorite table and the one we always try to grab when we come. For some reason, people whisper amongst themselves as we pass.

Why the hell is everyone acting so weird tonight?

"There you two are. I thought we lost you," Sally says as we approach.

"This place is packed." Penelope slides into the booth. "Is it usually like this?"

"Yep," we all say in unison.

"Got it," Penelope says. "What are you guys going to drink?"

"I'm going to order a beer. I can get everyone else's drinks too. What will it be?" I ask.

"Beer for me," says Dom.

"I'll have a Long Island iced tea," yells Sally over the noise.

"That sounds good. I'll have one too," Penelope says.

I want to stay by her side so no other men try to talk to her, but I also know that getting arrested two weeks before Christmas would put a damper on the holiday for Nora. Therefore, I need to put some space between us.

"Got it, be right back." I make my way to the bar.

"Brent! Hey man, long time no see," Alex says from behind the bar. "You here with Sally and Dominick? I saw them come in a few minutes ago."

"Hey man, it has been a little while. Yep, we're all here together and we brought a newbie whose car broke down in town. She's been staying at the inn while she waits for it to get fixed so we're showing her where we like to hang out."

"Oh nice, she hot?" he asks with a laugh as he smacks my shoulder.

"I haven't paid attention," I answer, lying through my teeth. "You know me, never looking for a relationship."

"True. We've all been trying to get you fixed up but it never works."

"Nope, not me. So, we need two beers and two Long Island iced teas."

"Coming right up." He goes to fetch the drinks.

Turning around and putting my back against the bar, I take in the room and all the people. Everyone is drinking, and there's a group of girls dancing in the middle of the floor. I laugh as I watch them stumble along to the beat.

My eyes inadvertently find our booth and I can't help but stare at Penelope. She's so beautiful, I can't look away. She's in conversation with Sally and Dominick, and I love that she gets along with them.

Just as I'm about to avert my gaze, some guy walks up to the table and addresses Penelope. Her gaze shifts from Sally to the guy, and I instantly feel jealous. Actually, I have an urge to punch him, but I'm an adult. That would be ridiculous.

Right?

I need Alex to hurry up with these drinks. I'm watching across the room as Penelope throws her head back in laughter at something this jerk says.

Is he actually a jerk? I have no idea.

I don't even know him, and I hate him.

"Here ya go buddy," Alex says, snapping me out of my jealous rage.

"Thanks man, can you open up a tab for us for the night?"

"You got it," he tells me as I grab the drinks.

I scurry back to the booth as fast as I possibly can. The guy is still standing there when I arrive, still talking to Penelope. I don't even care what his name is, I'm sticking to Jerk.

"Hey, here's our drinks." I stand at the table, right behind Jerk. He turns around and looks directly at me.

"Sorry man, am I in the way?"

He has to be visiting. I usually recognize most of the people in this joint.

"Yep," I force out.

He turns to the table and says, "It was nice to meet you guys, especially *you*, Penelope. I'm over there if you want to come hang out with me and my friends."

That was definitely directed at *her*.

Finally, he moves out of the way, and I set the drinks on the table.

"Who was that?" I ask. My voice comes out harsher than I intend. He's got me all messed up.

"No clue," Dominick says. "Sure seemed to like our girl Penelope here." He says it as a joke, but I ball my fists at my sides anyway.

"Shut up, Dom," Sally says as she punches him in the arm.

I glance at Penelope, whose face has turned bright red. Sitting down, I snatch my drink. We all start drinking, laughing, and talking. Except for Penelope. She quietly sips the drink I got her.

Maybe she isn't a big drinker? I didn't even think to ask before inviting her to a *bar*.

I lean down next to Penelope's ear so she can hear me. "Are you not enjoying your drink?"

"It's delicious, but I'll be honest, I don't drink. I haven't been drunk or even buzzed in years," she says sheepishly.

"Is there a reason? Or you just don't like it."

"I don't like feeling out of control, which probably sounds weird. I like knowing what I'm doing and being in control of the decisions I'm making."

"Doesn't sound weird at all. I like the taste of beer but haven't been drunk in a really long time either," I tell her honestly. "Especially since becoming a single dad. It's important to me that I'm on my A game for Nora."

"That makes sense. I'm actually not surprised by that." She places her hand on my arm as she says this.

"Hey, let's dance," Sally says to Penelope, pulling us out of the moment.

"Yessssss," Penelope yells.

It was nice to connect with Penelope on that deeper level, and it's only adding to my feelings. It's been a really long time since I've been jealous over a woman, and it's throwing me for a loop just how protective I'm feeling over her. My earlier jealousy about Jerk's attention on her is still lingering.

"Brent, move," Sally slurs. "We can't get out of the booth if you're blocking the way."

She's definitely letting loose tonight, which she deserves. That woman is at the diner everyday and has worked hard to make it a success.

As soon as I slide out of the booth and stand, the two women make their way through the throngs of people onto the dance floor. I settle back into my seat and look at Dom, who doesn't notice me.

His eyes are locked on one person: Sally.

These two drive me nuts.

I glance at Penelope, who's swaying her hips and moving to the music. She and Sally have their hands clasped with their heads tilted back, laughing as they move. I can't help but smile at the two of them.

They both look ecstatic.

When Penelope first arrived here in Winterberry, she was guarded. She would let little giggles out here and there, and pieces of her personality would come out, but she always seemed to carry the weight of the world on her shoulders.

But here, right now, with Sally on the dance floor, her inhibitions are down and I can see the *real* Penelope. There's a light in her eyes that wasn't there before. As I peel my gaze from her, I notice that I'm not the only one watching her dance with Sally. And I don't blame any of them for staring.

Out of the corner of my eye, I see Jerk heading toward the dance floor with two of his friends. He makes a beeline for the girls, and I immediately hop out of the booth.

"Hey, where are you going?" Dom asks as I stride away.

I head to where the girls are dancing. People I recognize try to stop me and chat, reminding me why I hate small towns. Everyone knows everyone, making it impossible to get somewhere fast.

By the time I make my way to Penelope, Jerk is trying to dance with Penelope, and I can tell she isn't feeling it. She's doing her best to ignore him by keeping her body turned to Sally, but apparently, he doesn't take a hint.

Turns out Jerk truly is a jerk.

I'm going to kill him.

"Hey Penelope," I say as loud as I can. I step between her and Jerk, practically pushing the guy out of the way. I put my arm around her shoulders, whispering, "Just go with it," so only she can hear.

"There you are, I was wondering when you'd get out here on the dance floor," she says, playing along. Her arms loop around my neck and her fingers caress the hair on the nape of my neck.

"Sorry, I kept getting interrupted but I'm here now," I say. "Hey dude, is there something you need over here?" I ask Jerk who's harassing her.

"Nah man, just dancing that's all." He puts both hands up, showing he's innocent.

"Well, I think we're done dancing here," I tell him as I look at Penelope.

I know I'm only helping her out of this awkward situation, but I like the feel of her small hands around my neck a little too much.

We stay like that for a few beats longer, swaying slowly to the music, the rest of the bar fading into the background. It takes a minute before I realize Sally left and it's just the two of us.

I move my hands down to the small of Penelope's back, gauging her reaction. When she doesn't make a move to pull away, I keep my hands there to stay in this moment.

She's staring at me intensely, and I see my own hunger reflected back. We sway gently as her hands slide down my neck to grip my shoulders.

Out of nowhere, the song changes, shattering the moment. Penelope pulls away. I do the same, following her lead.

"I need to use the bathroom. I'll meet you back at the table," she says breathlessly into my ear.

She kisses my cheek and quickly leaves through the crowd.

I'm rooted in the spot, in the middle of the crowded dance floor by myself, holding my hand where her lips just were. Damn it, I want nothing more than to feel those lips on mine.

Before I can think about it too long, or decide it's a bad idea, I push through the crowd and head in the direction of the bathrooms. When I get there, I see her standing with her back against the wall, trying to catch her breath.

I need her.

"Brent?" she asks, with desire written all over her face.

Without saying a word, I crash my lips against hers, reveling in the taste I've craved. The taste I've been thinking about ever since the night we first kissed.

My hands move up to her face, into her hair, and onto the back of her neck. I tilt her head back and deepen my kiss before pulling away. Her hands run through my hair as she gasps, working to catch her breath.

The bar is packed, and someone could walk around the corner at any moment and find us. All of Winterberry would know by tomorrow morning that I was caught kissing Penelope. The last thing I need is for people to talk.

"I'm sorry. I had to do that," I whisper, moving a stray piece of hair out of her face.

"Don't apologize. I've wanted to kiss you again since the other night. But I didn't know if that's what you wanted."

"Wait, what do you mean?"

"Once Nora was in bed, I thought that maybe you'd kiss me again, but you didn't. You just let me leave your house and you haven't tried to be alone with me again since. What was I supposed to think?"

Her cheeks are pink and her eyes avoid me. I can tell it's taken a lot for her to tell me this.

"Wow, I didn't mean to give you the impression that I didn't like the kiss or that I didn't want to do it again." I lower my voice. "Trust me, I liked it. Maybe a little too much. And I'm sorry I made you think otherwise."

"You have no idea how glad I am to hear you say that," she says, finally looking at me.

And in her eyes, I see someone who I'm starting to have real feelings for. Someone who fits perfectly in my life.

Someone who I was seriously considering punching Jerk in the face for.

I'm scared of those feelings, but at this moment, I can no longer deny them. So instead of pretending like they don't exist anymore, I bend down and plant a small kiss on her lips to let her know I mean what I say.

When I pull away, she has a small smile on her face—I want her to keep it forever.

"Should we go back to the table?"

"That's a good idea, Sally will probably be looking for me."

We walk back into the bar, with me following close behind her, and reach the booth where Dominick and Sally are deep in conversation.

"There you two are. Was my dancing too much for you?" Sally asks Penelope as we approach.

"Not at all. I haven't had fun like that in longer than I can remember. I just had to use the bathroom after Brent so heroically saved me from dancing with that stranger," she says, keeping her gaze locked on me.

"I did see that guy, he wasn't giving up was he?" Sally asks.

"Uh-oh, did I miss Brent here almost getting into a fight with a stranger?" Dominick laughs. "It's been too long since I've seen that."

Rolling my eyes, I punch him lightly on the arm. "Anyways, what's everyone doing for Christmas?" I change the subject.

"I'm planning to go to my parent's house after the Christmas Eve Ball and then come back for the log dimming," Sally says. "My sisters will both be there with their husbands and their kids so I'm excited about that."

"That sounds like heaven," Penelope says.

I know she doesn't have any family, so I'm not sure what her plans are, but I don't want to put her on the spot in front of Sally and Dom if she's not ready to share that with them.

"I'll be at the inn with the Harrisons this year," Dom shares. He doesn't have much family either so Mom invited him to spend Christmas Day with us before the log dimming. "I'm crashing their Christmas."

"Yep, for some reason Mom invited him." I laugh.

"What about you, Penelope?" Sally asks and Penelope stiffens next to me.

"I'll just be home in Manhattan. I might be traveling for work, I'm not sure yet. Once I get back home, I'll figure out my plans. I can't believe it's in two weeks."

"Where do you travel to?" Dominick asks her.

"All over actually. I do freelance work and it requires me to go to different places."

"Has anyone ever told you that you look like the actress from that superhero franchise?" Dom asks.

"Wait, you're right," Sally says as she looks at Penelope. "You do look like her!"

I glance between them, having no idea what they're talking about. I haven't been to the movies in forever.

"Actually, I get that all the time." Penelope laughs but her smile doesn't reach her eyes.

"Wait, isn't that actress named Penelope, too?" Dominick cuts in.

"Yep, what are the odds? I wish I were her, how fun would that be?"

"I would hate to be famous," I say. Seriously, being famous sounds like the worst way to live life. I don't even like to be recognized in the tiny town I live in, let alone all over the world.

"Why doesn't that surprise me?" Penelope elbows me in the ribs.

I spend the rest of the night nursing my drink, laughing at the three of them singing Christmas tunes off-key, and relaxing. I haven't had a night out in more than a year. This has been much needed. I try to keep my eyes off Penelope, fighting the urge to kiss her again. Sally would be so happy if she knew I was developing feelings, but the last thing I need is her in my business.

Sally yawns across the table.

Like always, she has to be up early in the morning to open the diner.

"Getting tired, Sal?"

"Actually, I am," she says through another yawn. "I'm having so much fun, but I'm fading."

"Is everyone ready to head out?" I ask the group.

She's right, this has been an awesome night, but Nora will also be coming home early tomorrow, and I'd like to be awake before she gets there.

"I am," Sally says. "I just got an Uber, and it will be here in a few minutes. Does everyone want to go together?"

"Sounds good," Penelope says, scooting out of the booth.

As we all stand and push through the partying crowd, I glance back at Penelope to make sure she's okay.

"All right guys, I have to pay the tab at the bar," I say. At the last second, I have a new idea. "Actually, Penelope, do you want to grab our own Uber back to the inn? Since we're going to the same spot?"

She looks over at me and I see her chest rise and fall with each breath she takes.

After what feels like forever, she says, "Okay, that works for me. I can order one now while you pay the tab."

"Are you kidding? I have to go with just *Dom*?" Sally rolls her eyes and crosses her arms over her chest.

I can't help but laugh at her pouting. It reminds me of one of Nora's fits.

"Oh come on Sal, you know you want to ride back with me." Dom puts his arm around her shoulders, and she immediately pushes him off.

"I'll sit in the front, you sit in the back. Great, it's here. Let's go, Dom."

Sally gives me a brief hug before kissing Penelope on the cheek.

"Why can't I sit in the front?" Dominick asks as he hugs Penelope and smacks me on the back.

As they walk away, I can hear them bickering like an old married couple.

"Those two crack me up," Penelope says, pulling me from my thoughts. I stride to the bar and pay the tab without introducing Penelope to Alex, because I just want to get out of here. "The Uber will be here in a minute, it's just around the corner."

"Perfect, let's head outside and we can meet them," I say. We start walking to the front door. "I have an idea. What do you think about making some hot cocoa and driving around to look at Christmas lights?"

"That sounds amazing." She stops in her tracks. "I used to do that when I was a kid, and it was one of my favorite parts of the Christmas season."

Her eyes mist over, and I can tell she's reminiscing about her childhood.

"Perfect, we can make cups at my place then head out. I nursed that one beer all night so I'm good to drive as long as that's good with you."

"Yep, I trust you."

I open the door and hold it for her, letting the cold air rush in. The car pulls up and we both climb into the back seat. Sitting closer than we probably need to, I rest my hand on her thigh, and she places hers on top of mine. We ride like this back to the inn, and when we get out, I can't stop glancing at her.

I'm more excited for this than I want to admit.

Chapter Twenty-Two

Penelope

As soon as Brent suggested going to look at Christmas lights, I tried to hide the joy that threatened to consume me. When I lived with Gran, we used to go to Dunkin Donuts to get hot chocolate, and then we would drive around the suburbs and admire the lights strung up on the houses.

I haven't done that since she passed, but when Brent had the idea, I immediately wanted to do it. We haven't had alone time since that night at his house anyways, and the thought of being with him makes my insides bubble with giddiness.

The inn is pitch black and it seems like everyone is asleep.

It's a clear night, and when I gaze at the sky, I can see an endless amount of stars.

In the city, there's too much light pollution to see the stars. But here in Winterberry, on cloudless nights, the sky stretches on forever, glittering with a billion stars.

A hand lands on my shoulder and I can't help but smile to myself before turning to face Brent.

"Ready to get some hot chocolate? I have a blanket you can wear, too, since I know how much you love that." He laughs at himself.

"You're never going to let me live that down, are you?" He shakes his head as we make our way into his house, where it's warm and cozy.

I sit at the table while Brent starts boiling water and takes down travel mugs.

"Do you want to use the bathroom or anything before we go?"

"That's a good idea."

I head to the bathroom to check my makeup and hair in the mirror. There are some black smudges under my eyes, so I fix my face and take a few deep breaths. After a few minutes, I hear the shrill screech of the kettle.

When I get back to the kitchen, Brent is pouring coffee creamer into the hot chocolate, just the way that I like it, and my heart swells.

"Drinks are ready," Brent says. "Blankets are next to the couch. Pick whichever one you want."

I pick the fluffiest one I can find and wrap it around my shoulders. Brent laughs and shakes his head.

"What? Are you embarrassed by my blanket cape?"

"Not at all. Whatever makes you happy." He laughs again. "Let's do this. I know the best streets to see the lights."

"I'm so excited," I say as we leave the house and head to his truck.

I settle into the cab of the truck and wrap the blanket around my legs. I'm comfortable, and when Brent gets behind the wheel and he hands me my cocoa, an involuntary sigh leaves my lips.

He backs out of the driveway, and to my complete surprise, he hits the power button on the radio and lets Christmas tunes fill the truck.

I smirk, but before I can say anything, he says, "Don't. Even. Comment."

"Nope, my lips are sealed." I mime zipping my lips and pretend to throw the key over my shoulder.

It's not that late, but there aren't many people on the roads. The sidewalks are mostly empty. Back in the city the streets would still be filled—people would be spilling out of restaurants and bars for hours to come.

We start our adventure on Main Street, taking in the stores that are decorated, before continuing to the residential streets.

The first one we drive down, there are white lights covering the trees lining the street, and most of the modest homes are lit up with decorations—nativity scenes sit in the front lawns and wreaths adorn the front doors.

"This is the street that I grew up on with my parents," Brent says as he looks around. "Right here was our house."

We pull up in front of a cute little cottage. The siding on the house is white, with black shutters on all of the windows, and flower boxes filled with winter greens. Similar to his current house, there's a small front porch with rocking chairs on it.

"How long did you live here?"

"Until I married Michelle and moved in with her. I loved it here, on this street, and in this house. My parents used to decorate those two trees in the front yard like a traditional Christmas tree and there were candles in each of the windows that my mom would light every night."

He appears lost in thought, and I don't want to interrupt his memories, so I stay quiet. I love learning more about him.

"That house across the street was where Sally lived, and we'd hang out all the time, playing in each other's yards and riding our bikes down the street. These trees along the sidewalk have been lit by the residents for as long as I can remember."

"That's amazing. What great memories you have. It looks like an adorable street to grow up on."

We sit there for another minute before Brent continues driving through the quiet streets in town. We sip our hot cocoa and listen to Christmas classics, and after half an hour speeds by, we pull into a development that takes my breath away.

"Brent, what is this place?" I try to take in the scene in front of me, but my eyes don't know where to look first. Each home is the size of a mansion, with three car garages, beautifully landscaped yards, and the most expansive collection of Christmas decorations.

"This is called The Woods," he says, as we slowly make our way down the first street. "It's the most expensive place to live in Winterberry and the homes are huge. Each one goes all out for the Christmas season, as you can see. It's my second favorite place to see the decorations."

"I can see why. It's gorgeous here."

Each house is bigger than the next and there's not a single one that isn't all decked out. My eyes stay glued to the windows, desperately devouring the sight before us.

We drive down the three main streets in the development.

"Can we go down the streets again before we leave?" I ask Brent when we see the last house.

"Sure, I'll go slower this time so you can catch everything."

"Thank you," I say, wrapping the blanket tighter around my legs and finishing my hot chocolate.

My favorite house in the development is one with giant wreaths with big red bows on each window, Santa's sleigh in the yard, oversized Christmas ornaments in the trees, and garland on the wraparound front porch.

Once we've gone down the streets again, and both our mugs are empty, Brent drives back through town and toward the inn. I know it's getting late, but I don't want this night to end.

When we park back at the inn, we exit into the cold.

"Thank you so much for tonight, Brent," I say. "This has been the best night."

"I'm so glad you enjoyed it. Do you want to come in for a little bit or are you ready to call it a night? I can light a fire."

I really am tired but this has been such a great night. Like a dream that has taken me back to my childhood. "I can come in," I say, wrapping the blanket back around my shoulders.

We enter his house. Only the lights on the Christmas tree are on, and as we take off our coats, Brent moves to the fireplace and lights it. Immediately, the comforting smell of firewood fills the room. The warmth feels amazing after being in the cold.

His house is so inviting, and I find it easy to take off my shoes and get comfortable.

"Do you want anything to eat?" he asks.

"No, I'm good. The fire is perfect. I can't believe how cold it is out there." I wrap the blanket tighter around myself and rest my head on the back of the couch.

Brent rustles around in the kitchen, opening drawers, and it sounds like he's looking for something.

"Do you need help in there?" I ask from the couch. My eyes are growing heavy, but I'm willing them to stay open.

"Nope," he says over his shoulder as he takes tealight candles out of a drawer.

Returning to the living room, he sets the little white candles on every surface. There has to be at least twenty of them. Grabbing a lighter from the mantle, he stops at each candle and lights them.

In a matter of minutes, the entire room is filled with the flicker of candlelight, and shadows dance on the walls. When he's done lighting the last one, he puts the lighter away in the kitchen. My eyes are barely staying open.

When he heads back into the room, he sits down on the couch next to me and wordlessly puts his arm around my shoulder. He pulls me close, and I rest my head on his chest. He slowly rubs circles on my arm, and I can't fight sleep any longer.

I let my eyes stay shut, and I feel him lean down and kiss the top of my head.

Chapter Twenty-Three

Brent

Light streams through the curtains, bathing my eyelids in orange. It can't be daytime already, can it? Damn, that's bright.

Opening my eyes slowly, I let them adjust to the light of morning. I feel the weight of Penelope's head on my arm. I glance down to see she's still sound asleep.

She's still wrapped in her blanket from last night, and she looks so cozy that I don't want to wake her up. Slowly, I move my numb arm out from underneath her and stretch it out. I know she needs to wake up soon, before Nora gets home, but I'm not ready for her to leave the couch yet.

She stirs slightly, before nuzzling back into the blanket. I get up, use the bathroom, and go to the kitchen to make us coffee.

I'm moving slowly this morning, even though I barely drank last night. As soon as the coffee machine spits out the caffeine, I pour two cups and bring them over to the coffee table.

Sitting down next to her, I can't stop myself from running my fingers down the side of her face.

She's even more beautiful when she's asleep.

Her eyes flutter open and a small smile creeps across her lips.

"Good morning, sunshine," I whisper. "I made us coffee."

"Oh, I'm so going to need that," she says as she sits up. "I think my neck is going to hate me for the next few days."

"Yep, my shoulder is not thrilled from having your head on it all night long. Not that I'm complaining," I say, locking eyes with her. "You passed right out."

"I was so comfortable, I don't even remember falling asleep."

"Penelope Smith, did you know that you snore?" A look of uncertainty flashes across her face but is gone before I know it.

"I do not!"

I can't help but laugh. "Trust me, I heard you last night. You fell asleep before I did and you were definitely snoring."

"Wow, that's embarrassing." She covers her face with her hands before pulling her fingers apart and sneaking a peek at me. She's so cute that another laugh escapes from my mouth.

I pick up her coffee mug and hand it to her. "Here, drink this. It will help you wake up." Both of us take sips of the coffee and sigh at the same time, locking eyes, and laughing.

"What would you like for breakfast? I can make eggs and bacon with hash browns."

"That sounds delicious," she says over the top of her coffee mug. "I'll help as soon as I use the bathroom."

She drags herself from the couch, scurrying down the hallway to the bathroom. I watch her go, and a small smile plays on my lips as I think about her sleeping in my arms.

Shaking my head to dispel the thoughts, I head to the kitchen to start breakfast. I crack the eggs into a bowl, get out the frying pan, and start making scrambled eggs before I feel Penelope's arms wrap around my waist. Her lips skim my arm.

"What can I do?" she asks.

"How about you turn on the oven and preheat it for the bacon. Then, you can sit at the countertop and talk to me while I cook."

"Aye aye captain." She salutes as she goes to the oven and turns it on.

Somehow, even though this is the first time we've done this, it feels so normal. So natural.

And that thought is scary.

Once the eggs are done and the bacon is in the oven, I get out the frozen hash browns, spray olive oil in a pan and cook them until they're brown and crispy on both sides.

"Mmm it smells delicious in here," Penelope says as she sits on one of the stools.

We wait for the bacon to crisp, passing time with small talk. We discuss our plans for the day and reminisce about how much fun we had last night at the bar. As soon as the oven beeps, I take out the bacon and make plates for us.

"You know..." I start as I take out silverware from the drawer and set them on the counter, stalling. "I've never had a woman here for breakfast. Well, since Michelle died."

She looks up from her plate, an expression I can't read on her face. "Oh yeah? How come?"

"To be honest, I'm not sure. I've gone on dates and spent the night with women but never like this. Never here."

I don't know why, but I'm embarrassed to be admitting this to her. But, for some reason, I want her to know that *this* means something to me. More than just spending the night together.

Slowly, I take the fork out of her hand and put it on the countertop. I turn to face her and move that one piece of unruly hair that's always in her face. Cupping her chin with my palm, I bring her closer to me and kiss her softly on the lips.

When I pull away, I rest my forehead against hers and notice the pink blossoming on her cheeks.

"I'm so glad we got to spend time together last night, just the two of us," I say before kissing the tip of her nose.

"Me too," is all she says, but the way her eyes lock with mine tells me she means it.

Taking a bite of my bacon, I let out a groan as the first taste fills my mouth. I would eat breakfast food for every meal if I could.

"Oh bacon, you're my favorite," I say as I bring another piece to my mouth.

Penelope laughs next to me. "Wow, I have some competition. I would be so lucky if you looked at me like you're looking at that bacon right now," she jokes.

If she only knew how little competition there was between her and anything else in my life, not counting Nora and my family. As soon as that thought creeps into my head and the reality of it hits me square in the chest, I turn to smile at her, masking my anxiety.

Side by side, we eat our breakfast and drink our coffee. It's as if this is something we do every day of our lives, and something we will do well into the future.

When we're done eating, we put our plates in the sink, and hop onto the couch like little kids. I pull her close and she rests her head on my shoulder. Giving her a small kiss on the top of her head, I grab the remote and put on "It's A Wonderful Life."

She curls her legs underneath herself and rubs her arms like she's chilly, so I get up and light the fire before grabbing the throw blanket and wrapping us up.

"I know this blanket is your favorite, so you can have it again," I say. We chuckle.

A few minutes into the movie, she nuzzles in closer, and when I glance down at her, she has a smile on her face. It tells me she feels exactly like I do—completely fulfilled.

At peace.

And perfect.

We don't make it even halfway through the movie when the alarm I set—so we didn't lose track of time—beeps. It makes us both jump, which is good because I was falling asleep.

Sitting up and stretching, she looks at me and we lock eyes. "Looks like it's time for me to go home," she says. "I mean back to the inn obviously." Her cheeks turn red as she corrects herself. But hearing her call the inn *home* hits me in the chest.

The thought of her leaving makes my heart constrict, and I already miss her. It's been amazing having her here, better than I thought it would be, and I didn't even realize how much I missed this.

The companionship.

Someone to eat breakfast with.

Someone to watch old movies with.

Don't get me wrong, I love my time with Nora, but somewhere along the way after losing Michelle, I lost the Brent part of me and shifted permanently into Dad mode. This, right here, moments like this, there are no words to describe it.

Instinctively, I pull Penelope close again, wanting to feel her warmth. I kiss the top of her head. "Is it okay with you that we don't let Nora know about this, whatever this is, yet?"

"Of course, Brent. I totally understand. I wouldn't want to confuse her especially when I have to go back to Manhattan." Her face looks pained. She starts to rise, suddenly ready to leave.

I put my hand on her knee, wanting to touch her, to reassure her that I'm fine with just having fun while she is here.

Or maybe it's to reassure myself.

Because to be honest, I'm not sure if I am okay with simply having fun and nothing more.

Chapter Twenty-Four

Penelope

B rent walks me to the door and kisses me sweetly on the lips before wrapping me in a hug, and I'm overwhelmed by the feeling of wanting his arms around me every day.

"Thank you for last night, and this morning," I say to him, smiling, before standing on my tiptoes to kiss his cheek. I need to sneak across the lawn and inside the inn without anyone seeing me—like I used to do in high school when I snuck out—so no one asks questions I don't want to answer.

I completely understand Brent wanting to keep this to ourselves.

Once my car is fixed, probably in a day or two, I'll be on my way back to my life. To Manhattan. To the loneliness I don't miss. To the next movie I'm filming. And to the photoshoots I have scheduled at the end of December.

"Brrr." The coldness of the morning slashes across my face as I creep across the lawn, making my way to the front porch. I peek in through the front windows and notice that Suzanne is already up, making coffee and a breakfast pastry for breakfast. "Oh no."

Okay, time for plan B. I wrap the blanket I stole from Brent's house tighter around me, trying to hide the fact I'm in the same clothes as last night. Then, I sit down on the swing and get comfortable.

This way, if she sees me out the window, she'll think I'm just taking in the cold air and the peaceful morning.

I swing for a few minutes, pushing off from the ground with my feet and pumping my legs back and forth. I'm so content, truly getting lost in the peace, when the front door opens.

"Penelope? Is that you?" Suzanne peeks her head out, wrapping her sweater around her body to ward off the cold.

"Morning," I say. "Sorry, I wanted to get out here before the town woke up and enjoy the silence."

"You don't have to apologize to me sweetheart, I just didn't hear you open the door. Have you been out here long?"

"Not too long. It's cold so I'm not sure I'll last much longer to be honest," I say with a laugh, pulling the blanket tighter around myself so she can't see what I'm wearing.

If she does, I don't know what I'll say.

But if she notices I'm lying, she doesn't let on.

"Well, come in when you're ready, there's coffee brewing and I have cinnamon buns in the oven."

"Yum, that sounds amazing. Thank you, Suzanne. I'll be in in a few minutes."

She closes the door, leaving me alone again. I take deep breaths to calm my racing heart. I don't like lying to her, but Brent doesn't want anyone to know, and that's the price to pay.

My mind wanders. What are me and Brent going to do when I go back home? Will he still want to see me? Is he interested in a relationship with me?

So many thoughts crowd my mind, stirring up my anxiety, so I decide to head inside. Once I'm in the cozy warmth of the inn, I rush upstairs to change.

I put Brent's blanket on my bed, burying my face in it and taking in the lingering scent. I know it sounds pathetic, but I'm probably going to sleep with the blanket tonight.

Quickly, I change, use the bathroom, brush my hair and teeth, and take in my reflection in the mirror. There's a light in my eyes that I haven't seen in a really long time and I know it's from my time spent with Brent.

Practically skipping down the stairs, I make my way to the kitchen. The freshly brewed coffee smells fantastic, and even though I ate with Brent this morning, my mouth waters at the sight of Suzanne's cinnamon buns.

"Suzanne, these look to die for," I say. This woman sure can bake. If they ever sell the inn, she should open up her own bakery.

"Thank you, Penelope. These are an old family recipe. I can give it to you if you'd like so you can bake them yourself when you get home."

Home.

That word doesn't feel the same anymore. Not since being here in Winterberry. I was hesitant about the small town when I first arrived, but now I feel like I belong.

"I'd love that," I say with a mouth full of the delicious pastry.

"What do you have planned today?" she asks as she sets the table.

Each and every morning, she puts out plates, silverware, napkins, cups, orange juice in a container, and fresh coffee for the guests.

She's a remarkable woman.

I hope one day I can be the type of mom, grandma, and person that she is.

"I think I'm going to walk down to the diner to have lunch with Sally and then stop in the boutique. I haven't gone shopping since I've been here and I want to see what I can find."

"That sounds like a great day. Will you be back for dinner, do you think?"

"I definitely plan to be. My car is going to be fixed soon and I want to soak in the time with everyone as much as I can," I say, trying to hold back my emotions.

She reaches across, giving me a big hug, and whispers in my ear. "You may go back to the city but this inn, this town, these people, we aren't going anywhere. And your room will be ready for you whenever you want to come and visit." She pauses. "You never know, maybe the parts won't come in and you'll still be here for the Christmas Eve Ball. Even if they do come in, you're more than welcome to stay. Just saying."

She laughs and I can't help but laugh with her.

If I had it my way, I'd make those parts disappear forever and stay here in Winterberry for good. Unfortunately, life doesn't work that way. And at some point, I need to return to my old life and my career.

When you're someone like me, you have to stay relevant if you want to stay in the game. No one cares about you if you aren't seen. With social media and tabloids, I learned a long time ago that if I didn't stay relevant, someone new would come and take my place.

And being here in Winterberry, celebrating the beautiful Christmas season, I'm not staying relevant.

Eventually, people will stop wondering where I am, and I'll fade into the background. Maybe they already have.

Is that what I want?

Or do I want to go back to my old life. Back to people who want to know everything I do and everywhere I go?

I pull away, bringing myself back to the present. "I'm hoping Ben will have an update soon. There's only two weeks until Christmas, so if I'm here for the ball, I'm going to need a dress."

"Lucky for you, I have an entire closet full of dresses," she says with a wink. "Although, I'm sure you'll want to be back in the city for Christmas. There must be people looking for you, right?"

"Only my boss and my best friend," I say, trying to play it off like it's no big deal, when in fact, it hurts my heart. Most of the world is looking for me, but the only person who *truly* cares or misses me is Georgia. Sure, my publicist sent me an email the last time I checked, but that was only to ask me how I wanted to spin the story of Drew's engagement.

And my agent didn't ask how I was, where I was, or when I would be home. He only wanted to discuss how I look to the press.

Of course, I don't tell Suzanne any of this. While I was in the middle of it, I never realized just how lonely and fake my life was. How the people in it were only there because of what I could do for them. Or how I could make them money.

This place, Winterberry, has helped show me that there are people who care about much more than looks, money, or power.

When I get back to Manhattan, things need to change.

"Well, I'll let you go. Are you going to hang out here for a little bit before you go to the diner?" Suzanne asks as some of the guests start to trickle down the stairs for breakfast.

"I think I'll read by the fire for a while if I won't be in your way," I say as she moves to say good morning to the guests.

"Absolutely not, sweetheart. Enjoy."

I smile at her as I grab a throw blanket from the basket by the door, plop into the big chair by the fireplace, and tuck my feet under me.

"Penelope! Hiiii!" Nora squeals as she runs down the stairs.

She throws herself at me, hugging me briefly, then rushes to the dining room table. Her eyes are locked onto those cinnamon buns.

"Good morning, sweet girl," I say. She climbs up into a chair, puts a napkin on her lap, and grabs a cinnamon bun from the middle of the table. Pushing the curls out of her face and licking her lips, she takes a massive bite, getting icing on the tip of her nose.

"Nora, you're making a mess you silly goose," Suzanne says as she walks into the room.

"Did I hear my little girl?" The deep voice stirs something inside of me. My palms sweat and my heart starts beating harder.

Brent.

"Daaaaaad! It's me, it's me. I'm in here, with the cinnamon buns," Nora yells.

"Of course you are, little one."

As soon as he walks into the room, he stops in his tracks at the sight of me curled up in the chair. My cheeks grow warm, and I clear my throat to try and hide the reaction my body gets just from the sight of him.

"Hey Penelope, you look cozy," he says, eyeing me.

"This. Is. The. Life." I say back, putting my head back in the seat and looking up at the ceiling. *Play it cool, Penelope, play it cool.*

"Nora, why don't you take that cinnamon bun to go? We have some errands to run today," he says, ruffling her curls.

"That sounds fun!" she says excitedly, wrapping her half-eaten cinnamon bun in a napkin and hopping off the chair.

She runs over to where I am, gives me another hug, and then runs and throws herself at her grandmother. "Thank you for the sleepover, Grandma."

"Anytime, my little pumpkin, anytime," she says. She turns to Brent. "Did you guys have fun last night?"

I can't even look at him.

"The bar was packed but we had fun. Penelope got to see a real dive bar," he jokes as our eyes meet. I see the same heat in his eyes that are in mine as we stare for a beat too long.

"That's great. And I bet Alex was happy to see you."

"He was, we talked for a little bit. I'm taking Nora to run some errands. Do you need anything while I'm out?"

"I think we're good here, but thank you sweetheart," Suzanne says, reaching up to give him a hug.

"Bye, Penelope," Brent says to me. "Will you be here for dinner tonight?"

"Yep, I'll be here. I'm going to the diner for lunch then doing a little retail therapy at the boutique on Main Street," I tell him, even though he didn't ask. What is wrong with me? Word-vomit much?

"Sounds like a great day. See you later tonight then." He waves as he and Nora leave through the back door.

I pay attention to the book in my lap, stealing a glance at him as he walks away. Just as he closes the door behind him, he looks back at me and winks.

This is going to be hard.

Chapter Twenty-Five

Brent

Dragging myself away from the inn, I shove the sight of Penelope, curled up in the chair, reading, out of my head. Looking down, I put my hand on Nora's head and pull her into my side for a hug. I had an amazing night with Penelope, but man did I miss my little munchkin.

My mind wanders as we walk and I picture what it would be like to have both Penelope and Nora, here, in my life. What if I told Nora that Penelope and I are more than friends?

"Did you miss me, Dad?" Nora asks as she looks up at me with those big eyes, pulling me back to reality. Of course that could never happen. Penelope will be going back to the city soon and I can't subject Nora to getting more attached and then hurt when she inevitably leaves.

"You know I did, my girl. How was your night with Grandma and Pop?"

"It was *fun*. We played board games and drank hot cocoa and then watched movies." She skips on the way to the car. "I love when I sleep there. Did you have a fun night with your friends?"

I try not to let it show on my face just how much fun was had. "I did. I think Penelope liked the bar and it was fun hanging out with Uncle D now that he moved back to Winterberry."

"Penelope is sooooo pretty. I'm going to miss her when she leaves." Her pout matches the same one I have when I think of Penelope leaving town, leaving my life.

"Me too, me too. But let's not think about that today. We have a few errands to run and we need to stop at the grocery store. I thought we could stop into Ben's Shop and check on Penelope's car too." To be honest, I don't want to hear that it's fixed and she's leaving. I want to pretend it isn't even an option, and that her departure from town isn't coming.

In the short time she's been here, she's changed so much in me. I never thought I'd be open to a relationship after Michelle. Especially not anything more than just a physical relationship. But with Penelope, I want it all.

I find myself looking for her, trying to impress her, and thinking of her everywhere I go. It's intoxicating. And I don't know what to do with that.

We hop into my truck, and I hit the button on the radio to turn it on, letting the sound of Christmas music take over the truck. Tapping my fingers to the beat on the steering wheel, I can feel Nora's eyes burning into me.

"Why are you staring at me?" I poke her in the arm.

"Dad, you're listening to Christmas music. In the car. And humming along." The confused look on her face makes me laugh. "Are you feeling okay? Do you need your temperature taken?"

She clearly gets her sarcasm from me.

"For some reason this year, I'm feeling the Christmas spirit a little bit. Not a lot, just a little."

"I like it." She smiles, singing along to Mariah Carey, and I turn my attention back to the road.

We make our way to Main Street and stop at the pharmacy to grab Nora's vitamins. After, we head to the public library to return our books and then swing by Ben's Shop.

I open the door to the shop and the bell chimes, signaling our arrival. Christmas music filters through the speakers, filling up the space.

"Hey Ben, how's it going buddy?" I ask as we walk deeper into the shop.

He's behind the counter, working on paperwork. When he spots us, he lights up, coming around the counter to give Nora a hug.

That girl has a hold on every single person in this town.

"Little lady, how are you? Why don't you stop growing already?" He laughs.

"Oh Mr. Ben, I can't do that!" She giggles. I can't help but smile.

Clapping me on the back, Ben shakes my hand, and Nora goes behind the counter to spin on his stool like she always does.

"Just coming by to check on Penelope's car," I say. "I know you talked to her not too long ago but I figured I could bring her any news when we get back to the inn."

"The parts should be here today actually," he says. "It should take a day or two for me to replace them in her car and then she will be on her way."

I try to wrap my head around this. In a day, maybe two, she'll be gone. What if I never see her again?

"That's good news, right, Brent?" Ben's voice brings me back from my thoughts and into the present.

"Definitely. I'm sure she can't wait to get home in time for Christmas," I say. I hope he buys it, because I sure as hell don't.

"But Dad, then Penelope won't be here for the Christmas Eve Ball," Nora whines. "I wanted her to see my pretty dress."

"What pretty dress?" I don't remember buying her a new dress.

"The one we have to buy, silly. For the ball. Duh."

This kid.

"Ohhhh that one." I play along, adding shopping for a new dress to my mental to-do list. The list is a million miles long and growing.

"Will you save me a dance at the ball?" Ben asks Nora, taking her hand and helping her down off the stool. "I want to see your pretty dress."

"Of course, Mr. Ben," she says seriously. "I will write it down so I don't forget."

Both Ben and I look at each other and laugh, shaking our heads. She's a 40-year-old trapped in a 7-year-old's body.

"All right, little one, let's go to the grocery store and then we can go back to the inn and tell Penelope the good news if she's there."

"Oooookay but it's not *good* news, Dad."

We both say bye to Ben and head back out into the cold and into my truck. The cold seeps through my jeans. I crank the heat as soon as I turn the car on.

As we pull into the grocery store parking lot a few minutes later, I go around to the passenger side door, take Nora's hand, and help her out of the truck. She holds onto my hand as we enter the store, swinging it as we grab a shopping cart and say hi to everyone we pass.

"Okay, we need cereal, waffles, eggs, bacon, pasta, and spaghetti sauce," I say as she climbs onto the back of the cart. I stand behind her, pushing the cart along. "You can pick out the cereal if you want."

"Yay! Thank you, Dad. You're the best."

It doesn't take long before we make our way through the store, finding everything we need. We only get stopped four times to chat, then we get in line at the register.

As we're waiting our turn to check out, I glance at the stupid tabloids. My body goes rigid.

"What the hell," I say a little too loudly. I pause, taking a closer look.

"Dad, you cursed. Do we need to start a curse jar again?" Nora asks me as she follows my line of sight. "Omigosh is that *Penelope* on a *magazine!*?" She squeals, standing on her tiptoes to grab it off the rack.

Why is Penelope on the front of a tabloid? And why does it say "Spotted: Penelope Maxwell In Small Town Bar?"

Penelope *Maxwell*?

"Hey, baby, can I see that for a second?" I ask Nora, taking the magazine out of her hands and opening it up. I scan the table of contents, find the page number for the article, and stop in my tracks.

Skimming the page, I keep mentally processing the name Penelope Maxwell.

Maxwell hasn't been seen in two weeks, since the news of her fiancé Drew Henry's affair. Penelope hasn't posted on social media, and most recently, her ex-fiancé is newly engaged. Now, we know that Maxwell is hiding out in a small Vermont town.

When will she return to New York City?

My heart stops.

I don't understand. This must be some kind of mix-up. Has she been lying to me this whole time?

"Dad, I want to be in a magazine too!" Nora says, taking the tabloid back from my hands and admiring the photos of Penelope.

In some of them, I barely recognize her. The woman I know is down-to-earth, naturally beautiful, and wears a smile that lights up any room she walks into.

The woman in these photos has more makeup on than I knew existed, clothes that show off more skin than not, and a smile that doesn't even show her teeth.

All of a sudden, moments come crashing into my mind. That first day at the diner, Sally said she thought she recognized her from somewhere. And at the bar last night, Penelope had seemed unsure in the crowd, especially when everyone was staring at her. Even Dom and Sally thought she looked like someone famous. I can't believe she doesn't just look like that actress, she *is* the actress. Did other people know she was a famous actress? I'm guessing someone recognized her. That must be how this trashy tabloid knows where she is.

I'm the biggest idiot. Here I am, thinking I've met someone special, someone who I really like and who my daughter adores. But the whole time, she's been keeping a huge secret.

Would I have cared that she's famous? Maybe at first, but not once I got to know her.

To me, she's just Penelope. I don't care what her last name is or what she does for work. But to *lie* about it? Even after we got close? *That* I'm not okay with.

I grab two more magazines off the rack and add them to my cart. My head is spinning, and I need to figure out what's going on. Wiping my sweaty palms on my pants, I try to act as normal as possible, so Nora doesn't realize something is amiss.

There's still two people in line before us. One of them is Miss Emily and I know she likes to chat, so it'll be a while. I take out my phone and send a text to Dominick. I need his help to make sense of what I am seeing.

Me: You home?

Dom: Yeah man, just doing some work in the office. What's up?

Me: Mind if me and Nora stop by? I need to talk to you.

Dom: Sure. I'll make some coffee and a grilled cheese for the kid. When will you be here?

Me: We're in line at the grocery store then coming over... that cool?

Dom: See you then

"Hey Nora, wanna stop by Uncle D's before we go home? He said he'll make you a grilled cheese sandwich."

"Yummm. Uncle D is the best," she says with a huge smile on her face.

"Hey, I thought you said I was the best," I tease.

"Ummm, you both are, duh." She makes me laugh even when I don't want to, like in this moment.

If Miss Emily could hurry up, that'd be great. I need to get out of here and talk this out.

Finally, after what feels like forever, the line starts moving and we unpack the cart onto the belt. I hope I can pay for the tabloids without anyone noticing.

"Hey Mr. Harrison, hi Nora, long time no see," the young kid at the register says. I recognize him from here at the store. "Doing some tabloid reading, Mr. Harrison?"

Of course he noticed *and* asked.

"Yeah, sometimes these magazines suck you in when you're standing there waiting," I say.

I'm restless and it's taking too long, so I start bagging our groceries myself. I don't want to be rude, but I can't wait much longer. I feel like I'm going to burst.

"I can do that, Mr. H," he says to me.

"That's okay, you bag enough groceries in a day. I've got it."

As soon as I pay, I grab the bags and practically bolt from the store. My adrenaline is pumping so hard I could probably run a marathon right now.

"Daaaad, what's the hurry? Jeez," Nora scolds as she struggles to match my stride.

"No hurry, sweetheart, I just don't want your sandwich to get cold. Uncle D is expecting us," I say.

I place the grocery bags on the floor of the truck and help Nora jump in and buckle up. We're on the road in seconds, and thankfully, Dominick doesn't live far.

I'm definitely speeding, and I hope the sheriff isn't doing speed checks or I'll be getting a ticket. Normally, when Nora is in the car, I'm a cautious driver. But right now, I barely even notice the trees as we go by.

We pull into Dom's driveway. My truck is out of place in this neighborhood. This old beat-up thing definitely doesn't fit in here.

"Wow, it looks like a castle," Nora says in awe as I turn off the engine. "This is *soo* much bigger than our house, Dad."

My little one has no filter.

"It does look like a castle, huh. Let's go knock on the door and spend some time with Uncle D."

She runs up the long driveway and knocks on the door before I'm even next to her. In seconds, Dominick opens the door and Nora throws herself into his arms.

"Uncle D, is my grilled cheese ready?"

I chuckle. At least she has her priorities straight.

"Well nice to see you too, munchkin." Dominick laughs, putting her down and letting her run into the house. "Your sandwich is on the table," he calls after her.

"She just loves me for my food, doesn't she?" Dominick asks as I get to the door. I don't reply, gripping the magazines tightly in my hands. "Whatcha got there?"

I shove them at his chest and wait for him to take in what's on the cover. Freezing, he looks at me, then back down at the magazine.

"Is this who I think it is?" he asks after a few seconds of scrutinizing.

"That's what I'm trying to figure out."

"Where did you see this?"

"At the checkout lane in the grocery store, you know where the racks of tabloids are. Miss Emily was ahead of me so I started browsing and saw this on the cover." I walk further into the house and head to the kitchen where I smell coffee brewing.

"Who's Penelope *Maxwell*?" he asks as he follows me in.

"Dude, I don't even know. I don't have any social media and I didn't get the chance to Google while I was in line. Can we use your computer?"

"Let me pour you a cup of caffeine and then we can go into the office. Is Nora good out here by herself to eat?"

"I'm good, Uncle D," Nora says from behind him.

"Little ears," I say as we both laugh.

Dom grabs two mugs, pours the coffee and creamer, and we head into his office. It's right off the living room, so he stops at the huge flat screen TV and turns on cartoons for Nora.

"Hey Nora, you can come watch TV on the couch when you're done if you want. I put on cartoons," he yells.

"Thanks, Uncle D," she answers. "This is such a good sandwich. Can you teach Dad how to make one like this? His are always burnt."

"Nora! That's not true!" I say defensively. I feel attacked.

"Sorry, Dad, the truth hurts sometimes. Isn't that what you always tell Grandma and Pop?"

This kid is always listening.

As soon as we enter Dom's office, I look around at the leather furniture, the huge oak desk, the plants around the room, and the wall of windows overlooking the lake. This place is gorgeous. He's one lucky man.

"Okay, let's see what we can find," he says as he wakes his computer up.

I pull up a chair next to him. My palms grow sweaty again. I don't know what we're going to find, and honestly, I'm scared to even look.

Dominick brings up Google and types "Penelope Maxwell" into the search bar.

The second he hits *enter*, hundreds of articles pop up with her name and photo. I can't believe it. Penelope Smith, who's staying at my parent's inn, who I've had around my daughter and in my home, is a celebrity.

And her last name isn't even *Smith*.

"Wow, Brent, that's her," Dom says in disbelief as he scrolls through the pages. There are so many pages that my mind can't comprehend. "I *knew* she looked familiar. Why don't we check out Instagram. If it really is her, I'm sure she'll have an account."

A part of me wants to stop right here, not look up another thing, and forget I saw any of this. But I know I can't. Not now.

Dominick opens his Instagram account and searches Penelope's name. Her account is the first one to show up, with a blue checkmark next to her name. I have no idea what that means. All I do know is it's definitely her in that profile picture, and in all the other pictures Dom scrolls through.

"Wow" he says as he keeps scrolling. "I don't even know what to say."

"She's been lying to me. To us. To my parents. Why would she do that?"

"I don't even know man. Maybe she was worried you wouldn't want her to stay with you? I'm surprised no one recognized her while she was here. Although, I did think she looked like someone famous. Remember when I asked her? She played it off like she hears that a lot."

"Not many of us here in Winterberry care about movie stars or celebrities. How did someone get a pic of her from last night at the bar?"

Dominick clicks on something on her Instagram page and a bunch of photos show up. The first dozen look like they were taken last night while we were out.

"What are these?" I ask Dominick. I don't know a single thing about social media, and I have no idea what I'm looking at.

"These are photos other people posted and tagged her in. I guess people at the bar recognized her," he explains.

The way people stared at her that night makes sense now.

I sit there completely speechless. I really thought I was falling for her. For a woman who's apparently been lying to my face, pretending to be someone she's not.

"What's going through that head of yours?" Dominick asks. He turns in his chair to look at me. "I can see the wheels spinning from here."

"I honestly don't even know what to think. If she can lie about her own name and what she does for a living, what else is she lying about?"

"It looks like she had her heart broken," he says as he clicks back to Google and starts opening articles.

As we read, we find out that the man she was engaged to, some famous asshole, was caught cheating on her the day after Thanksgiving. At least that part of her story was true. But how can I believe a single thing that's come out of her mouth since I've known her?

"She told me that her fiancé had cheated on her when I found her crying outside the inn," I say, thinking out loud. "I wish she'd told me the whole truth."

"Maybe she was trying to get away from the spotlight. Didn't you say she doesn't have a cell phone on her and no one has tried to reach her since she's been here?"

"Yeah, that's what she told me. But now I'm second guessing every single thing she's said," I say, shaking my head. I'm mad. And confused. And hurt. "If I'm being honest, I was actually falling for her."

"I could tell, man," Dom says, putting his hand on my shoulder. "The way you looked at her last night... I haven't seen you like that with anyone since Michelle."

"Yeah, and now look. I don't even know Penelope's real name."

"What are you going to do?" he asks me hesitantly.

"I'm going to go back to the inn and talk to her. What else is there to do?"

"Do you want me to go with you?"

"Thanks, Dom, but I think I need to do this by myself. I want to give her the benefit of the doubt, but I don't know how I could ever trust her after this. You can't start a relationship with a lie."

"I'm sorry, man. Text me after you talk to her, and we can go grab a beer. I feel like you need one."

"Yeah, maybe two or three beers for me. Or a whole pitcher," I tell him. "I'm going to get Nora and head back to the inn. I need to get this over with."

"You got this, man. If you need backup, you know where to find me."

We stand and head to the living room. Nora is laying on the couch, cuddled up with a pillow, living her best life watching cartoons.

"Hey sweetheart, time to go home," I say as I kiss the top of her head. "Grandma and Pop are going to be looking for us."

"But Dad, look how comfortable I am." She looks up at me with wide eyes.

"How about when we get home, I'll cover you up with a blanket on the couch and you can put another movie on before we go to the inn for dinner. Will that be comfortable enough?"

She takes a few minutes to think about it, mulling it over in her little head. "Ooooookay. That can be comfortable." She hops off the couch and runs into Dominick's arms. "Thank you for the sandwich, Uncle D, and for the movie. Can you make me another one soon?"

"Of course I can, sweet girl. You can come have a sandwich and a movie whenever your dad lets you."

"All right, little one. Let's go. Thanks for letting us crash your day, Dom. I'll text you later." I bro hug him and lead Nora out to the truck.

My stomach is in knots, and I feel like I'm going to throw up. I'm terrified to see what Penelope has to say. And how it will change things with us, with me.

This could be the longest ride home ever.

Chapter Twenty-Six

Penelope

After a few hours of reading, and maybe a few minutes of napping, if I'm being honest, my stomach starts rumbling. It must be time to head to Sally's Diner.

Suzanne has classic Christmas tunes playing in the kitchen while she bakes cookies, and it fills my heart with such warmth. The inn always smells delicious. It has the perfect cozy vibe that makes me never want to leave.

And makes me feel safe from the outside world.

It's the complete opposite of my cold, lonely penthouse, which I thought I loved before. This town has truly changed me, a fact that both excites and scares me. I always believed I was living the life of my dreams. Famous, rich, living in a penthouse in Manhattan with a closet to die for. That's every girl's dream, right?

But since I've been in Winterberry, I'm rethinking everything.

Peeking my head around the corner, I catch Suzanne twirling to the music and singing into her spatula. As she spins, she sees me and stops in her tracks.

"I didn't see you there! Well, now you can't let me dance alone," she says, with her hand outstretched to me. "Come join me!"

Laughing, I step into the kitchen and take her empty hand. I twirl with her, swaying my hips and singing at the top of my lungs.

I have a terrible singing voice but we're both belting out the lyrics and laughing so hard, it doesn't even matter.

"*All I want for Christmas is youuuuu.*" We sing in unison, pointing at each other.

"Hey, did I miss the invitation to the concert?" Tom says as he enters through the back door.

Completely out of breath, we both collapse onto the floor. With cheeks that hurt from smiling so big, I put my head on Suzanne's shoulder.

This is by far my favorite Christmas season ever.

"Sorry honey, we forgot to send it out to the shed," she says to Tom. "Next time we'll give you more notice."

I stand, offering her a hand to help her up, and I pull her into a huge hug.

"Thank you for that," she says into my hair.

I fight back the tears filling my eyes. "I'm going to miss you when I go home," I whisper.

"Me too, honey, me too. Remember, the offer still stands. You don't have to go if you don't want to."

After a few seconds, we pull apart and she gently places her hand on my cheek. "Off to the diner?" she asks.

"Yep, my stomach is yelling at me for not putting food into it. Sally is going to make me my favorite, her BLT. I swear, she puts something addictive in that sandwich."

"Ohhh that is a good sandwich," she says, releasing me and rubbing her stomach. "Well, tell her hi from us, and tell her she needs to come by the inn for dinner one night. We haven't had her over in so long. She's always so busy at the diner."

"I'll tell her! See you both later for dinner," I say over my shoulder as I make my way to the front door, grab my coat off the coat rack, slide on my UGGs, and wrap a scarf around my neck.

Each day, it gets colder and colder as Christmas inches closer. Today, the distinct smell of snow lingers in the air again, promising a white Christmas. It's a scent I've come to cherish.

It doesn't take long for me to walk to Main Street, and instead of going right to the diner, I trek through the town square park and stop at the gazebo.

As usual, there are people milling about. Some rest on the benches, others admire the massive tree. Some warm their hands at the fireplace. Couples walk hand in hand along the sidewalk, and kids run around playing tag.

Whenever the fire gets low or the wind blows it out, someone appears and lights it again.

Everywhere I turn, people stop and say hello, asking me how my car is and how I'm enjoying the Christmas season in Winterberry. And the feeling that consumes me, that settles in my heart, is a feeling of home.

I've found a place where I finally belong. Not as Penelope Maxwell, but simply as *Penelope*.

The thought crosses my mind that maybe, just maybe, I don't have to leave.

Maybe I could live here permanently.

My home base can really be anywhere, what matters is where I go when I film. And in today's world, I could reside anywhere and still have meetings with my agent, go on casting calls, and update my social media.

Would Brent want me to move here?

Or would that be too much, too soon?

My stomach growls before I can ponder that question. I need to eat, and Sally is waiting for me.

I make my way down the street, stopping to look at the decorations in the windows of the shops as I pass. Opening the door to the diner, the delicious smell of food and the sound of laughter reach me.

When I close the door behind me and step into the foyer, the conversations fade into silence and people turn to look at me.

Do I have something on my face? Did I accidentally slam the door?

I notice Sally in her usual spot behind the counter and wave. She locks eyes with me, her face grim. She holds up a finger to signal she'll be there in a minute, then quickly glances away

That's weird.

Usually she's happy to see me and I'm greeted with a big hug. Her affection is something I've come to look forward to.

As I look around, people are still staring at me and I feel completely self-conscious.

It takes a few minutes before Sally comes out from behind the counter and walks toward me.

"Hey girl!" I say as she approaches me. She has a menu in her hands but her eyes never meet mine. Instead of her usual smile, her mouth is set in a straight line.

"Hey, normal seat?"

"Uh... yeah, that would be great."

I have no idea what's going on, but I really don't like it.

I follow Sally as she leads me to my favorite people-watching booth. The hustle and bustle of the season is definitely here in Winterberry, and I can't get enough.

As I slide into the booth, Sally hands me the menu. "Do you want your usual sandwich? Or do you want to check out the menu for something different?"

"I'm going to go for your famous BLT," I say with a laugh. But she doesn't even crack a smile.

"Sounds good," she says and walks away without another word.

Now that I'm alone, I notice people are still eyeing me as they eat. Hushed whispers go up around the diner, but I can't make out what anyone is saying.

No one could have found out about who I really am, right? I haven't noticed anyone taking photos of me. Wracking my brain, I try to figure out if it's possible someone recognized me and just didn't come up to me.

"Here ya go," Sally says a few minutes later, placing my sandwich in front of me.

Before she can turn to leave, I say, "Hey, is everything okay? I feel like everyone is staring at me."

"We all know, Penelope." She says it so seriously, so matter-of-factly, that my heart stops beating.

Oh my God. I try to swallow but feel like there is something stuck in my throat. Someone recognized me and now everyone knows I'm not Penelope Smith.

"What does everyone know?" I whisper, fidgeting with my napkin.

"Your last name isn't Smith and you've been lying to every single one of us." She crosses her arms.

Instantly, my cheeks get hot, my breath hitches in my throat, and my hands start sweating. How does she know?

"Sally... I can explain..."

"I can't wait to hear this one," she whispers.

"Can you sit for a minute? I'll tell you everything."

She hesitates for a moment before slowly lowering into the seat across from me and resting her hands on the table. There's a sadness in her eyes as they fill with tears. I need to come clean.

I wasn't ready for this. I was hoping I'd be able to tell her on my own timeline, and I wanted Brent to be the first to know. I wish I knew how she found out, even though that really isn't important.

"My name is Penelope Maxwell and I'm an actress," I start, swallowing hard to try and dislodge the lump sitting in my throat. "When I broke down on Main Street, when Brent found me in my car, I had come straight from Manhattan. The morning after Thanksgiving, I was having coffee at my table when I saw the cover of a tabloid with my fiancé's picture on the front. He was kissing someone else."

I stop, trying to get a handle on my emotions. I feel like I could either sob, throw up, or pass out at this very moment. But Sally is my friend, and she deserves to know the full story, so I continue.

"I was heartbroken and embarrassed. I made the rash decision to pack my bags, put my phone and laptop in my closet, get in my car, and drive until I ran out of gas. Little did I know, my car would stop working and break down right here in Winterberry."

She doesn't say anything for a few minutes, and I fully expect her to get up and walk away from me, just like most people in my life have done.

"Why didn't you say anything when Brent met you?" she eventually asks. "Why did you lie?"

"To be honest, I panicked. Not a lot of people want to deal with someone who has paparazzi following them all the time, and for once in forever, I wanted to feel normal. Like everyone else. So, I told him my last name was Smith. And I have been scared to tell him the truth since."

"What did you think would happen if you did?"

"I don't know. I didn't think I'd love it here, that I'd even be here past the night, and that I'd feel like I was home in Winterberry. Or that I would have feelings for Brent and that they would grow." I pause, catching my breath before continuing. "And then, it never felt like the right time to say anything. I was scared I'd lose him, and you, and Nora. I was scared you'd look at me the way you are now."

"I can understand that Penelope, I truly can. But you've been here for two weeks now and I can't help but feel betrayed."

She's right. I hurt her and I feel so terrible.

"I know. I know I messed up and I should have said something that first day. I'm so, so sorry, Sally. If I could take it back and be honest about who I was when Brent found me crying in my car, I would. But I can't. All I can do is apologize for lying."

Despite trying to hold them back, tears stream down my face. I dab at my eyes with a napkin and take a deep breath to try and relax.

It doesn't work, and my shoulders shake as the sobs escape my lips. I'm full on ugly-crying now and the tears won't stop.

Sally gets up, comes to my side of the table, and slides into the booth next to me. Slowly, she puts her arm around my shoulder and pulls me against her.

"I'm so sorry, Sally. I've only ever had one other friend like you in my life and I ruined it," I say through sobs.

"Penelope, I'm hurt, so hurt, but I'm still your friend. Real friends don't run just because of your last name or what you do for a living. I only wish you would've told us." She grabs another napkin and hands it to me.

"I wish I had too," I tell her honestly. "Do you think Brent knows?"

She hesitates. "I don't know, but I'm going to assume yes."

"Can I ask you how you found out? Is it only on social media?"

She pauses before she answers my question. "I saw it on Instagram—a picture of you at the bar. Someone I went to high school with shared it to their account. But some people said they saw a photo of you on the cover of a tabloid at the grocery store, too."

I groan, burying my face in my hands. "Brent was running errands with Nora today. What are the chances he doesn't know yet and I get to tell him myself?"

"If I'm being honest with you, probably slim to none. I don't think there's anyone in here right now who doesn't know. If he's seen anyone today, or gone into the grocery store, then I'm sure he knows. I'm sorry, I know that isn't what you want to hear, Penelope."

She rubs my shoulder and gives me another napkin to wipe the fresh set of tears that are now streaming down my face.

We sit there for a few minutes in silence, before someone calls for Sally.

"I have to get that. Will you be okay?" she asks me before she moves to stand up.

"Thank you for understanding, Sally. I can't say I'm sorry enough. I'll regret not telling the truth forever." I grab her hand and squeeze. "I'll be fine. Can we talk later about this?"

"Of course we can," she says as she walks away. "If I were you, I would try and talk to Brent as soon as you can. He isn't always the most understanding person on the planet," she calls over her shoulder.

I wipe my face with the napkin again and try to pull myself together. I can still feel the lingering stares, but I try to block it out. I should be used to this, people scrutinizing me.

But now it feels uncomfortable. So wrong.

After a few minutes, I decide I can't just sit here. I need to find Brent and I need to do it fast. I'm scared of what he's going to say, and if I'm being honest with myself, I don't think he'll be as understanding as Sally was.

I don't want to lose him.

I mean, I may have already lost him for all I know, but I need to try and make things right.

But his disappointment in me, his rejection, it might just break me.

I'll go right to the inn and find him as soon as possible. The less time that goes by, the better my chance of being the one to tell him.

Thankfully, Sally heads back to the table to check on me a short while later. "Can you wrap that up for me?" I point to my uneaten sandwich. "I'm going to go back to the inn and hope that Brent is there so I can talk to him."

"I'm proud of you, Penelope. That's really brave," she says as she takes my plate and walks over to the counter to put the food in a box. "Don't worry about paying for it, you can whenever you come back in. Just go find him."

"Thank you, Sally. I'm so sorry, for everything."

A flash goes off through the window, and I jump.

I turn to see where the light came from and notice a man outside with a bag over his shoulder and a huge camera in front of his face. The light flashes again as he snaps a few photos.

"What in the world?" Sally mutters.

"Oh, God. The paparazzi... they found me," I say as flashes continue to go off. This can't be happening.

"Okay, deep breaths, I'll go out there and tell him to go away, providing a distraction so you can sneak out the back door," Sally tells me. "I hope you can find Brent, Penelope." She pats my hand.

"Thank you, Sally, I'm so grateful for you. You have no idea."

"Don't mention it. I guess this is what happens when you have a famous friend." She chuckles.

"*Best* friend," I amend.

She gives me a soft smile then heads for the door on a mission. As soon as Sally approaches the man, I take the opportunity to scoot out of the booth.

"Penelope..." Someone touches my arm as I stand. I recognize her from Nora's school. "I get why you didn't tell the truth. I'll go with Sally and create a distraction, too, so you can leave."

"Thank you so much, I really appreciate it, and I'm sorry," I say loudly, so every single person in the diner can hear me. "I'm so sorry for lying to you all."

People nod, murmuring their understanding. A few residents even join Sally outside, aiding the distraction. It takes me a minute to get control over my emotions before I scurry behind the counter, through the kitchen, and slip out the back door into the alley.

I take a second to get my bearings before walking in the direction of the inn.

It's not that far, but I find myself looking over my shoulder every few steps. I don't want anyone following me and taking photos of the inn. The last thing I need is for Brent's family's business to be in a tabloid.

I feel bad enough as it is without putting them through any of this. Suzanne and Tom have been amazing to me, and I want to protect them.

As I get closer, a different man appears, calling out my name. He has the same telltale bag and camera as the man from the diner.

Crap.

Without thinking, I make a sharp turn and run through the bushes. Thorns prick me, scratching up my jeans and jacket, but I keep going. I hide behind a tree, only peeking out when I think the coast is clear.

It dawns on me just how much I've changed.

If this had been just a few weeks ago, I would've been all dolled up, purposely seeking out the paparazzi so they could take my picture.

Now, I'm hiding like a wild animal, desperate to *not* get my photo taken.

A delirious giggle escapes me.

Who even am I?

When I'm confident the paparazzi is gone, I make a run for it, creeping onto the back of the inn, opening the door, and sneaking inside.

Chapter Twenty-Seven

Brent

My attitude sucks and I'm snapping at Nora. I shouldn't, but I can't help it. I feel so betrayed and I'm trying to process those feelings before seeing Penelope tonight.

She'll be at the inn for dinner—at least she's supposed to be—and I need to be prepared. I have no idea what I'll say to her or how mad I'll be when I see her infuriatingly gorgeous face.

As soon as we get home, I let Nora put on the movie I promised and busy myself cleaning. Does the house actually need to be cleaned? Nope.

But my nerves have kicked up a hundred notches and I can't sit still.

Moving to the kitchen, I let my hands get soapy and start washing dishes in the sink. My mind wanders back to the first moment I saw Penelope. The day I walked up to her car and was completely struck by her beauty.

And then every moment in between, from how she interacts with Nora and the look on her face at the tree lighting to the way it felt when I kissed her for the first time.

We've made so many amazing memories in the few short weeks Penelope has been in Winterberry. Now, I'm questioning if any of it was real. Or were those moments as fake as the last name she gave me.

"Dad, when are we going for dinner? My tummy is making noises and talking to me," Nora looks comfortable, laying on the couch, her head propped against the cushion, and a blanket wrapped around her legs. Her curls are wild, and she pouts at me. "I'm hungry."

To be honest, I'm hungry, too, but I've been too nervous to eat. Now I'm stalling before dinner.

I know I'm putting off the inevitable, but I don't care. I'm not ready to face Penelope. A big part of me is furious at myself. I never should've opened up to someone I only met two weeks ago. Someone I hardly know.

"I know, Nora-Bean, I am too actually," I say. "Grandma said dinner will be ready around 6:00 so we'll go over then."

"When is that? Like how many minutes?"

"Well, right now it's five so that means we have an hour before going over. Do you know how many minutes that is?"

"Um... I think that's 60 minutes, right?"

"That's right!" I can't help but smile. My little girl is intelligent, and I can tell how proud she is just by the look on her face. "Good job sweetheart." I rinse my hands off, dry them, and go to sit with her on the couch.

I may have a hard time sitting still right now, but my little girl centers me, even when the fiercest storm is raging inside of me.

She's completely engrossed in the movie that I use the opportunity to take a shower.

"Will you be fine by yourself out here while I'm in the shower?" I ask her. Sometimes she gets scared when she's in the living room and I'm in the shower. "I can leave the door open, or you can come sit on my bed and watch TV while I shower. What do you think?"

"The TV in your room sounds good, Dad. Can I watch the movie in your room?"

"Sure you can. I'll put it on for you in there." I haul her off the couch and throw her over my shoulder. She squeals with laughter as I carry her into the bedroom, tossing her on my bed. She scrambles to nestle into the pillows.

I turn on the movie for her and kiss her head before going into the bathroom.

Once I'm under the spray of water, I develop a plan for confronting Penelope. I don't want to come on too strong, but man am I pissed.

I can't imagine why she would lie to me, to Sally, to the entire town. I never would have cared if she had told me who she really is.

I've never even seen her movies—I haven't been to the movies in years—and I don't have social media, so it probably wouldn't have meant anything to me. In fact, most of the people in this town wouldn't have known her, even if she had shared her real name.

Even though some people thought she looked familiar, in all the time she's been here, no one recognized she was a famous actress. This town just isn't like that. Sure, there are people in Winterberry who care more about taking a photo for their social media and looking good than anything else. But most of us are just living our lives. We don't get starstruck when a celebrity comes into town to see the snow. And the one time a famous singer stayed at the inn for a week, he was just another guest. No one in town treated him differently.

It would've been the same with Penelope, if she'd been honest.

Now, I have to decide if I can move past her lies. Or if she'd even want me to.

Admitting to Dominick that I was falling for her was hard to do, but it was the truth. The time I've spent with Penelope has meant so much to me. More than I've even admitted to myself until right now.

Washing my body, I decide that I'll wait for her to tell me when we get to dinner. I want to see what she'll say, if she'll be forthcoming with the truth. And if she doesn't bring it up, then I need to figure out how to handle it. Either way, a conversation needs to be had.

Turning off the water, I wrap a towel around my waist, dry off my hair with a second towel, and place my hands on the sink, staring at my reflection.

"I can do this. I can do this," I say to myself, pumping myself up for what's to come.

Moving to my bedroom, I see Nora still in the same exact spot in the middle of the bed, completely entranced by Frosty, and I go into my closet to pick out my clothes.

Casual seems like the way to go, so I dress in jeans, a white t-shirt, and a zip-up hoodie.

"Nora, time to get dressed so we can go for dinner," I say, waving my hand in front of her face to get her attention.

"Daaaad the movie is almost over. Can I just finish it?"

"Okay, only a few more minutes sweetheart. Do you need to change your clothes before we go?" I sit next to her on the bed.

"No thank you. Will Penelope be there?" she asks without looking away from the TV.

"That's what she said this morning. Can I finish the movie with you?"

"Duh, Dad, get comfy." She rests her head on my chest.

We stay like this until the end of the movie, singing the "Frosty the Snowman" song together when the credits roll.

From the bedroom, I hear a knock on the front door. I have no idea who it could be.

"I'll get that," I tell Nora. "Be right back."

As soon as I get to the door, I quickly yank it open to reveal Penelope standing on my porch.

"Penelope..."

Chapter Twenty-Eight

♥

Penelope

As soon as I enter the inn, the warm air hits my face and I smell the evergreen tree and live garland. The sounds of "Have Yourself a Merry Little Christmas" play in the background and soft Christmas lights fill every room.

I close my eyes, taking it all in. It's so beautiful.

I make my way into the kitchen and find Suzanne in her usual spot, rolling out dough on the counter with a rolling pin.

"Suzanne, it smells amazing in here," I say as I approach. "What are you making tonight?"

"Hi sweetheart, I'm making a loaf of bread so we can have garlic bread with dinner tonight. Then, I'm going to take a portion of the dough to make homemade cinnamon buns for breakfast. I'm making spaghetti and meatballs for dinner, one of Nora's favorite meals."

"That sounds delicious. Have you seen Brent?" I saw his truck in the driveway so I'm hoping he's home.

"I haven't yet. I told them to come over at 6:00 for dinner so it will be a while. How was Sally?"

For a second, I think about telling her the truth, but the words won't come out of my mouth. She's been so amazing to me since the moment I stepped foot inside her inn. I feel terrible for lying to her.

And I feel like I need to tell Brent before I talk to anyone else. He deserves an explanation, and I don't want to wait any longer.

"She's good," I say quickly. I'm trying not to be rude but I want to find Brent. "Hey, I'm going to get some air, the cold felt so nice earlier."

I make my way out the back door before she has the chance to respond. With my heart racing and my palms sweating even in the cold, I practically sprint across the yard to Brent's front porch and knock on the door.

"Please be home. Please be home," I say under my breath, looking around to make sure there's no paparazzi. The last thing I need is Brent's house being plastered across a tabloid or on Instagram.

After a few seconds, he opens the door. His eyebrows are pinched together, and his scowl is back.

"Penelope, did you come to hang out with us before dinner?" Nora yells as she comes running from the other room and jumps into my arms.

Over the top of her head, I see Brent lean against the door frame. The heat of his gaze reaches deep into my soul, and I get the sinking feeling that it's too late.

He knows.

We lock eyes and my heart threatens to burst. I have to set Nora down, out of fear of collapsing.

"Nora, can I talk to Penelope for a minute? Why don't you go get ready for dinner," he says without peeling his eyes away from me.

"Okay, Dad," she says. She runs off, her curls bouncing as she goes.

"Brent..." I start before he cuts me off.

"Don't. Whatever you're going to say, unless it's the absolute truth, keep it to yourself."

Okay, this isn't going to be easy.

"I'm sorry for lying and for giving you the wrong last name, but I can explain. Can we go outside so Nora doesn't hear me?"

"It's freezing outside," he says in a flat tone. "I like being in the warmth."

"I know, and I'm sorry, but I want to be able to explain this all to you without her walking in."

He takes a few seconds to study me before pushing off the doorframe and wordlessly stepping onto the porch. He stands there and waits for me to break the silence.

"Well, let's hear it, Penelope Maxwell," he says.

I want to literally turn around and run, but I need to face this, so I stand my ground. He closes the door behind him. He's right, I can see my breath, and a chill works its way down my spine.

He crosses his arms across his chest, leveling me with such a serious look that I almost shrivel up on the spot.

"You're right, my real name is Penelope Maxwell and I'm an actress who lives in Manhattan, has paparazzi following me around all the time, and has more money than I know what to do with," I start.

"When you found me in the middle of Main Street, I'd found out through the tabloids the day before that my fiancé was cheating on me with someone random. I decided to pack my bags, leave my phone and computer in my penthouse, and drive until I wanted to stop. I didn't want the paparazzi to find me." I rub the edges of my coat in between my fingers to calm my nerves so I can get through this.

"I had no idea that my car was having issues, I have a driver in the city, and it broke down here in Winterberry."

"So, why the lie?" he asks. "Why didn't you tell me who you were when I first came up to your car?"

"I wanted to be anonymous for the first time in years. And I wanted privacy to nurse my heartbreak. So, when you asked me what my name was, it just came out." If I could go back in time and tell the truth on that very first day, I would. My lie will be something I regret forever.

"As the weeks went on, I fell more and more in love with this town and felt like if I told the truth, I'd be looking at the same face you're giving me right now."

"I just don't understand," he says. "You've been around my daughter, my parents, my lips on yours..." he stumbles over his words, like he's trying to make sense of everything. "You had so many opportunities to tell me the truth and you didn't."

"I know, and I'm so sorry for that. I didn't expect to be here any longer than a night and now, I can't imagine leaving Winterberry." I cup my hands in front of my mouth and blow into them, trying to warm them up.

It takes everything in me to say those words and to finally be honest. I don't know what he's going to say, but I have to lay it all on the table.

"Brent, in the weeks I've known you, and your family, my feelings have grown. *Real* feelings. I know you don't have a reason to believe me right now, but I need you to know that how I feel about you is real. The night we spent together was real."

He looks at me like he wants to say something, but nothing comes out. I'm dying to know what he's thinking, if he feels the same.

When he finally speaks, he says, "Penelope, I'm sorry, I just don't know what to believe from you anymore."

"I deserve that. And I understand," I reply. Tears build in my eyes, and I need to be on my own.

Because I did this to myself.

I could've had it all, but I chose to lie, and that's on me.

I turn to leave, but Brent grabs my hand to stop me walking down the steps and off the porch. I turn around, as he grips my hand, and look up at him.

"Brent..."

Click. Click. Click.

"What is that?" he says, dropping my hand. We both turn toward the sound.

My blood runs cold when I realize what it is.

The paparazzi found me again. The man from earlier is standing on the front lawn of the inn, with a long lens on his camera, snapping photos of me and Brent.

I thought I'd lost him.

"Hey, get off the lawn!" Brent yells.

The man ignores him, continuing to snap photos.

"Brent, no, don't say anything to him. He'll use anything you give him and spin a story out of it."

"Is he paparazzi? He's taking photos of my parent's inn. How is that allowed?"

"These people don't care about any of that," I tell him. "Get inside quick before he can take any more. I'm so sorry."

We open the front door to his house and slip inside.

I rest my head against the door for a minute to get my bearings. "This is why I lied," I say. "These vultures will find someone anywhere if they get enough for a story or some photos. And as soon as it's out that this is where I am, they'll be swarming the place."

"We need to tell my parents," he says. "They need to know someone is taking photos of the inn."

"You're right. We need to tell them now. This is a mess and it's all my fault."

Stepping inside the house, he calls for Nora and tells her to get her coat on so we can leave for dinner. Neither of us tells her what's happening. Instead, we act like everything is normal. As soon as she's all bundled up, we head to the inn. Brent walks in front of me with Nora, and he doesn't look back once.

When we get inside, we shake off our coats and Nora runs into the dining room where Suzanne and Tom are relaxing before dinner.

"Grandma! Pop! We're here for dinner!" Nora says as soon as she sees Suzanne and Tom.

"Hi silly goose. It isn't dinner time yet. I told your dad to be here at 6:00 but it'll be ready soon," Suzanne says as Nora climbs into Tom's lap. She gives him a peck on the cheek and snuggles him.

"DAD! Why did we come early? You said it was time for dinner?" she says.

I follow Brent into the dining room where his parents are. One look at my face and Suzanne notices something is wrong.

"Hey, you two," she says, glancing between us. "Is everything okay?"

"Of course it's okay, Grandma," Nora says. "Dad is probably just hungry and wants to eat early. Right, Dad?"

We stand there for a beat as Suzanne and Tom study me and Brent.

"That's right sweetheart," Brent says in a monotone voice.

"Hey Nora, why don't you come with me to the office. I have a game on the computer I think you might like," Tom says.

"Ohhhh that sounds fun." Nora bounces off his lap and follows her grandpa into the office. Tom puts his hand on Brent's shoulder and gives it a squeeze. As soon as they're out of the room, I feel like I might throw up.

"Mom, there's something Penelope needs to tell you," Brent says, throwing me right under the bus.

My tongue sticks to the roof of my mouth and I wipe my sweaty hands on my jeans.

"My name is Penelope Maxwell and I'm an actress. I've been in some big movies and the paparazzi tend to follow me around everywhere, trying to get my photo," I say. "When Brent found my car broken down, I didn't want anyone to know who I was, so I lied. I'm so sorry I deceived you, Suzanne, and I get it if you want me to leave." Tears well in my eyes. Blinking, I force them away and clear my throat, ready for whatever answer she gives.

"Wait, I don't understand, so your last name isn't Smith?" she asks.

"No, I'm sorry." I pause, taking a breath. "I should've told you who I really was. I just didn't want anyone to find me, and I found myself loving it here more and more the longer I've been here."

The dam of tears bursts. I can't stop them from falling, and if I could be anywhere but here, I would be.

Standing up, Suzanne walks over to me and wordlessly pulls me in for a hug. She rubs my back in circles for a few minutes until my sobs subside and I can breathe normally again. Taking my hands in hers, she walks me over to the couch and we both sit.

"To be honest, I'm shocked. I'm not really sure why you lied," she says softly. "Who you are and what you do for a living makes no difference to me or anyone else here. I wish you would've told us the truth. But it doesn't change who you really are, in your heart, I hope you know that."

"Thank you, Suzanne, you have no idea how much that means to me," I whisper. "Once I got closer to you all, I knew that if anyone found out who I was, the paparazzi would swarm the town. Which is the next thing I need to tell you. The paparazzi did find me, and they're outside the inn trying to get photos of me to sell to the tabloids."

I cover my face with my hands. "I'm so sorry, you guys, I never intended for this to happen. I was hoping no one would recognize me while I was here so you didn't have the paparazzi or flocks of people coming to the inn, snooping around."

"Oh no. Are they outside right now?" Suzanne asks as she gets up and peeks out the window.

Sure enough, two more paparazzi have joined the original man, and they're trying to peer into the windows from the sidewalk. I can't believe this.

"What do we do?" Suzanne asks, looking directly at Brent. "Are we able to ask them to leave?"

"You can, but they don't have to," I say. "Not if they stay on the sidewalk. I'm so sorry, Suzanne. As soon as my car is ready, I'll leave and they'll be out of your hair, I promise."

She comes back to the couch, wraps her arms around me and I rest my head on her shoulder. Her affection hits me deep in my core and I long to stay here, wrapped in the warm embrace of the town and these people. I sniffle, willing the tears to stop falling.

The truth is, the life I've found in Winterberry is everything I didn't even know I wanted.

"It's okay, Penelope, you didn't mean for this to happen. It's not your fault," she says into my hair. "You don't need to leave sweetheart."

She pulls away and I turn around to look at Brent, to gauge how he's feeling. The way his eyebrows pinch together tells me his feelings haven't changed. When this realization hits, fresh tears threaten to fall.

"Penelope, are you okay?" Nora asks as she comes out of the office and hugs my leg. "You look so sad. It's okay."

"Sorry." Tom grimaces. "I thought the coast was clear."

"I'm fine, sweet girl," I say as I wipe my face and hug her back.

"Well, the cameras aren't leaving right now anyway, so let's try and enjoy our evening," Suzanne says. "Brent, that sound good to you?"

"Wait, what cameras?" Tom asks, clearly confused.

"I'll fill you in later, dear," Suzanne says, winking.

"Sure, sounds good, Mom," Brent responds without lifting his eyes.

I stay in my seat and Nora climbs up on the couch to sit next to me. She nudges closer, so our shoulders touch. The warmth of her little body next to mine helps me relax a bit. But the knowledge that I've ruined what Brent and I had weighs on my mind.

Conversation flows, with Nora exuding excitement for the upcoming holiday, but I can't focus on any of it. My mind wanders. I don't want to leave Winterberry, but *now* I have to.

And that crushes me.

Ring, ring.

The landline rings, interrupting the conversation. Suzanne gets up to answer it.

"Hi Ben," she says. "Sure, she's right here, hold on one second... Penelope! Ben is on the phone, he says he has news about your car," she yells.

I look up, catching Brent's eye before he averts his gaze.

Accepting the phone from Suzanne, I say, "Hi Ben, you have news?"

"I have the news you've been waiting for, Miss Smith," Ben says. "Your car is all fixed and ready to head back to Manhattan. I even took it for a little ride to make sure it's good to go. The keys will be in the safe box out front if you want to grab them tonight. The code is 112123."

Wow. I don't even know what to say.

This is what I wanted, right? Now, I can be out of everyone's hair, and they won't have to worry about the paparazzi snooping around.

So, why do I want to cry harder?

"Amazing!" I say, trying to muster up energy. "Ben, you're the best. Thank you so much for letting me know."

"You're so welcome, Penelope. Winterberry will surely miss you when you leave. Make sure you come back and visit us, okay?"

"I'll miss you, too, Ben." I give him my address so he can send me the bill. "Thank you for all you did for me."

I hang up the phone and stand there for a minute before heading back to the dining room. I take a deep breath, smoothing down my clothes and shaking my shoulders to let out the tension.

"Looks like my car is all fixed! I can pick up the keys whenever I want to," I announce to the room, feigning excitement.

"Nooooooo Penelope, don't leave!" Nora yells.

"I know, sweet girl, I'll miss you, but I do need to get back home," I say.

I glance at Brent. He lifts his head up, locking eyes with me, and his expressionless gaze tells me all I need to know.

He's ready for me to go.

Chapter Twenty-Nine

♥

Brent

Not long after Ben calls, Mom goes into the kitchen to finish making dinner with Penelope and Nora, which leaves me and my dad alone. Thankfully, he doesn't ask what happened. He pulls out a book, puts on his reading glasses, and gets lost in his story.

The voices of my three favorite women echo from the kitchen, and a sharp pang of longing hits my chest. Moments with Penelope over the past two weeks fill my mind. They're bittersweet memories now.

Once dinner is ready, we eat, acting like everything is normal. Like a huge bomb wasn't just dropped, and the woman who's stolen all of our hearts hasn't lied to us.

But I shouldn't be surprised. Acting is what Penelope does best, after all.

As soon as the plates are cleared, I bid a goodnight to everyone, including Penelope, and usher Nora home. I need to be alone.

Now that we're home, Nora hasn't stopped asking questions about Penelope leaving. I keep reassuring her that Penelope won't leave without saying goodbye and that she'll come visit.

Is that what I want? I don't even know anymore.

The fact that she lied, and then brought the paparazzi to the door of my parent's inn, has thrown me for a loop.

I can see it in her eyes that she was sorry, that she truly regretted it, but what's done is done. Now, as I stare out my front window, I notice a crowd has formed on the sidewalk. More cameras flash, additional paparazzi having joined the group.

"Don't these people have anything better to do?" I mutter. I guess I say it a little too loud because Nora bolts out of her room and joins me at the window.

"Who are all those people, Dad?"

"Come here for a second." I sit on the couch and pat the cushion next to me. Once Nora sits, I run my fingers through her curls and think of how to word this so she understands. "Penelope is not only a really great woman, she's also a famous actress. Remember how you saw her photo in the magazine at the grocery store?" She nods. "Well, those people are the ones who take those photos, and they want to get more of Penelope."

"Hmm, that's weird. But okay." She's just as confused as I am. "How long are they going to be out there?"

"To be honest, I'm not even sure," I say to her honestly. "Hopefully not too long."

"Hopefully." She pauses, appearing to ponder something. "Dad?"

"Yes, my love."

"Is she going to leave now that her car is fixed?"

That's the question I've asked myself since that phone rang with the news from Ben. If I'm being honest with myself, which I'm trying to be, I'm not ready for her to leave. And I may never be.

As that realization hits me, my mind replays the moments with her.

Seeing her on her walks.

Dinner at the inn.

That fun night out at the bar.

I want to have more of those moments, but I'm not sure if I should tell Penelope that.

Do I try to convince her to stay? Or do I let her walk away and get back to her life?

Now that I know she's rich and famous, I doubt she'll ever be happy in a town like this. Sure, she seems at ease here, but it's like when you're on vacation. It's not real life and won't last forever.

Small-town life isn't for everyone. Hell I don't even know if it's for me, but someone who's famous is used to fancy dinners, expensive shopping, and high-rise apartments. Not local diners, tiny stores, and a little house that could probably fit inside a penthouse closet.

Nora yawns and rubs her eyes, the telltale signs she's tired.

"Okay little one, let's get you ready for bed," I say.

"But Dad, I'm not tired," she says through another yawn.

"Uh-huh, so that yawn is just something you do all the time?"

She giggles in response. "Okay, you got me, I'm feeling sleepy, but I don't want to go to bed yet."

"I know, but you need to. Here, hop on my back and I'll give you a ride to your bedroom."

I get up and she stands on the couch so she can reach my back. Wrapping her little arms around my neck, she climbs on. I give her a piggyback ride to her room, depositing her on the bed.

"Okay, you get changed into your pajamas and I'll get your toothbrush and hairbrush ready in the bathroom. Meet you in a few," I say over my shoulder as I leave her bedroom.

I'm trying to act like everything is normal, so that Nora doesn't feel my anxiety, but my stomach is in knots. I head into the bathroom to get everything ready for Nora's nighttime routine.

She comes galloping in a few seconds later, her curls flying around. She climbs up on her stool so she can see in the mirror. She may be seven, but she's short for her age, a trait she got from Michelle.

Once she's done brushing her teeth, I braid her curls, and tuck her into bed. I wrap the blanket around her like I always do, and kiss her goodnight.

"Sweet dreams, my love," I say as I leave her room. "See you in the morning."

I change into my sweatpants and pour a glass of scotch before bed. Today has been exhausting. From finding out who Penelope really is to the paparazzi and her car being fixed, my mind is all over the place.

Taking my glass, I sit by my Christmas tree, attempting to calm my racing thoughts.

If Penelope had told me who she was the first day I met her, would I have given her a chance? Probably not. As much as I hate the fact that she lied, I understand why she did it. I don't like it, but deep down, I do understand.

I sip my drink, letting my thoughts wander, and by the time the glass is empty, I've made a decision.

Tomorrow, I'll go to the inn and talk to her. Tell her that I forgive her. That I wish she hadn't lied, but I don't want her to go.

Satisfied with my decision, and eager to talk to Penelope tomorrow, I put my glass in the sink. The men still gather on the sidewalk with their cameras around their necks.

Don't these people sleep?

Shaking my head, I turn off all the lights except the subtle glow of the Christmas tree, and head to bed. The faster I go to sleep, the faster I can have a conversation with Penelope.

And hopefully sort this all out.

I just hope it won't be too late.

Chapter Thirty

Brent

"Dad! Wake up sleepyhead." I hear the screeching before my eyes are even open for the day. "Daaaadddd it's not Christmas break yet, you need to take me to school, silly goose."

I put my pillow over my head to block out the sound, but my little spitfire decides to jump up and down on my bed.

"Okay okay, I'm awake." I groan. "Go get some cereal and I'll be there in a minute."

"Okay, Dad, see you out there." I hear her feet pad out of the room.

As soon as I open my eyes, I'm assaulted by bright, white light. Sunlight bounces off the fresh layer of snow, and it's practically blinding. I spent most of the night tossing, turning, and dreaming about what today will bring.

"Daaaaddddd, there's snow on the ground!" Nora screams from the kitchen.

"That's awesome baby," I yell back.

Maybe that means that the paparazzi aren't still outside, and I'll be able to take Nora to school in peace.

I climb out of bed and stride to the window. Sure enough, there's at least four or five inches of snow on the ground.

Closing the curtain, I make my bed and throw on a pair of jeans and a hoodie to take Nora to school. As soon as I'm back, I'm going to the inn and see if Penelope is awake.

Making my way out of my bedroom, I move to kiss Nora on the forehead. She sits at the island, eating a bowl of cereal and swinging her legs. I can't wait for Christmas break when I don't need to be up at a certain time, and I don't need to pack her lunch.

Looking at the time, I notice we only have a few minutes before we need to leave.

"All right little one, let's go get you dressed and brush your teeth. We need to leave the house in five minutes, think we can do it?"

"Oh, we can do it," she responds, giggling and climbing down from the stool. As soon as her feet hit the floor, she carefully puts her bowl in the sink and bolts down the hall into her bedroom. She gets dressed in two minutes flat and meets me in the bathroom where I'm waiting for her, so we can brush our teeth together.

"T-minus three minutes," I say.

Putting way too much toothpaste on her toothbrush, she quickly brushes her teeth and rinses. "Let's go, Dad, hurry up."

She throws the toothbrush back into the holder and turns to stare at me, crossing her arms.

"Do you need me to go faster?" I ask.

"No, Dad, I need to use the toilet." She giggles.

"Really? Well okay then, I will finish brushing *my* teeth in the kitchen sink." I rush into the kitchen to rinse and spit.

I grab Nora's backpack, holding it out for her once she gets her shoes and coat on. I also wrap a scarf around her neck since I'm sure it's freezing out.

"All right, let's do this," I say, peeking one more time to make sure there are no cameras pointed at the inn.

We're in the clear, so we hurry to my truck, where I blast the heat and Christmas tunes.

We have to drive slower because of the snow. There are already so many people walking around town, and I can't help but keep an eye out to see if Penelope is taking her daily walk, but so far, no sight of her.

I pull up to the curb outside of school, not late for once, and walk Nora to the entrance. Kissing her goodbye, I tell her the usual thing I say before each school day: "Have fun, be good, learn something!"

"Love you, Dad!" she yells as she runs up the steps and into the building.

As soon as she's inside safely, I head back to the truck and try not to speed on my way home. So many thoughts swirl through my mind.

I get to the inn a few minutes later and notice one of the paparazzi is back. I carefully pull into the icy driveway and park. When I get out of the truck, the paparazzi yells at me, desperately asking where Penelope is.

Instead of responding, I duck my head and go into the inn's back entrance. Quickly closing the door behind me, I shake off my boots. They're covered in snow, and I don't want to trek that into the house.

"Mom?" I say, as I stride through the house and catch her sitting at the dining room table by herself. She glances up at me, her hands wrapped around a coffee mug, and I can tell by her deep frown that something's wrong.

"What happened Mom?" I put my hand on her shoulder and squeeze, sitting down next to her at the table.

"She's gone," she says as she wipes a tear from underneath her eye. "Penelope is gone."

Chapter Thirty-One

♥

Penelope

Before my head even hit the pillow last night, I knew what I needed to do. So, when I got back to my room after dinner, I packed all my things and set my suitcases by the door. I noticed the paparazzi left when the snow and darkness fell, so I formulated a plan before getting much needed rest.

I won't say goodbye, I'm really not good at those, but I write a note to Suzanne and Tom, as well as Sally and Nora.

I'll forever be grateful to each of them for making Winterberry a home and giving me a holiday season to remember.

Is it the right thing to do, leaving before everyone gets up? That I don't know.

But the one thing I do know is the look Brent gave me, and the coldness in his demeanor, tell me he's rethinking everything that happened between us.

Before the sun wakes, I tiptoe down the steps, my bags trailing behind me. I'm careful to avoid the squeaky steps, pausing every so often to ensure no one has woken.

I set my bags down by the dining room table and take the notes out of my pocket. I'm filled with a brief surge of regret and guilt, but I push it aside. I need to leave this way. I place Suzanne's note on the dining room table, where I know she'll see it first thing, then I take a few minutes to study the inn, committing everything to memory. I never want to forget the feelings of peace, comfort, and family that the inn evokes. I never want to forget the time I spent here for the holiday season. I walk over to the Christmas tree and gently caress the branches.

I feel terrible for bringing the paparazzi to their front door and the only way I know how to fix that is to remove myself. It's what I've always done in the past.

How dumb I was to think I could truly live anonymously in a small town and have a quiet Christmas. All I've done is bring stress and pain to the people who have been nothing short of amazing to me.

Making my way to the front door, I glance over my shoulder one last time before stepping outside and shutting the door on the life I never knew I wanted.

The freezing wind slaps across my face and I grit my teeth as I walk down the steps. The snow is absolutely gorgeous, especially in the dark of the early morning. The lights from the inn make the snow glisten, even at this time of the day. I wrap my scarf across the bottom of my face to keep it warm.

At the end of the driveway, I turn back to look at Brent and Nora's house. The lights are all off, except for the soft glow of the Christmas tree and the fairy lights on the front porch.

Blowing a final kiss at the house, I grab my bags and drag myself toward Main Street.

Next, I stop at Sally's Diner. It isn't open, but I leave her letter in the mailbox. She checks her mail each morning before opening the diner, so I hope she'll see it.

And I hope she won't hate me.

I trudge through the snow, struggling to keep a hold of my luggage, and pass by the gazebo and the fireplace. It's out for the night but I'm sure in an hour or two it'll be lit again. I love what this fireplace represents, and it's another memory I'll always hold onto.

Town is completely quiet, with not a soul around. It's tranquil yet eerie, and a little bit depressing. I guess it's fitting that as I leave, back to my old life, I'm all alone.

My arms start to ache from the weight of my luggage as I make my way through the inches of snow. Why did I have to pack so much crap?

Next, I head to Ben's Shop to grab my car keys.

My keys are where Ben said they'd be, and I easily locate my car in the lot. I finger my keys, turning them over in my hand and breathing deeply. Anxiety blossoms in my chest. Hauling my bags into the trunk, I quietly close it then climb into the driver's seat.

The smell of my expensive perfume and a lavender air freshener hits me in the face and almost makes me cry. For the first time, I feel like a stranger in my car. The memories of Manhattan that flood my mind feel like they're from someone else's life.

How am I ever going to go back to Manhattan?

I climb in, turn the car on and am both relieved and disappointed when it works. Guess it really is time to go.

Pulling out of the lot, I decide to take one more tour around town. I drive past the shops on Main Street, smile at the large bows on every lamppost, and take in the lake one more time. Lastly, I roll past the inn. It's still completely dark inside. With an ache in my chest, I slowly drive by before heading out of town, passing the "Come Again Soon" sign.

"Bye, Winterberry. I will truly, truly miss you," I whisper to the empty car, tears streaming down my face.

The trip back to New York isn't too bad. Thankfully, traffic is light until I hit the Holland Tunnel a few hours later. This is always the worst part of the drive into the city. I open my window to let some of the cold in and am immediately hit with the smell of smog and car fumes. That, I didn't miss.

The sun rises into the sky, signaling that the day has officially begun. Cars with out-of-state license plates clog up the tunnel, from people visiting the city this time of year. The lanes of traffic are at a complete standstill. Little kids peer out of backseat windows, sharing looks of awe.

From the ice skating at Rockefeller Center to the decorated window displays on Madison Avenue, there's so much to do in the city this time of year. But honestly, I'd choose Christmas in a small town over the city any day.

It takes a while to finally cross into the city but once I do, I navigate to my building. I carefully pull into the parking garage, showing the employee in the booth my parking pass, and make my way to my designated spot.

The garage is filled with high-end cars. Various nameless neighbors rush to their vehicles. Most are dressed in suits or heels. Some yap on their cell phones. I wave as I drive by, and only one person gives a confused wave back.

I guess I'm not in Winterberry anymore.

As soon as I park, I grab my bags out of the trunk and head inside. It's not as cold in the parking garage, since it's technically underground, but the chill lingers and I'm desperate to get inside.

It takes me a few minutes to wheel and carry my luggage to the entrance. The doorman opens it and lets me inside.

"Miss Maxwell, it's so nice to see you again. Did you have a nice trip?" he asks with a huge smile. Maybe he thinks I was on vacation.

"Good morning. I did. Thank you so much," I say as I walk through the huge foyer. The gigantic chandelier glints overhead, marble floors shine underfoot, and gold accents touch almost every inch of the space. Residents mill about, and no one spares me a second glance.

"Do you need help getting to the elevator, Miss Maxwell?" the doorman calls after me.

I must look like I'm struggling as I lug my bags through the building, but I'm fine on my own.

"No, thank you," I say over my shoulder. "Have a great day." I muster a fake smile to hide my sadness.

As soon as I enter the elevator, I drop my bags and am finally able to breathe. I was only in that space for less than five minutes and I felt like I was going to burst. Seeing the cold looks and the rush of everyone around me is a stark contrast to the warmth and slow pace in Winterberry. It's going to take some getting used to to get back into my old routines.

The elevator dings and the doors open to my foyer.

I quickly lug my bags into the space, with tears streaming down my face, and pause. Looking around at the place I call home, I can't stop the unhappiness from taking over.

The tears from streaming.

The sobs from escaping.

I lean against the door and slide down, pulling my legs to my chest. I rest my chin on my knees and let it all out.

How am I ever going to call this place home again?

Chapter Thirty-Two

♥

Brent

"What do you mean she's gone?" I ask, staring at my mom.

The wrinkles on her forehead grow deeper and she slowly shakes her head in defeat. I put my arms around her shoulders and hug her tight. There's a piece of paper on the table with a few ink smudges, like something wet splattered and dried.

"Here, she wrote it all here." Mom hands me the note. "I need to get breakfast for our guests. Take your time." She gets up from the table, patting my arm and making her way into the kitchen.

Sitting down in the chair, I slowly unfold the letter and read.

Dear Suzanne and Tom,

I'm not sure how to say this, and I'm not good at goodbyes, so I'm choosing to do it this way instead. The past few weeks in Winterberry, here at this inn, have been the best of my life. I came here, trying to be someone I'm not, and in the process, I found who I really am.

I'm so sorry for lying to all of you. It wasn't my intention to cause any pain, but I realize I have. I also apologize for bringing the chaos of the paparazzi to your front door.

I want you to know that you will forever hold a piece of my heart, all of you, and I will always remember this Christmas.

To Nora: You are so beautiful, kind, funny, and I hope you always keep your love of Christmas. I will miss you.

Brent, all I can say is I'm sorry. Hopefully one day you can forgive me.

I hope you have a successful Christmas Eve Ball at the inn and a memorable Christmas. I wish I could be there.

If you're ever in Manhattan, I would love to see you all.

Love always,

Penelope

Setting the note down, I take a moment to let it sink in, then I pick it up and read it again. I can't believe this.

I can't believe that she's gone. Back to New York. Without even a word.

Slowly standing, I walk into the kitchen clutching the note and stare at my mom from in the doorway.

"She's really gone," I say to her back as she whisks eggs.

"Unfortunately, she is. I wish she would've stayed. We all forgave her already, right?" She turns around and stares at me.

I nod, unable to speak.

"She didn't leave a phone number or a way of contacting her," I say dejectedly. "She says we should come visit if we're in Manhattan, which never happens, but didn't leave us a way to find her. Why would she do that?"

I work to keep my face neutral, but my jaw clenches and I furrow my brow. I feel like my mom can see right through me. I guess I suck at being an actor.

"I'm not sure, sweetheart," she says. "But I guess she felt like she needed to go home. I'm going to finish getting these eggs ready. Do you have a lot of work to do today?"

I take her question as a sign she's moving on from the conversation. "Yeah, I actually do have some to catch up on," I say. "I'm going to take Nora shopping tonight for a dress for the ball, do you want to come with us?"

"I'd love to! That sounds fun. Your dad may need your help tonight, figuring out when we should start moving furniture for the ball."

"Sounds good. After we go shopping, we can come back here for dinner, and I'll be here to help Dad out with whatever he needs."

"Great. Want to come pick me up after you get Nora from school?" Moms asks, turning around from the stove with a smile on her face. I can tell it's forced but I don't point it out.

Because if we're being honest, mine is forced too.

"Yep. I think I'll go to the diner for some breakfast then work from the office today. I need to focus so I can wrap things up before the madness ramps up for Christmas." I walk over and place a kiss on the top of her head. "I love you, Mom."

"Love you too, son." She pats my hand and returns to her cooking.

I head out the back door to my truck. Those damn paparazzi are on the sidewalk again, rapidly screaming questions and snapping photos. I almost forgot they'd been there, waiting for a shot of Penelope.

"Where's Penelope? Is she coming?" Two of the paparazzi talk over each other, as if battling to get their questions heard. "Are you two dating? How long is she staying here?"

"Hey jerks," I yell. "Penelope went back to Manhattan. So you can take your cameras and get off the sidewalk."

Talking amongst themselves, they lower their cameras, but don't leave.

Don't they have anything better to do with their lives than follow people around?

Does she always have to deal with this?

No wonder she lied about who she was. If these vultures are always harassing her, she probably just wanted to breathe in peace for once.

Shaking my head, I climb into my truck and turn it on, backing out of the driveway and heading to the diner. I have to tell Sally that Penelope left. She's going to be heartbroken.

But the person I'm most scared to tell is Nora. She adores Penelope and I don't know how she's going to take the news.

I drive down Main Street, passing the town square gazebo and trying to avoid eye contact with the people who are walking or shopping. I'm not in the mood to talk to anyone other than Sally right now. She'll get what I'm going through.

Finding a parking spot, I turn off the truck as fast as I can and head into the diner with my head down. As soon as I open the door, the sounds of people chatting, Christmas music, and the clattering of silverware fill my ears.

"Brent! Hey! What are you doing here?" Sally says from her spot behind the counter.

She's smiling, but her red eyes and pink nose indicate she's been crying.

Does she already know about Penelope?

"Hey Sal, I'm here for some breakfast and to talk to you. Have a minute?" I ask, striding over to her.

"Yeah, give me a second. Meet you in the office?"

She has an office off the kitchen in the back, and though she doesn't use it often, we'll have some privacy.

"Sounds good," I say, making my way into the kitchen. I enter the office and take a seat in one of the big leather chairs across from the desk.

The door creaks open a minute later, and Sally joins me. "Sorry, I got caught chatting," she says. "Everyone is excited for the Christmas Eve Ball. Do you and your folks need help moving anything or setting up tables?"

"That'd be awesome. I'm taking Nora shopping for a dress today with my mom, but after that we're going to order a pizza and start planning. It'll be here before we know it. If you want, you can come over and help."

"I'm there," she says before an awkward silence fills the room. "So... I'm assuming you're not here to talk about the ball or the weather. Did you get the note from Penelope?"

"Wait, she left you a note?" Am I the only one who didn't get a note directly from her? Yes, she mentioned me in the one to my parents, but she didn't say anything personal to me. It felt like I was an afterthought.

"She did..." she says slowly. "Didn't you get one?"

"Nope." I cross my arms over my chest.

Wow, I guess I really meant nothing to her. Our time together, the connection we had, meant nothing.

"I'm sorry, Brent, I just figured she would've left you one, too," she says. "I found mine in the mailbox this morning. Do you want to read it?"

"No, that's okay. I'm sure she meant for you to read it. Just tell me, is she all right?"

"I'm not sure to be honest. She didn't say in the letter. I can't believe she left. Did you say anything to upset her?" she asks me accusingly.

"Really, Sally?" I get up from the chair and start pacing. "No, I didn't say anything to her. I was actually planning to talk to her today, and even though I'm mad she lied, I didn't want her to go. I guess it doesn't matter now though."

"I'm so sorry, Brent. I wish she'd stayed. I'm really going to miss her."

"Me too," I say. "I'm actually not feeling very hungry. Can I get a sandwich to go? I need to get some work done at the office."

"Are you sure? I could get you a booth in the back so no one bothers you."

"Nah, thanks though. I'll order a turkey club and fries to go."

We head back inside the diner and Sally puts in my order. I stand off to the side, hoping no one talks to me, as I wait.

Luckily, only a few people stop and say hi but I think they can tell I'm not interested in conversation because they move on quickly.

"Here ya go," Sally says, handing me a bag over the counter. "What time should I come over tonight?"

"How does 6:00 sound? We'll be home by then."

"Sounds great. I'll see you then." I quickly head to my car and drive to my office. I spend the next few hours working, trying to keep my mind off Penelope, and only eating when the hunger pangs become unbearable.

Before I know it, my alarm goes off and it's time to pick my little girl up from school. Dress shopping is the last thing I want to do today, but the smile on Nora's face will make it worth it.

I'm going to tell her about Penelope before we get my mom from the inn, so hopefully the shopping and decorating will take her mind off it afterward.

As soon as I pull up outside the school, I get out and Nora barrels down the steps with her friends.

"Hey, Dad!" She throws herself at me, wrapping her arms around my neck and pulling me close.

"Hey, munchkin, ready to go get a new dress for the ball? Grandma is going to come with us so we are going to grab her now. Sound good?"

"Yeeeeees," she squeals in my ear. I help her into the truck. I'm not looking forward to this conversation. Closing the door once she is settled in her seat, I walk around the front of the truck, open the driver side door, and get inside.

"Hey Nora, I have to tell you something really quick before we go," I say cautiously as she turns in her seat and looks at me. "Penelope left this morning back to Manhattan, back home. She wanted to be there for Christmas."

"She did?" Nora starts to cry. I knew this would happen. "But what about the ball? And Christmas here with us?"

How do I put this? "Honey, unfortunately she needed to get back to work. But it's okay, we'll see her again, and the ball will be amazing as usual."

"Okay, Dad," she says, whimpering and wiping her tears. I lean over, using the sleeve of my coat to dry her face. "I'm going to miss her."

"Me too, Nora-Bean, me too." And that's the truth. "Let's go get Grandma and take you shopping, little lady."

We pull away from the curb and make our way back to the inn, honking in the driveway to let my mom know we're there to get her. I notice that the paparazzi are gone, and I sigh in relief.

"Hey guys. How was school, Nora?" my mom asks when she slides in next to Nora.

"It was good, I can't wait for Christmas break," Nora says, giving her a kiss on the cheek. "What color dress should I get?"

"Hmmm, maybe a pretty red one?"

They get lost in conversation about dresses, shoes, and jewelry until we get to Main Street and park. For the next two hours, we browse the shops. I follow them around, carrying their bags. Luckily, Nora is so distracted that she never once mentions Penelope. I'm so relieved that I don't even care how much of my money they're spending.

My mood never lifts. Anger and heartbreak still course through my veins, but I fight to bury it, faking contentment instead.

As soon as we get home, Nora runs inside our house to put the shopping bags down. Mom ordered pizza on the way home, so it won't be long before it arrives.

Running back outside, she meets us in the driveway, and we all make our way into the house to wait for the food and start on the planning.

"Grandma, can I help plan too?"

"Of course you can sweetheart. Dad said Sally is coming to help, isn't that right Brent?"

"Yes, I am!" Sally says as the back door opens, and she blows in with the cold wind. "The planning committee is here!"

"Yayyyy let's do this," Nora yells, clapping her hands. This little girl just loves Christmas.

"Brent, ready to help me?" Dad calls from the living room where he's probably reading his book.

"Yep," I say. I'm not in the mood for anything Christmassy, but I promised I'd help, so here I am.

Together, Dad and I pull out a blank piece of paper from behind the check-in desk and figure out a timeline to get ready for the ball. We need to move a lot of the furniture out into the shed and there will be a company bringing in tables and chairs for people to sit. Nora, Mom, and Sally are zero help as they sit in the kitchen and talk about what they're wearing to the ball. But I don't mind. Nora is busy with the people she loves, which is what she needs right now. It's what we all need.

"Let's get as much planned as we can tonight so I don't have to do this again," Dad says, chuckling. He doesn't hate Christmas, but he isn't as much of a fan as Mom and Nora are.

We finish the to-do list just as the door chimes, signaling the arrival of pizza. I answer the door, grab the pizza, and head to the dining room where we all sit down to eat.

Once we're in our seats, with our plates filled with pizza, and the air filled with comfortable conversation, I glance at the empty chair to Sally's right. It's where Penelope always sat.

It's where she should be sitting now.

Christmas won't be the same without her.

And I'm worried it never will be again.

Chapter Thirty-Three

Penelope

The next few days begin the same. I wake up in my California King bed, with my 400-thread-count sheets and down comforter. I press a button on the remote on my nightstand, and the shades lift, letting the morning light leak in.

This bed should be more comfortable than it is. I shouldn't feel like a stranger in this room, but I do.

It's like I'm living in someone else's apartment, wearing someone else's silk pajamas, and staring at a face I don't recognize in the mirror.

I contacted my agent and publicist the day I got back, trying to resume my life.

Yesterday, I even stopped at a corner tree lot and bought myself a Christmas tree. I don't have any lights or ornaments yet, but it's a start. The interior of my penthouse is bland, so I need to go shopping for decor. Maybe that'll make me feel better.

Each morning, I walk down my street. It's not as peaceful as Winterberry—no one says hi and the air isn't as fresh—but it's something. I even found a diner I like. It has nothing on Sally's Diner, but the food is decent enough. Every evening, after I eat dinner by myself, I light my fireplace, snuggle into my couch, and read. It's become my new routine and I'm really enjoying it.

It reminds me of who I was in Winterberry which warms my heart.

But I'm still so unhappy.

And I don't know how long it's going to take before that feeling goes away.

I stayed off social media the first two days I was home, and the moment I signed back in, the notifications went wild. There were thousands of them. It took me hours to get through only half.

And most of them were discussing the same thing—Drew and his fiancée's upcoming wedding.

At first, I couldn't believe it. But after seeing hundreds of tags and mentions on various articles, I finally accepted that it was true. My ex-fiancé is soon walking down the aisle with a woman who isn't me.

Boy, did I dodge a bullet.

I thought seeing the official news and hearing about it nonstop would break my heart all over again. But to be honest, it did nothing. I had come to grips with the end of that relationship while I was in Winterberry.

Leaving Winterberry hurt more than leaving Drew.

One of the first things I did after I slogged through the overwhelm of notifications was call Georgia. Hearing her voice was like a warm hug. I didn't even realize how much I missed her.

"Pen!" she screeched. "When I saw your pic in the tabloids I was going to come to that town and save you. How miserable were you?"

I hesitated. "Actually, I loved it."

"Wait, what?"

"It was the best place, filled with the nicest people and the best Christmas traditions. I miss it so much."

"You can't be serious. Penelope, you are not a small-town girl. You're a famous actress who women all over the world wish they could be. Do you... do you want to go back there?"

"I do, Georgia." I gulped. It felt weird to say it out loud. "I wish I never had to leave. I also, um, met someone."

"Okay, I need to come over!" she yelled. I had to hold my phone away from my ear. "Give me an hour and I'll be there."

"I'm actually still trying to relax since being home," I said. "How about we get dinner soon? My treat." I faked a chipper voice.

"Are you sure? You're kind of scaring me."

"I'm sure. I'll call you," I said before hanging up.

After that, my phone wouldn't stop going off. I was spammed with notifications from every social media app, bogged down by an incessant stream of texts and calls, so I only lasted one day with it on. I turned it off, put it away in a drawer, and ordered myself a brand-new iPhone.

Complete with a new number.

I only gave my new number to my agent and Georgia.

And it's so much quieter ever since.

The day before Christmas Eve, the urge to stay in bed pulls at me, but I force myself to get up.

Making my way across the room, I head into the en-suite bathroom to wash my face and fix my hair. The bags under my eyes are evidence of my lack of sleep, so I put on eye cream and try to make myself look presentable.

I don't know why. I don't plan on leaving the apartment today other than for my walk, but Winterberry's Christmas Eve Ball tomorrow is on my mind.

Will everyone be getting the inn ready today? What does Nora's dress look like?

Maybe I'll find something to distract myself.

Maybe I'll go to a movie or view the Rockefeller Christmas Tree.

I put Pop-Tarts in the toaster then mix eggs for scrambled eggs. I brew a cup of coffee, with sugar cookie creamer, to get in the Christmas spirit.

While I sit at the table, I look long and hard at my bare tree and decide that today will be the day I get ornaments and lights. That should take my mind off what I'm missing.

Once I'm done eating, I get dressed, lace up my sneakers, bundle up, and go for my daily walk. Once I'm on the street, I smile at everyone who passes, resulting in a few weird looks thrown my way.

I walk for as long as I can tolerate in the cold, then I hail a cab and ask the driver to drop me off at Target. Since I've been home, I haven't used my driver, preferring to walk or catch a cab instead.

As soon as I get to Target, I make a beeline for the Christmas section, buying as many ornaments as I can fit in the cart and four strands of twinkle lights. Some people recognize me—good thing I brushed my hair—so I take a few pictures and sign autographs before checking out.

I went a little overboard, so I apologize to the cab driver who picks me up. The bags barely fit in his car.

When we pull up at my building, the doorman comes out to help me with my bags. He takes half while I take the other half.

"Miss Maxwell, I can come back and get the rest of these, you don't need to carry all of that."

"Oh, that's okay, I don't mind," I say. Together, we get into the elevator and take it straight to my floor.

"Do you have any plans for Christmas, Miss Maxwell?"

"Actually, I don't. I finally have ornaments and lights to decorate my bare tree and I'm thinking of going to the Rockefeller Tree tonight. But no other plans. How about you?"

The surprised look on his face tells me that he might not get asked about himself often. "I work in the morning here and then I will be home with my family for dinnertime."

"I'm so sorry you have to spend the first part of the day away from them," I tell him sincerely. I guess I never even realized that no matter what holiday it is or what day of the week it is, they're always here to open the door and greet us.

What kind of person have I been that I never noticed?

"Oh that's okay, Miss Maxwell, my family understands. We move our celebrations to later in the day," he says.

What a sweet man.

It saddens me to know he's away from his family Christmas morning, all to open the door for us. I make a mental note to order him food tonight, so he can have something special while working through the holiday.

Once we reach the top, he helps me carry the bags into the apartment. I thank him, giving him a generous tip before he heads back downstairs.

Before I start decorating, I put on a Christmas playlist from Spotify, hooking it up to my surround sound, and I find myself belting out lyrics at the top of my lungs.

Slowly, I begin to decorate, starting with the lights on the tree, and then moving onto ornaments. I chose a pink-and-silver theme, something different, with a large silver star on top of the tree.

After about two hours, I stand back and admire my handiwork. There's barely an inch of the tree that doesn't have something hanging from it or lighting it up. I love what I see. This is the first year I've decorated a tree in this apartment, and I'm so glad I did.

When my stomach growls, I grab a pizza from the freezer and pop it in the oven. I light cinnamon-scented candles, to lend to the holiday spirit, and I keep the Christmas music coming.

While the pizza bakes, I change into a pair of sweatpants and my favorite fuzzy socks. I throw my hair into a bun atop my head.

When the oven dings, I pull the pizza out, slice it up, and sit down at the table to eat.

I'm about to take my first bite when the intercom by my front door buzzes.

Confused, I wipe my hands on a napkin and rise. I push the *talk* button. "Hello?" I say into the intercom.

"Miss Maxwell, sorry to interrupt you, I have someone here to see you. Would you like me to send them up?"

It's probably Georgia here to surprise me. I sigh. "Yes please."

I've only talked to her once since I got my new phone, and she hasn't been thrilled about my recent introversion to say the least. I know I should see her; she's my best friend, after all, but I just don't feel like myself yet after returning to the city.

After a few minutes, I hear the ding of the elevator. I go to greet Georgia as the door opens into the foyer. "Hey, Geor…"

I freeze.

It's not Georgia.

"Brent?" I ask, disbelief lacing my tone. "What are you doing here?"

"It's nice to see you, too, Penelope," he says as he stands in my doorway, holding what looks like a garment bag. "Can I come in?"

Moving aside, I open the door wider so he can enter.

Chapter Thirty-Four

Penelope

"Wow, some place you have here," Brent says as his eyes sweep over the penthouse. For some reason, I'm embarrassed by the size of the place. Closing the door behind him, we both stand there awkwardly. I'm not sure what to say or do.

He walks over to the couch and carefully sets the garment bag down, turning to look at me.

The scents of citrus and cedar fill my home as he walks through, and I can't help but take a deep breath and soak it in. It's one of the things I've missed about Winterberry. Along with the man currently standing in my living room.

"Do you want something to drink?" I ask.

"Really? I show up at your door and that's all you say?" He raises his eyebrows.

"To be honest, I have no idea what to say right now. How did you get my address?"

"Well, you didn't leave it in the notes to my parents or Sally, so I had to strong-arm Ben into giving it to me. Don't worry, I went easy on the old man." We both laugh. "Once he gave it to me, I decided to get in the car and come see you."

"Why?" I manage to croak out.

"You left in such a hurry, and I didn't even get the chance to talk to you." He stares at me, and I feel my cheeks heat.

"I'm sorry I left like that, but I knew I'd messed up and it would be better if I wasn't there. The paparazzi would have never left the inn if I didn't. And I'd already screwed up with everyone."

It's strange seeing him here in my space, among my things, completely out of his element. My penthouse is wildly different from his home in Winterberry. I fight the urge to run into his arms and never let go.

Instead, I stand frozen in the foyer and stare at him. Desperate for something to do, I make my way into the kitchen and busy myself with making coffee.

I can feel Brent's presence behind me.

"How is everyone in Winterberry?" I ask as I turn around to see him leaning against the counter with his arms folded over his chest. His hair is a little bit shorter than it was since the last time I saw him and I like the way it looks.

"Everyone's good. Mom told me to tell you hi and Nora was jealous I was coming here to see you without her. She's on Christmas break from school and getting ready for the ball."

"I miss her little face. What does her dress look like for tomorrow night?" I want him to tell me so I can picture it in my head.

"Maybe you should come and see it for yourself."

Wait. Hold on. Did he just say what I think he just said?

"You... you want me to come back?" His statement takes me completely by surprise and I almost can't get the words out.

Brent pushes off the counter and crosses the room to where I'm standing. He reaches out and rubs my arms before pulling me against his chest and wrapping me in a hug. The warmth radiating from him is almost too much to bear, and against my better judgment, I let my tears fall.

Once the dam breaks, the flood doesn't stop. My tears stain his shirt but he doesn't seem to notice as he holds me. After a few minutes, I stand back and wipe my face with my shirt. How many times have I imagined him, right here, saying he wanted me to come back?

Back to Winterberry.

More times than I can count.

But, now that it's really happening, I don't even know what to think.

As soon as I pull away, he tucks a piece of hair behind my ear and tenderly plants a kiss on the top of my head.

"I've wanted you to come back since the moment you left," he says. "Listen, I was mad when I found out you lied. I didn't understand at first, but I get it now. No matter what, I didn't want you to leave. No one did."

I'm not sure what to think right now, and I can't stand still. Everything I've been feeling since I've been back home pours out, and I start pacing like a caged animal.

"Brent, I don't know what to say. I thought you hated me." My mind's going a mile a minute and I walk into the living room to center myself. The lights from the Christmas tree twinkle back at me and I can see my reflection in one of the ornaments.

"You got a tree, huh?"

"I did. I couldn't be here, in my home, without Christmas this year. Not after being in the Christmas capital of Winterberry," I say, trying to infuse lightheartedness.

"That's true, it changes you."

"In more ways than one," I whisper.

Turning around, I catch Brent picking up the framed picture of Georgia and me.

"Who's this?"

"That's Georgia, my best friend I told you about. That picture was taken not long after we moved here to Manhattan and were trying to get our life together," I tell him as he sets the frame back down and picks up another photo. This one is of me as a little girl, with my arms around my Gran and a smile that reaches my ears.

"Is this your Gran?"

"It is. She was the best woman I ever knew, that is until I met your mom. Suzanne is a force of nature who I'd one day love to be like."

He turns around, locking eyes with me. "You're more like her than you think."

I can feel my pulse speed at the compliment. Glancing away so he doesn't see my eyes glistening again with a fresh set of tears, my sight lands on the bag he placed on my couch.

"What's in the bag?" I ask. I think I know the answer, but I want to hear him say it.

"I wasn't sure if you'd need a new dress for the ball, so I picked one out for you," he says sheepishly, rubbing the back of his neck. "You don't need to open it now."

"Brent, that's so sweet. But… I can't accept that." My voice shakes as the words leave my mouth.

"You're not coming back with me, are you?" His shoulders slump and he shifts his weight to his other foot.

I shake my head and wrap my arms around myself. "I'm so confused right now. I can't make a decision that fast. This morning I woke up thinking I'd never see you again, and now, here you are, and I just don't know what to think. I need some time. I hope you understand."

"Wow. Well, this isn't how I thought this was going to go." His eyebrows pinch together, and a flash of pain crosses his face. "I shouldn't have come. How dumb of me to think a famous actress like you would want to be with someone like me or live in a town like Winterberry."

"Brent, that's not what this is at all. I *love* that little town and I'd be lucky to be with a man like you. I'm just taken by surprise, that's all."

I close the distance between us and reach out to touch his arm before he pulls it away and strides toward the elevator door.

"Don't leave Brent. Let's go get something to eat and talk. Please."

"That's okay, I should get home. I need to help get ready for the ball. I'll tell everyone you said hi." His voice hitches as if he's trying to hold it together.

"Please Brent. Don't go like this," I practically beg.

"Goodbye Penelope." He presses the elevator button. "Merry Christmas."

And with that, he turns and enters the elevator, letting the doors shut between us.

I fall to the ground and fold over myself, rocking back and forth and trying to breathe. What have I done? How could he expect me to just come back with him? Did I just make the biggest mistake of my life?

Spotting the bag he left on the couch, I stand up on shaky legs and pull myself to where it sits. I drag the zipper down to reveal the most stunning dress I've ever seen. A gorgeous red shade, it has a small slit up the front and sparkles in the light. I take it out of the bag, walk to the full-length mirror in my closet, and hold it up to see how it looks on me.

It's breathtaking.

My emotions take over again, and as I look at myself in the mirror, the mental image of Brent's back as he left replays in my mind.

I'm such an idiot for letting him go.

I know what I have to do.

Manhattan has been my home for so long, but it doesn't feel like where I belong anymore. Placing the dress back in the bag and closing it, I go back to my closet and choose a pair of shoes, a small gold clutch, and a pair of earrings.

I head to my bedroom and take down the same luggage I had with me the first time I found myself in Winterberry. I had no idea how my life would change in the time I was there, and now, I can't imagine myself anywhere else.

I may have made a mistake not leaving with Brent, but I can make it right. I know I can. With the utmost confidence in my decision, I fit as much as I can into my bags and turn off the tree in the living room. It's still a little early, but I'm going to bed. I need to be rested for the drive back to Winterberry tomorrow.

It's time to go home.

Chapter Thirty-Five

♥

Brent

"My girl, look at how beautiful you are!" I say to Nora as she spins in front of the mirror, smiling.

When I got back into town last night, everyone expected Penelope to be with me. When I returned to the inn alone, their disappointment mirrored my own. Now, it's Christmas Eve and I need to focus on my little girl. Penelope doesn't want to be with us, and I have to respect that.

"Thank you, Dad. I love this dress," she squeals. "I can't wait for the ball. It's going to be so much fun. I just wish Penelope was here to go with us."

"I know little one, I do too. But let's get over to the inn to help Grandma and Pop in case there's some last-minute stuff that needs to be finished before everyone arrives," I say, ruffling her hair.

"Dad, don't touch the hair, it's perfect," she tells me as I laugh.

"Sorry, sweetheart. I wasn't thinking."

She runs out of the bedroom, and I take another second to look at myself in the mirror. With a black tux on and gel in my hair, I look pretty good.

"Dad! Come on!" Nora yells from the other room.

As I walk down the hall and into the living room, I hear her humming "We Wish You A Merry Christmas" under her breath and twirling as she puts her coat on.

I grab my coat, throw it on over my tux even though we're only walking a few feet, and we make our way outside.

Music trickles from the inn, spilling into the yard. Caterers rush inside, carrying trays of food.

There may be a lot of events in Winterberry leading up to Christmas, but this is the biggest one, and almost every resident will stop by tonight, if only for a moment. Each year, my parents put this ball on for free.

We enter through the back door and the hustle and bustle hits me in the face.

"Grandma! Pop! We're here!" Nora calls.

Mom rounds the corner, and I'm struck by how beautiful she looks. She doesn't dress up often, in fact this might be the only day of the year she does, and she looks amazing.

"Hello, gorgeous girl, look how pretty you are!" she says, giving Nora a big hug and taking our coats. "And look at you, my handsome son." She cups my cheeks in her hands.

"Thanks, Mom. What do you need help with?"

"Could you help your dad get the rest of the food set up? The caterers are bringing them all in now."

"Sure thing," I say.

I head to the living room. We moved all of the furniture out and added a few tables with chairs, so everyone can sit and eat. We did the same in the dining room, where the table is adorned with platters of food, lit candles, and winter greens.

"Hey, Dad, what can I do to help?"

His black tux matches my own—I know Mom made him wear it—and he looks really great.

"Hey, son, if you could just tell the caterers where to go when they come inside, that would be great," he says. "Guests should be arriving in a few minutes." By the sweat pooling above his upper lip and the way he keeps running his fingers through his hair, I can tell he's stressed but everything will be fine, just like it always is.

This year, I'm more into the Christmas season than I've been in years, and it feels like everyone can tell. But, with the rejection from Penelope still fresh in my mind, I'm hoping I can muster up my festive spirit without letting the weight of my pain show. What I wouldn't give to have her by my side tonight.

Before I know it, guests start arriving. I have to admit, each person looks amazing. Dressed in suits, ties, tuxes, and ball gowns, the whole town is dressed in their best. Every person stops and says Merry Christmas, bringing trays of homemade desserts like every year.

After a while, the party is in full, loud swing, with some people eating and others dancing to the Christmas music. Ben and his wife twirl past, and I smile.

I stand off to the side by the Blue Spruce, taking it all in.

"Dad! Dance with me!" Nora yells as she comes running through the room. She's in her element.

"Sure, honey," I say.

She reaches out and takes my hand, pulling me to the dance floor. She jumps around, moving to the music, and I try to keep up with her moves. Grabbing onto her hands again, I twirl her around before picking her up and moving her all over the dance floor as she squeals in delight.

She's something else, this daughter of mine.

Loud voices and movement by the kitchen catches my attention. I stop dancing to peer through the crowd of people to see what's going on. My parents might need my help with something, so I tell Nora I'll be right back and walk toward the kitchen. The crowd parts, letting me pass, but I only make it a few steps before I freeze.

There, standing in the doorway to the kitchen, is Penelope. She's an unbelievable vision in the red gown I bought her, wearing her brown hair curled and that red lipstick I'm so fond of.

What is she doing here?

We lock eyes, neither of us moving or saying anything. My pulse quickens. The whole room seems to hold its breath.

Slowly, she walks in my direction, but I stay in my place because apparently my legs forgot how to work. As soon as she's in front of me, the smell of her perfume invades my nostrils and my heart thumps wildly against my chest.

"Hi, Brent," she whispers, sounding as nervous as I feel.

"Penelope, you look beautiful. I'm so happy to see you."

"Can we go outside for a minute and talk?"

"Penelope? Is that you?" Nora yells from beside me. "You're here, you're here. Best Christmas present ever!" She squeals and jumps into Penelope's arms, wrapping her arms around her neck.

"Hi, pretty girl, oh I missed you so much," Penelope says, as she closes her eyes. I can't help but study her face and notice her take a deep breath. Burying her face in Nora's curls, she holds onto her, and tears form in my eyes.

"Nora, honey, me and Penelope are going to talk for a second alone, okay?" I say to Nora when Penelope puts her down.

"Okay, Dad, but don't be too long, I want to dance with Penelope!" Nora says as she bounces off.

"Want to go out front?" I ask. I want to be alone with her and away from the prying eyes of the town. I need to hear what she wants to say and to try and convince her to stay. Now that she's here, I can't let her leave again.

"Sure," she says.

My hand instinctively goes to the small of her back as I lead her out the front door and onto the porch. She starts shivering almost as soon as we're outside in the cold, so I take off my jacket, wrapping it around her shoulders to keep her warm. I bring my palm to her cheek, rubbing circles with my thumb, and look her in the eyes.

"So, what did you want to tell me?" I ask, my hand still cupping her cheek.

"After you left yesterday, I felt like I'd made the second biggest mistake of my life," she says. "The first biggest being when I lied to you. I should've packed my bags and came back with you yesterday, Brent, but I was scared. I still am, if I'm being honest."

She takes a deep breath.

"While I was here in Winterberry, it changed me. I'm not the same woman I was when you found me in the middle of Main Street. And that thought is terrifying. But I like the woman I have become. And I know I may live a different life back in the city, and my career isn't traditional, but I want to try and make it work here in Winterberry. Because... I love you."

She looks at me through her eyelashes and time seems to stand still. Clearing her throat, she continues. "I've been in love with you since the first night we kissed. I'm so in love with you. And Nora. And Winterberry. This is my home."

Her words hit me directly in the heart. In the two weeks since she left, I've wrestled with wanting to go to Manhattan and bring her back to Winterberry. I missed her since the second she left. But, when I put myself out there and went to the city, she turned me down.

Now, here she is, standing in front of me, admitting she's in love with me. And I want to tell her the truth—that I'm in love with her, too—but a part of me is scared. She left without saying goodbye once, what makes me think she won't do it again?

"I want to believe you, Penelope, but I'm scared to. You broke all of our hearts when you left. I can't do that again to Nora... or myself."

The tears start spilling down her face and I know immediately that she's telling the truth. Those tears, the emotion written all over her face, that's real.

No, I'm still not over her walking away without saying goodbye, but I've fallen so in love with this woman that I'll do everything I can to move on and let go of that pain.

Instead of saying anything, I pull her into my arms and hold her. It feels like she's home, with me, in Winterberry.

And I never want to let go.

"I love you too, Penelope," I say into her hair.

She lifts her head, gazing at me, and I brush the fallen strand of hair out of her face.

"I love you," I repeat, in case she didn't hear me the first time.

Reaching up, she grabs the lapels of my tux jacket and pulls me closer.

"I am so in love with you, Brent. I want to come back," she says.

"Yes, come home, Penelope," I whisper. She smiles through the tears. "Come home."

Using the sleeve of my jacket, I wipe her face. We stand there for a few seconds, letting the world around us fall away. It's as if we're the only two people on the planet.

Pulling my gaze from her, I glance at the yard to notice snow is freshly falling. Taking her hand, I walk her toward the steps so she can see the snow too.

When we stop, I look up. The mistletoe hangs overhead.

"Penelope," I say, as she looks away from the snow and into my eyes. "Look up."

Slowly, she notices the mistletoe and starts laughing. Putting my hands around her waist, I pull her against me and whisper in her ear.

"Kiss me under the mistletoe?"

"Yes please," she says.

Her lips meet mine. It's the perfect kiss, soft and gentle, with so much love exchanged between us.

"What would I have done if you weren't the one to find my car in the middle of Main Street that day?" she asks against my lips, causing me to smile. "If I didn't meet you in Winterberry?"

"I don't know, Penelope, and I don't ever want to find out," I say as I kiss her again. "Merry Christmas, baby."

The End

Epilogue

♥

Brent

One year later

"Nora? Are you ready for the ball?" I ask my little girl.

She comes running out of her bedroom into mine. This year, she chose a gold dress with glitter all over it, the same color as Penelope's dress.

Penelope returned from shooting a movie in New Jersey last night and brought Nora's dress with her. She's been staying there during the week and coming back home to Winterberry on the weekends. I hate when she leaves, but I love that she's still able to follow her passion while making this little town her permanent home.

Not long after the ball last year, we officially moved in together. Nora loves having her here. The two of them are thick as thieves.

"I'm ready," Nora says.

I stop in my tracks when I see her. She's only eight, but she looks so grown.

"You look gorgeous!" I say, spinning her around so I can see how pretty she is. "Penelope, you ready too?" I call into the bathroom. She's been getting ready in there for what feels like hours, even though she doesn't need a single bit of makeup to look beautiful.

"Yep, ready too," she says, coming out of the bathroom. Her long hair is up in a bun this year, with dangly gold earrings that skim her shoulders, and tall black heels.

My God, my girl is gorgeous.

"Wow, look at you two," I say to them. I'm the luckiest man in the world.

I help them both into their coats before putting mine on, kissing Penelope in the process. We head across the lawn to the inn. Guests have already started to arrive, and everyone looks great, as usual. We get inside and my mom gives Nora and Penelope a hug, then holds them at arm's length to get a good look at them, in typical mom fashion. My parents love Penelope. She's seamlessly become a member of our family.

Once all the guests are inside and the party is in full swing, I take Penelope by the hand and lead her outside onto the front porch. It's freezing out, but it's my favorite place to be with her. It's filled with so many amazing memories.

"My God, it's cold out here," she says. I take off my coat and drape it over her shoulders. "Did I tell you how handsome you look?" She pulls me in for a kiss.

"You did, but I don't mind hearing it again." I laugh. "Penelope, I wanted to tell you something." My hand goes to my pocket, searching for the box I've been carrying around for days.

"When you left Winterberry last year, I never thought I would see you again," I say, working to keep my voice steady. "And I wasn't sure if I'd ever be able to heal from a second broken heart. After Michelle died, I hadn't given my heart to another woman, and I never expected to, until you came along. You're everything I could want and more. An amazing role model for

Nora, the best partner, an inspirational businesswoman and a great friend. And I'm so lucky to call you mine."

I kneel down, pulling out the ring box. Her hands fly to her face when she realizes what I'm doing.

"Penelope, I love you with everything I have. Will you make this family official and become my wife?"

For a second, she stares at me silently, her mouth agape. A small smile spreads across her face as she nods. "Yes! Yes Brent, I will marry you! Omigod I'm so surprised!"

As soon as the word *yes* comes out of her mouth, I slip the ring on her finger and stand up, pulling her in for a kiss. We pull apart and she glances down, admiring the ring. She holds up her hand, moving it around, taking it in from every angle.

"Oh Brent, you make me the happiest I've ever been," she says, kissing me again. "Should we go tell Nora the good news?"

"I already know!" Nora squeals from the doorway where everyone from the party has gathered to watch me propose.

Nora pushes through the crowd, running up and throwing her arms around our waists, holding on for dear life.

This, right here, is all I need in my life. And I know that Michelle is looking down, smiling.

"Merry Christmas, you two," I say to my girls, holding on as tight as I can.

You know, maybe Christmas in Winterberry isn't so bad, after all.

Acknowledgements

First and foremost, I want to thank you, the reader, for taking a chance on a new author and picking up my book. This has been a dream of mine for as long as I can remember and I can't believe my little book baby is out in the world, and in your hands. Writing this has been such a joy!

To my husband Joey, none of this would be possible without you. From all the long nights that I sat at the computer writing and you took care of our little family to the hours spent listening to me bounce ideas off of you, thank you. You are the best thing that has ever happened to me and my favorite love story.

To my daughter Olivia, you are my inspiration in life and everything I do is for you. I love you to the moon and back.

This book wouldn't have happened without my amazing editor, Miranda, who helped take a rough manuscript to an actual story. You are the best!

A huge thank you to my cover artist, Jillian, for bringing my vision to life.

Taylor, my writing partner, who has spent hours with me as I wrote this story and kept me accountable, you're next! Whitney, I'll always be grateful you came into my life. Thank you for pushing me, spending forever on Facetime making content for social media, and listening to me talk about this book for months.

To my parents and my sisters, thank you for always pushing me to conquer my dreams and cheering me on. I did it!

I have been so lucky to have amazing friends who have been on this journey with me from the beginning. Rachel, Laurel, Lyssa, Sloane, Jeanne, Alicia, Kate, Lauren, Christine, Catrina, Heather, Rana, and all the Jokers moms, you all mean so much to me. Last and definitely not least, to my book club ladies, my biggest fans, I can't wait until you read this!

About the Author

Karen Liszewski lives in New Jersey with her beloved husband, sweet daughter, and fur babies. She always has her nose in a book, and it's been her lifelong dream to be an author. Meet Me In Winterberry is her debut novel.

Connect Online

Instagram: authorkarenliszewski

Facebook: Author Karen Liszewski